THE
DOOM
THAT CAME TO
ASTORIA

THE
DOOM
THAT CAME TO
ASTORIA

NORTHWEST TRILOGY BOOK ONE

CRAIG RANDALL

MORRIGHAN PUBLISHING

where your words come to life

ISBN: 978-1-7342355-4-8

Library of Congress Control Number: 2021903849

This is a work of fiction. Names, characters, incidents, and dialogues are products of the author's imagination and are not to be construed as real. Any resemblance to actual events pr persons, living or dead, is entirely coincidental.

First published in the United States in 2021 by Morrighan Publishing.

Printed in the United States of America.

Morrighan Publishing

www.morrighanpublishing.com

"Where wilt thou lead me? Speak."

—William Shakespeare, *"Hamlet"*

PROLOGUE

In a house far removed from the well-traveled roads of the common man, in a room, further yet removed from any natural light, sat a man with great internal struggle. He wished to move mountains, to raise his hands to the stars above and bring them careening down in one vehement and righteous strike.

That would show them, he often told himself as a deep and bitter rage swelled within him. *That would show them all.*

For years, this man had followed the breadcrumbs laid out by those who came before, those whose bold and dark steps shook the very heavens. Yet, through some unknown failure, no amount of inquiry could quite pinpoint what went wrong; the purposes of his predecessors were left unfinished and in need of resolve. This man had spent his entire life searching for a *key* that would make it all work. That one *thing*, a *person* who had, for years, managed to elude his grasp.

Time was running short.

He knew they would need to redouble both their efforts and their reach if they were to succeed. The divide he created within *The Order* with his defiant search for what the others had always referred to as 'his fruitless dream' must be redeemed. He would tear the sky in two if he had to make it so.

A headache formed while his thoughts mulled over, yet again, all their failed attempts. A thousand times he'd gone over everything they'd tried, but he would go over them a thousand more if that's what it took.

His ghost-white hair had gone wild with how many times his hands had passed through it, his inadvertent attempts to stave off the headaches that plagued him. They were occurring more frequently as of late, especially given how close the project was to completion, and yet how impossible it would be to fully complete without that *one* person. The *key*. The foundation of it all.

His headache moved, concentrating itself in the left frontal part of his brain, when a knock came at the door. Without warning, it swung open.

"Sir?" The man who entered was out of breath.

"What is it?" There was an obvious, disdainful agitation in the man's voice.

"Sir, I thought you'd want to know right away. We found him at last, Sir!"

The man looked up in disbelief. His headache immediately began to fade.

This will show them, he thought. *This will show them all.*

ONE

It had been years since Charlie West had thought of and truly dwelled on his father. Years. Memories and images would pop into his mind from time to time, but they were nothing he couldn't push away or move on from. Over time, he had learned not to dwell on them, not to brood or allow them to become an anchor preventing him from moving forward. Which is why this particular morning was so peculiar. There was *something* different. A feeling, really. And Charlie found himself unable to let it go. This morning, his father's shadow loomed over him and his many thoughts like a storm, ominous and foreboding, pushing its way upriver against the wind. It scorched itself into the recesses of his thoughts and mind, hovering over him as if it were a cloud directly overhead waiting to burst from the mounting stratospheric pressures and rain down upon him, muddying the soil of which Charlie was trying to build his life.

Today, for reasons he couldn't figure, Charlie wasn't able to stop thinking about his father. The memories lingered, not allowing his mind to find rest, even for a second. Arcane and hollow pangs built up in his lower gut. He took them as nothing more than the average warnings his mind and body provided whenever he made an attempt at *anything* new. That's what today was all about after all: leaving, moving on. Every alarm system within his body was telling him not to go; warnings that he always listened to without question and had rarely ever failed him.

A few months before, Charlie had been offered a job, sort of out of nowhere, teaching ninth grade at a small school in the tiny coastal town of Knappa, Oregon. It was a small logging community just outside of Astoria, which he'd at least heard of because of all the films from his childhood that had been made there: *The Goonies. Kindergarten Cop. Short Circuit. The Road,* to name a few.

He had finished his master's degree in teaching the spring prior but, given the economic state of things nationwide, the prospects of getting a job right out of the gate were low. He still applied for anything that popped up.

Charlie had just finished convincing himself that it would be okay to simply substitute teach and keep stocking shelves while he lived at home to save money when he received a call that would truly test his resolve. The superintendent of a very small school district he'd never even heard of called him, a rarity in the world of teaching, telling him that he'd come highly recommended by his professors at PSU, and that he would love for Charlie to come for an interview and tour of the school.

"Knappa?" his mom had asked.

"Yeah," Charlie said. "Right outside of Astoria. You know, on the coast."

Right from the start, Charlie's mother had been very nervous about it, but would never express why.

Even though Charlie felt that he'd botched the interview completely and really had given the worst first impression, at the end the principal had still reached his hand across the table and said, "We'd love to offer you a contract to join us out here if you're interested, Charlie."

Am I interested? Charlie remembered thinking. *Of course I'm interested!* He thought anyone would be crazy not to take this.

10

On top of it all, the district said they could recommend a great apartment for him, only if he wanted the help, him not being from around town and all. The principal had some friends in town who were looking to let out their basement and Charlie moving to the area and needing a place to stay seemed to fix both of their problems.

Though he was at first weary of the prospect of living with people he didn't know, in the end the undercutting price of rent compared to whatever he'd find anywhere else clinched it for him.

Immediately, he began planning his new life and dreaming about the opportunities he hoped it would bring. He could finally branch out and move on. Maybe he could finally make some lasting friendships, something he'd never been able to cultivate under the hovering pressures of his father – his childhood and adolescence had been incredibly lonely. And finally, Charlie could really pursue his true passion of writing, which had been one of the truest forms of therapy in his life. That and reading were the two biggest sanctuaries, places he could always go to find solace.

So, Charlie signed the contract for his first *adult* job, as he called it, and he was set off on his new course of life.

Any warnings his insides sent him about the situation, he buried. Still, deep down, there were parts of him screaming *no!* His body and mind had worked together to protect him his whole life, and they were converging then to tell him he should stay home, that he should stick with his initial plan of subbing and stocking shelves.

But this move was something he had thought long and hard about. He had fought for this new life, mostly with himself but also with his mother. She was the confusing part, always encouraging him to grow, to try new things. She had always wanted him to *go*, to *live*, but she never really wanted him to *leave*. And strangely, ever since his plan to move started to take shape, she seemed dead set against it.

It doesn't make any sense, he told himself over and over.

And she never actually made any arguments about his not leaving. Whenever the conversation got that far, she'd stop herself.

It was as if something else was holding her back, like she *couldn't* speak. For Charlie, it was infuriating.

Either way, it did make sense to him that, on this morning of all mornings, his long-forgotten scars resurfaced and that he could feel his chest and mind constricting, as if the whole room was wrapping itself around him.

It had been a long time since he had experienced these physical manifestations.

Looking back, he remembered some of the breathing exercises he'd learned in therapy and, with a rote efficiency, he began them.

Breathe, Charlie... one... two... three... four... hold... one... two... three... four... slow exhale.

He felt the pressure ease ever so slightly.

When he was younger and panic attacks were a more regular occurrence in his life, he'd been able to use these breathing exercises to keep them from getting out of hand if he caught them early. And as the years progressed, he learned to master certain exercises and pathways of thinking to remove the majority of his anxious thoughts and symptoms from his life almost entirely.

They came and went, but at much lower intervals and with much less severity.

Charlie breathed and walked himself through two more cycles of the exercise, hoping to quickly re-cultivate his hard-won peace.

Breathe... two... three... four... hold.

Opening his eyes, Charlie found himself still in the attic of his childhood home, the ruins of a time he would rather have forgotten. The warning signs of leaving were still present, but much less pronounced.

He took another deep breath and reminded himself why he had gone up to the attic in the first place.

Just get the damn picture, Charlie! He reminded himself.

Of course, he'd waited until the day he was leaving to sift through the many jumbled boxes of miscellaneous goods that had survived the fractured years of their former lives, but it was important to him. It was a photograph of he and his mother, a memory of hope, and one of the few tangible relics of his childhood that he could reach to and remember that it wasn't all pain. It was of the two of them dressed up on Halloween, one where Charlie's father must have been away. She had hastily thrown together their costumes out of old, shabby sheets – crude by any standards. Most people would have thought very little of the moment but, to Charlie, it was a treasure.

His father had been a tyrant, inflicting terror and enforcing his rule wherever he could.

He had only passed down two things to his son, so Charlie would say: pain and a recurrent temper. Over the years, Charlie had learned dozens of strategies to at least suppress his temper   but, in reality, it had never really left him. He always felt it there, deep down, brooding, almost waiting. It never felt very far below the surface.

And right then, as he stood rifling through the attic, that temper was bubbling in him, slowly smoldering to the surface.

He couldn't explain it.

He looked through one box after another, cursing himself for not doing this sooner. His anger was still rising slowly. Each box he sifted through was filled with a multitude of objects. Each triggering one-minute eruption of anger after another. Each pushing him a little further from control.

He found his chest once again beginning to constrict.

Breathe, Charlie, he thought to himself. *Just breathe.*

He began his search again and at last found a box marked *Charlie* on its side in big Sharpie letters.

Maybe this one, he thought. He reached over another smaller box and picked it up.

Inside, he found it filled with many random objects from Charlie's life, most of which were of very little consequence. But amid it all, he found a stack of photos. Sorting his way through them, he finally came to what he'd been searching for so desperately.

Ah, yes! The sudden burst of excitement gave him a momentary reprieve from the rising levels of tension in his body. It only lasted a second before the anger ebbed back and gripped him once again.

What the…? he started to wonder, still unable to reason out why he was feeling so agitated.

Amidst the tumultuous rising and falling of his emotions, Charlie looked down at the photograph and smiled. He remembered the freedom he'd felt that night, the hope that had existed. It was the first and only time Charlie had ever been allowed to dress up for Halloween; his father would never allow it. Even now, standing there holding the photo, he felt like he was getting away with something.

Charlie hoped the photo would become a reminder to him, a seed of where his future would lead, that he would be able to outgrow the years of pain and all that had held him back for so long. That that small and brittle flame of hope he'd so long held onto would finally have a chance to bloom and break free of its constant strain.

Charlie's father had died when he was 12 in a car accident on Highway 30 as he was heading toward the Oregon Coast. Ironically, that was the same road Charlie would be traveling on today. This was a consistent cause for agitation when Charlie and his mother discussed his leaving, but she always seemed to lose the ability to articulate or express what she was thinking. She always stopped herself right before she would say anything concrete. He never pushed her, but he suspected that there were always things she wasn't telling him, that she knew more about than she was letting on. That was another point of contention.

The greatest disappointment, though, after Charlie's father's death, was that Charlie had assumed he and his mother's lives would be relieved of the burden of his rule. That they would be free of his constricting regiment and expectations. But no matter how much time passed, the precision of his shadow still loomed, and hope was always kept at a distance.

The entirety of their lives had been ruled by his father. Maybe the routines were too deeply imposed or maybe it was just too hard for them to change. Maybe his mother was simply too broken-down to enact the necessary change, and this is why it took Charlie so long to leave, even though she had always encouraged it.

Neither of them would ever dare to upset the balance of *his* expectations or order, even after his death. Over the years, especially as Charlie got older, he learned simply to not speak at all about his father. And most of his life was just that: unspoken. The majority of his interactions with the world took place with at least an arm's length of distance. Anything or anyone *new* was considered dangerous, and he knew he'd have to fight that in the coming months. Like the people he observed around him, he would have to accept the things that took place in his new life. He'd been driving home the fact that he would have to try ignoring those warning signs in his body and just accept the world around him. He would learn to trust and if he didn't feel that trust, he would assume it and see where life took him.

Charlie's father's shadow hung over their house, long after his footsteps ceased. It clung to Charlie and his mother, to their lives, like wet grass on old shoes.

Charlie was so focused on these thoughts now, so derailed from his purpose, he was unaware of how they were affecting him.

His anger was still rising; his fingers had been twitching against the sides of his legs; pressure building within him, churning whatever anxiety was already there into something he might not be able to contain.

Out of nowhere, a wave of guilt washed over him as he remembered his reaction to his father's death. *How did I get so lucky?* He'd thought. And no matter how much he justified it, it always blanketed him in shame. It was his *father*, after all, no matter how much the man had terrorized him.

He tried to push the thought away, as he had so many times before, but this time, for whatever reason, it didn't work.

His agitation spiked again, his whole body wincing as the shadow of his late father seemed to be looming over him somehow.

"Charlie!" A yell came from downstairs.

"Fu—" he jumped, startled by his mother's call. It had jolted him back to reality and made him realize how long he'd been upstairs. Surprisingly, he noticed the quick burst of anger that flared through his body, as if she was infringing upon his time.

Confused, he shook his head and attempted to push the thought away.

15

"Be right down, Mom!" he yelled, still unsure as to where the burst had come from but becoming minutely aware that a cold sweat had wrapped itself around him despite the sweltering August heat.

He tried to push aside the feelings that were starting to overwhelm him and, once more, looked down at the picture he held in his hand.

Again, he felt the anger flare within him, the warmth of it stretching out all the way to the ends of his fingers and toes. It was followed by a subtle prickling in his gut and a heightened awareness that Charlie was all too familiar with.

Anxious pangs thundered through him and he looked down at the picture in his hand only to have his thoughts interrupted by flashes of memories of his father standing over the both of them.

Come on, Charlie, he found himself thinking. He always knew this day would be difficult, but still, he hadn't expected something like this. Certain ghosts just won't let go.

He could feel the panic swarming, surrounding him, getting ready to sink its grip into him.

His whole body tensed.

Sharp pain fired through his mind, settling into a dull ache; memories began to flood and flow through him, slowly at first, but picking up speed gradually, none of it seeming to be in his control.

Come on, he tried to encourage himself. He needed to reel himself back in, and soon.

Charlie did what he could to push each thought aside as they came in turn. But still the undermining voices came.

Why leave Portland? they would ask. *You don't know anyone there; you probably wouldn't cut it anyway; might as well just stay where you are.*

He had heard this all before since deciding to go, but never as forcefully or in such quick succession.

Something seemed to wrap around his lungs and twist; it tightened even harsher than before and the panic was beginning to mount in full.

Another image of his mother – all alone – popped into his mind. A tangled sheet of guilt folded over him, followed by a quick and smoldering surge of anger

The room swirled around him.

The part of Charlie's mind he still felt some autonomous control over frantically spun, trying to figure out what was happening to him and why. After so long a time without incident, why it was coming on so strong? Yes, even these thoughts were taken over.

His body wrenched itself, becoming trapped in the assuming mistake that the physical can overpower the mental, and he quickly lost his hold on anything concrete.

Charlie's anger continued to flare as the image of his mother lingered in his mind, weak and in need. His fear of needing to stay in Portland to take care of her exploded, scrunching his face up in pain as he fought against it. But, like quicksand, the harder he fought, the faster he fell.

His mind flailed as his body settled into a state of steadily gripped rage.

Straining against the rising onslaught of tension, a thought occurred to him out of his rote practice well beyond the confines of reason. His body, as if acting out of its own will, began to carry him through his regimented breathing pattern.

Breathe... two... three... four... hold... two... three... four... breathe...

But it was no use.

He kept trying, consciously now, but still nothing.

With all his strength, Charlie gripped and fought against the pressure. It was like fighting against a falling sky. Then, without warning, something slipped, as if the gears of whatever mechanized tether that that was holding him together jumped the rail and fell out of place. His mind, his heart rate, and his thoughts exploded, well beyond any pace he could keep up.

Waves of pings and prickles followed along the currents of his anxiety's rising tide, edging their way up his arms and legs, down to his feet, his fingers, to his skull and mind – his discomfort was exponential – and he quickly lost whatever little control remained of his sensory functions. Fidgeting, his fingers and hands tapped and bounced off his legs and stomach.

The pressure surged again and flared in wave after wave; the room was in a tailspin; images of his past flooded his mind; of his father, of himself, of his mother, of he and his mother's inability to fight back against his tyrannical presence; a montage of screams punctuated each memory; doors slammed; the echoes of a hand coming down hard, then a body hitting the floor; his childhood blitzed through his mind and the pain grew, fueling the torrents wresting their way through him.

Finally, an image flashed before him of his mother lying on the floor. She had just been struck while he, Charlie, had been cowering in the corner, powerless and unable to come to her defense. Then, in his mind, his father's looming presence turned and began making its way toward him an—

Charlie couldn't help but yell out. The echo of his flailing reverberated off the attic ceiling. It was too late.

He was triggered.

His perceptions morphed; he felt the room tumbling through the sky, his whole body tensed and he was trapped for what felt like forever, even though it only lasted for very few measurable moments; it was as if reality was passing through him, coursing; fear and worry ripped through the entirety of who he was, body and mind, like a virus.

Images flashed through him even quicker than before: his father standing over them both, raging; Charlie and his mother quivering, hopeless, without defense; then, his mother was lying lifeless on floor; Charlie saw himself walking over to her and kneeling down, shaking her, calling out her name; he heard footsteps and turned; he father stood over him again, his angry, devilish face glaring down at them both; Charlie screamed and covered his face with his hands.

Panting, Charlie opened his eyes to find himself on his knees, buckled over, propping himself up with both hands out in front of him. He was layered in a thick coat of cold and sticky sweat, desperate for a full breath of air.

His mind cleared, and he felt the strain loosen but not leave.

Aside from the heaving sounds of Charlie straining for breath, silence held dominion over the room.

Charlie grasped for reason, for understanding. It had been years since he'd had a full-on panic attack. What had brought it on now? But he still couldn't quite keep his thoughts connected.

This was something he had hoped to leave behind as he pressed forward in this new season of life, that these ghosts would no longer haunt him nor stalk his nerves. Now, he was unsure.

He needed to leave, right then. He needed, so desperately, to get out, to find a new context. To leave it all behind: the pain, the loss, the haunting memories, and his...

Mom...? Charlie thought, his stomach turning over within him, again.

He'd been through this debate with himself so many times before. He'd be leaving her alone.

But... I have to go... he would tell himself.

She had been and was still his one reservation. The one thing that left him nervous and unsettled about leaving.

Leaving is going to break her, he thought again.

And right then, she was the only thing that stood between him and walking to his car. He would have to go through her.

Just as he was turning to leave, as he was shaking away the barren and unsettled feelings that were still swirling within him, something else caught his eye. The frame of a picture inside a box Charlie would have sworn he'd never seen before, right next to where he'd found the box with the photo in it. There was something odd about the frame, something *otherworldly* that he couldn't explain, as if it somehow was able to strain the atmosphere around it.

Reaching down to pick it up, Charlie shuddered and left it where it sat. He rubbed the tips of his fingers that had touched the object with his other hand as if that would rid himself of whatever eerie feeling that had invaded him sooner.

It was freezing to the touch. And after he'd taken a step back, he noticed that, while everything else inside the box carried years of

19

dust, *this* object did not. That was impossible, of course, because of how everything was arranged within the box. It was obvious, with everything else resting on top of the frame, it must have been in there just as long.

Both intrigued and confused, Charlie considered this strange object.

And reaching down again, he grasped it and lifted it out of the box. It carried with it an electricity, an almost imitation of life that brought with it a heightened sense of discomfort.

A subtle wave of chills echoed through Charlie, knocking at the door of his ever-darkening thoughts, followed by the slightest creeping ripple of anxiousness.

He was about to put it down when something about the photo struck him: there were four men in the photo, older, and standing together. It was an old photo by its look, so Charlie was sure these men were long dead. They wore thick wool, black three-piece suits. They looked old in the classic sense and each wore a matching medallion around their necks, the likes of which Charlie had never seen before. He brushed the image out of his mind and moved his attention to their faces, their expressions, or the lack thereof. They each shared the same blank and eerie look, void of any emotion.

Charlie brought his attention back to what had originally struck him.

The man on the right, his vacant look, like an icy winter wind, pierced Charlie, like someone had left a window open and the cold had crept in, covering every inch of his exposed skin.

Charlie took in a deep breath and held it as his brain tried to make sense of what he was looking at.

He'd seen those eyes before, but only in one other person.

It couldn't be…

But as he looked closer, Charlie was sure. They were the same eyes that had looked on him throughout the entirety of his childhood. Those that haunted him and had left deep scars.

As Charlie stood staring down at the photograph, he was frozen by the fact that it appeared that his father was staring back at him.

He brought the frame closer to get an even better look and gasped. As he exhaled, a part of him deflated.

Again, images began to churn slowly in his mind; carousel wheels of thoughts screeched back to life; the faintest hues of color faded from Charlie's cheeks and his chest tightened as breathing grew difficult once more.

He hadn't seen those eyes in years, except for in nightmares – waking or not.

Slowly, Charlie covered the man's beard with his thumb and let a small whimper escape.

It was *his* father, or an identical being.

What the fu— That's... that's impossible, he told himself. *It can't be... it ca—*

His breathing picked up speed.

Closing his eyes, he held them tight, and focused on breathing.

Not again, he thought. *Oh, please... not today.*

His body constricted, and his mind started to spin again. If he could have thought clearly, he would have agreed that he was more worried about the panic than anything else.

Memories and fears played again in his mind, and his arms grew tense.

Charlie trembled and, *Shit,* he thought, as the frame slipped from his fingers and fell shattering to the floor. Glass shot everywhere and the frame itself broke into several jagged pieces.

But, to Charlie's benefit, it had pulled him out of whatever anxious trance he had been slipping into.

A prickle of frustration flared again as he knew he would have to clean the mess up before he left. Kneeling down to pick up the shards, something else caught his eye.

The photograph, having been freed from its frame, was now lying face down in the mess, and Charlie noticed a series of scribbles and scratches written across it. He picked it up and brushed away the glass.

21

"Charlie? Are you there? Is everything okay?" his mom called out to him. "I heard noises. What's taking you so long?" her tone was filled with worry.

Anger shot up in Charlie again, but he was more concerned with what he'd just found. Distracted, really.

Fairly annoyed, he called down that he would be there in a second and that everything was fine. Then he went back to his investigation.

He was growing used to the rising level of agitated worry in him.

The photo was icy to the touch and faded at the edges, worn with age. The words were written in a washed-out ink, scribbled longhand — calligraphic in style — difficult to read by modern standards.

Most of the script was illegible, but he could make out a few words. There was a signature at the bottom that read: *Mr. Johann Ashcroft Wilkes.*

Flipping the picture over again, Charlie attempted to discern which man was which, but he wasn't sure.

Maybe it was the man standing next to the one he had mistaken for his father. *He* stood a bit more regal than the rest, with patterned clothing and rings on most of his fingers, and his hat was taller — details that spoke of wealth.

Turning the photo back over, Charlie continued his perusal of the scribbling lines. His eyes were drawn to the opening salutation.

"What?!" Charlie said, aloud. He re-read the words several more times to be sure of what they said.

"To Mr. Lester B. West."

Charlie's brow scrunched in wonder and confusion.

"Who the hell is Lester B. West?" he wondered aloud.

Charlie had never known much about his family history on either side. In fact, he didn't know much beyond the fact that he was his parents' child. It was one of the many unspoken topics of his life.

So, this came as an interesting and unexpected shock to him.

Charlie flipped the photograph over again and looked down at the man with his father's burning eyes.

Who are you? He thought, as his quickening heartbeat seemed to wind up whatever had been cinching around his chest. He struggled for a few quick breaths.

There was only one other string of words on the back of the photo he could make out, just below the names in the corner. It was mostly gibberish, but underneath it in a larger scrawl were a series of larger letters, much bolder, that read: *The Order.*

The Order? Charlie thought. *What is the–*

"Charlie! Are you okay up there?" his mom yelled up again, startling him back into the reality that he needed to be leaving.

He checked his watch, noting the tenseness of her tone – it was lined with worry. It was 2:15.

He felt his mind crease at the realization that it was much later than he'd hoped to leave.

He took one more look at the strange picture in his hand, then down at the broken glass that littered the floor, still torn between the two conflicting urges to stay and go.

Come on, Charlie! You've been through this. Just go!

He took a moment to clean up the broken glass; it wouldn't be right to leave it for his mother. Today was going to be hard enough on her already.

Brushing the glass shards onto a piece of paper, Charlie hastily dumped them back into the mysterious box they had come from. *Better than nothing,* he thought as he picked up the pieces of the frame and dropped them in as well, onto the pile of papers situated on top. They landed harshly on the pile and the weight shifted, disturbing the orientation of everything inside the box. Its contents each settled into new positions within their tiny world.

Lastly, Charlie slid the photograph of the four men into a slit at the edge, away from where he'd put the glass. In doing so, he rubbed his fingers against another object, one that he hadn't seen as it had been concealed deep beneath the pile of paperwork and files.

It was icy to the touch as well, more so even than the frame had been.

Charlie flinched as a strange, feverishly chilled shiver shot through his whole body. He pulled his hand back quickly as if he had burned him, as if it had been coated in some sort of liquid nitrogen and would not allow itself to be held without causing damage to the holder.

Ouch! What the— Charlie began, but stopped as a tingling shadow seemed to wrap itself around his mind.

He was shaking his head to push it away when his mom yelled up for a final time, "Charlie? You're running late!"

"I'm coming!" he yelled back down.

He looked back at the box and wondered at what he had felt. But he really had to go – whatever it was in there would have to wait.

He felt his back pocket to ensure that the photo he had gone up there for in the first place was still there. It was. Then, he rushed out of the attic with the hope he was leaving those clinging memories behind for good.

He ran down the stairs and through the living room to where his mother stood on the front porch. She was facing his car with her arms crossed, as if physically trying to hold herself together.

The further he got away from the attic, the more he felt something loosening in him, as if whatever it had been that had been holding onto him finally released its grip.

"Hey, Mom," Charlie said, his tone gentle and controlled.

He knew he needed to be careful here. How she reacted to his leaving would dictate the tone of their ongoing conversations. His chest tightened and he tried taking a deep breath.

Before she even turned or said anything, her chin sunk and with it so did Charlie's heart. This was a motion he knew all too well, and one that normally spelled tears and distress.

"Mom…" he started to say, reaching out with his hand and feeling nothing but the weight of her thoughts. The weight of her months of silence in regard to why she didn't want him to move to Astoria. She didn't seem to be against his moving, but Charlie got the impression that she would have preferred him to move anywhere but there. It was like she expected to never see him again. He couldn't quite wrap his head around it.

At last, she turned to him and, with longing concern, said, "I love you, Charlie, and—"

Again, she cut herself off.

Charlie's head raised at the conjunctive wording, and he hoped that today he might finally hear some reasoning or logic for her contrary feelings.

In the softest and most tender tone he could manage, as if to bridge her hesitancy, Charlie asked, "And?"

She stood there for a moment, mouth open, as if she had finally found the strength to tell him what she was thinking but, to Charlie's disappointment, all that came out was a quick, "Nothing. I just love you and I hope you have a nice trip." Her words were frail and brittle, like raindrops that froze in midair and shattered as soon as they hit the ground.

The whole scene seemed to hold its breath amidst the tension. They stood apart from each other, neither of them ready to admit what was taking place.

Charlie, who needed to leave but knew how much it would hurt his mother, stood there with pursed lips, accepting her continued silence, while his mother, who needed to let him go but knew she didn't have the strength to do so – especially given what she feared was waiting for him out there – stood there trying to hold herself together.

Charlie's mother had many reasons for not wanting him to go, but none she'd ever felt able to express. For there were many secrets in their family that she'd spent so much of his life keeping him safe from.

As he got older, she'd always meant to tell him everything, but it never seemed the right time or place. And after he had announced he'd accepted the job and would be moving, she'd found herself so overwhelmed by the prospect of losing him, any means of telling him seemed lost in the mass of plaguing and jittering fears that steered her.

"I love you too, mom," he said, unable to completely hide his disappointment.

Tell him, she told herself. *You need to tell him now before he goes. What if you don't get another chance? What if it's—you have to tell him about* them!

She went to speak but found herself unable and instead burst into tears.

"Mom?" Charlie stepped forward, breaking the plane that separated them, and wrapped his arms around her. She disappeared into him, like a child. "Mom, what is it? What's wrong?" He asked. "And what aren't you telling me?"

Charlie held back his exasperation as best he could.

She considered how long it would take to explain everything, why she hadn't said anything before, how she'd been paralyzed by fear, and why now—

No, she thought. *It's been settled, he's already set to go. I can't do this to him right now.*

Instead, she pushed it aside and looked up at him. "I'm… I'm proud of you, Charlie." Her tone was shaky and robotic, but there was a hint of sincerity in it, even if weak. This, Charlie could feel.

Still, her silence was her prison.

"Thanks, Mom, but—"

She just shook her head and tightened her own arms around him. She couldn't speak any further, not in front of him, not right then. She would have collapsed, and no matter how much she didn't want him to leave, she couldn't do that to him. She had to keep it together so he could go, then hope for the best.

For a time, they just held each other in the quiet.

"I love you, Mom," Charlie said at last.

"I love you, Charlie," she replied in a barely discernable whisper.

After some time more, it was Charlie who spoke up again, saying, "I'll call you first thing?"

His mother nodded to him and, understanding the cue, released her embrace.

"It might take a little longer," he told her. "The drive's two hours but I want to take highway 30 so I can swing by the school again just to take a look."

She seemed to flinch at the mention of the road that had taken Charlie's father's life, pushing away whatever frightful images had overtaken her mind about her son, and gripping herself to keep back the coming tears.

A few more moments, she told herself. *For Charlie. You can do this.*

"And I'll drive safe. I'll let you know if anything happens, and I'll make good choices," he said, the last bit more of a quip to bring some levity to the moment.

Something deep within Charlie's mother was telling her, *tell him! Tell him, now! You have to at least warn him!* But even the thought of opening her mouth to speak was crippling. The years of not saying anything had trained her too well.

At last, Charlie said to her softly, "Well, I'll be off then."

She strained a smile at him and did her best to feign excitement for her son, but a single tear did manage to escape the confines of her eyes and slid slowly down her cheek.

Charlie leaned in for one last hug.

"I love you, Ch—" she managed before the words grew raspy and became caught in her throat.

They each let go of the other and Charlie walked over to his car. He opened the back door and tossed his backpack and suitcase before opening the driver's side door to get in. He removed the photograph from his back pocket and set it gently on the passenger seat. Then, leaning in, Charlie stepped into the car and shut the door behind him.

He looked back and waved to her one last time and, with a nervous finality, turned the keys over. The engine roared to life.

Without looking back, Charlie's car sped off down the road, leaving behind everything that he hoped would no longer haunt his steps, everything he needed be set free from.

Curiously, in the shadows that overtook the attic when Charlie left, when all was silent and still, the faintest flicker of unearthly light gleamed from inside the box where he had found the old photo. As if willed to life, it came quickly but then died out again. Then its faint glow would flicker once more and reach out beyond the confines of that lowly box before fading as it did before and shrivel back to into nothing.

Back and forth, the light and the shadows fought. And each time it ebbed back, the illumination grew, eventually spilling out over the edges of the box from which it came. It was a soft amber at first, with gentle swirls of crimson at its edges. It continued to grow and die down again, caught in an endless fluctuation, as if the room was breathing.

Then, out of nowhere, as if it had been gathering its strength together, this light exploded outward, filling the room entirely with hues of splintered ambers and crimsons. No shadow or darkness could stand before its radiance or show of strength. Every centimeter of the room was touched by its power.

It emanated from inside the box Charlie had found the picture; consequently, from the very same object Charlie had brushed his hand against. He would have seen it too, had he only taken that moment to investigate what had filled him with that chilled and icy feeling. He would then have witnessed, firsthand, this phenomenon.

Underneath the stacks of files and papers, underneath the broken glass and picture frame, rested a chain of bronze, thick and ancient in look and ware. Attached to it was a medallion of sorts, several inches long and rectangular at one end, semi-circular on the other. On the rounded end rested a jewel that was currently set ablaze like an alabaster sun, majestic and terrible, exactly like the medallions worn by the men in the photograph.

Just when one would have thought the room couldn't stand amidst its shine any longer, the light vanished as quickly as it came, like someone had flipped a switch. As if the light was sucked out of the room and sent back to wherever it had come from.

And it was gone.

The room had been plunged back into darkness and shadow, and once again, all was silent and still.

Upon reaching the highway, Charlie noticed that he was feeling much better. Whatever had gripped him was, by then, completely gone. *It* had let go.

He couldn't correctly explain it, but now that it was gone, he wasn't going to push the subject further. He was just relieved. His brain felt like it was back in his control now, and he was able to breath in and out with ease. *Finally*, he thought. *It's all behind me. I can finally move on.*

These were his final thoughts before he turned up the stereo and placed his focus on the road ahead.

Charlie's car pulled away. And as soon as it was out of sight, his mother's footing gave way, and she stumbled backward, as if suffering a bout of vertigo or shock, and collapsed in through the front door of the house.

She'd been feeling strange all morning but assumed it was merely a biproduct of Charlie leaving.

It was part of the process, she'd told herself. Part of the grieving.

Since he'd told her about accepting the job, she'd felt torn in two.

On the one hand, she wanted nothing more than her son to experience the norms of growing up, of moving on into adulthood. She wanted him to thrive and be free. But on the other, she felt like she needed him. She'd grown accustomed to him helping her keep the house. He was all she had. They were bound to each other by a singular pain, like two broken bones that hadn't been set correctly and had healed wrong. They had twisted around each other and fused together. And as Charlie's car had driven away, these bones had been ripped apart. The front porch was littered with the splinters.

Worst of all for Charlie's mother was how ill-prepared she felt she'd left her son.

Astoria? She thought again, like so many times before. *After how hard we worked to get away...*

All she'd ever wanted was to protect Charlie from harm, to keep him safe from the life she had lived. The life his father had lived. To spare him pain, she'd kept so much from him, and now it felt too late. He was gone.

A hundred times she wanted to tell him everything about what they'd ran away from, about what they – Charlie's father included – had saved him from, but whenever she went to open her mouth, nothing came out. Something ingrained left her paralyzed, telling her if she opened that door, Charlie wouldn't understand, or he'd be furious that she hadn't told him earlier.

Even though so much of his experiences in life would have made more sense if he'd known the truth. If he had known what it was that had shaped his father into the man he had become. But she never dared disrupt the balance and peace they had found. After so much hardship, she couldn't lose it. She couldn't lose *him*.

Now that he was gone, the grief struck her in full force, rendering her incapacitated at the front door.

I'm so sorry, Charlie! she thought, tears streaming down her face. *I'm sorry I never told you... I never warned you... about them.* The tears came harder and harder. *I didn't prepare... I... your father and I... we... got away... I thought he... would change... but...*

Her thoughts grew more unclear as something seemed to reach up and grip the reins. *And now... now you're headed right... back... there... toward them...*

She sat there shaking, her back leaning against the open front door of the house, trembling and overtaken by a violent dizziness. Oxygen was becoming difficult to come by, and her focus was failing completely. So much so that, in the midst of it all, she failed to notice a faded-yellow truck's tires screeching against the pavement as it sped suspiciously in the direction of Charlie's car.

"I'm so… sorry, Charlie," she said after some time. Then, through a heavy and cathartic exertion, "I… I should have told you. I should have warned you…"

After a while, all Charlie's mother could think about was sleep. She was so tired, but aside from the grief, she couldn't figure out what had come over her. So, for whatever unspecified amount of time – she wasn't quite able to reason it out – she lay there, too weak to get up. Simply too tired. Too shattered by grief.

She missed dinner, but she couldn't fathom eating anyway.

Eventually, she did manage to drag herself up the stairs to bed. It took a great amount of effort and, once there, she wrestled her way through one of the most restless and shallow sleeps she had ever experienced. In the morning, she would wonder if she'd even slept.

All night she tossed and turned, flinging out random cries and calls for Charlie.

Before she had drifted off into her growing delirium, she also failed to notice the faint and fragile crimson glow coming from underneath her bed. The same eerie herald that was the mark of Charlie's family's haunting past.

The faded-yellow Chevy with paint peeling off most of the panels hummed its way down the freeway, trailing behind Charlie's equally run-down burgundy Honda. The driver kept his distance well, always leaving a few cars between them. In doing so, he ensured two things: first, that Charlie didn't notice him, and second, that he never let Charlie out of his sight. His timing was patient and practiced. By the time Charlie had left a stop sign or a light, the truck would just be rounding the corner and was able to check whatever direction was needed to keep the tail.

After weaving its way in and out of the back streets of North Portland, they made their way north on I-5. He had been Charlie's shadow, and would continue to be so as long as it took. Where Charlie went, he went. What Charlie knew, he knew.

Once they were officially outside Portland, the driver picked up his phone, clicked on the recent calls list and hit the number at the top.

Several seconds passed while he waited for the other line to pick up. All that could be heard beyond the ringing was the rumbling of engines and other cars on the freeway, entities, really, moving past one another with an acute unawareness of each other's comings and goings — *beings* really only concerned with themselves.

The phone picked up.

"Hey," said the driver.

There was a slight pause as he waited.

"Yeah, it's me."

He paused again.

"Uh-huh. Yeah. I got it. Yeah, he's taking 30." The conversation pinged back and forth this way for a few minutes with regularity. "Yup, I'm snuggled right up behind him now. Yeah, he won't suspect a thing. Uh-huh. Yeah, I got it."

After one last pause, the driver nodded his head in agreement.

"Understood. I'll check in when he gets there. Yeah, I'll send a message. Absolutely. Bye."

He hung up the phone and, with an annoyed look on his face, tossed it onto the empty seat next to him, never once taking his eyes off Charlie's car.

It's nice to have a job, he thought, *especially one that takes care of me as much as this one does, but I fucking can't stand* that *guy.*

He knew he didn't have much to complain about; he was a glorified errand boy, a go-fer, only every once in a while did he have to do more extended jobs like this one, and they took care of his whole life. His house, phone, a pretty decent salaried wage – he wanted for nothing. And that's more than most people with his past could say.

It was a family job, one might say. His father had done it before him and, as he grew up, he had taken it for granted. Like a lot of guys growing up in Knappa, he hadn't really put much planning into his future, always assuming he'd end up working at either the mill or in the woods logging, he didn't really push himself to excel in school so he would have other options. So, when regulations were passed that put quite a strain on those trades, he was, like so many, left without a lot of options.

Eventually, his father had passed away – they had become estranged sometime before that, to the driver's regret – and by that point, he had fallen down the only path really left for him to make money: drugs. Over time, the floor grew very thin and, from a careless mistake, he'd found himself locked up for what should have been a fairly lengthy stint.

That was when Mr. Wilkes had shown up. When an alternate route, one beyond his normal desperate reach, had presented itself. One that couldn't be turned down.

Several years had passed since then and the driver had rather enjoyed his time steering clear of the law, being able to breathe what he perceived to be fresh air as he lived a life he had defined as comfortable.

But sometimes he wished Mr. Wilkes would just call him himself instead of having his assistant call him.

Mr. Booth, the driver scoffed, *what a fucking a-hole.*

That had been, for most of his experience, how his directions had been given: second hand via Mr. Booth so as to disassociate any connection. Today was no different.

Everything is in motion now, he'd been told. Of course, he hadn't revealed the whole plan. The driver was never given the whole plan and he was fine with that. As long as they kept taking care of him, he would keep doing whatever they needed him to, regardless. He wasn't about to throw away his easy life.

It seemed a pretty easy job anyway. He just had to follow this kid to his new place and await further directions. And the kid seemed an oblivious type – a boy, really, who wouldn't ask any questions. Someone who didn't have much fight in him. *He's a city boy, after all,* the driver had said. That's what he'd taken from his instruction, anyway. *Not tough.*

Whatever is was Mr. Wilkes wanted him for, it wasn't anything to the driver. He was another mortgage payment, another month of groceries, another reason to stay out of jail. Charlie was another opportunity for he, the driver, to stay above the sinking sand that so many of his friends had fallen into.

He did wonder at who the kid was though. He'd *never* seen people kicking up such a fuss at the manor before, everyone whispering to one another, fearful of any secrets spilling out. It was quite a circus.

Stay focused, he told himself. The blandness of the open road was getting the better of him.

All that mattered now was that he had a job to do and he would do it well, no matter what. He had never let Mr. Wilkes down before and he wasn't about to start now.

Smiling underneath his sunglasses, the fresh air pouring in through the window, he thought: *Alright, Charlie-boy, let's see where this all leads to.*

TWO

The first half of Charlie's drive was uneventful. He had pushed his way up the straight, carved-out I-5 corridor, which took him all the way to the city of Longview, where he had stopped off for some gas and a quick bite. He considered calling his mom, then decided to give it some more time. It had only been an hour, after all. He needed to start training her to not expect him to be there all the time.

After fifteen more minutes, he finished a bag of chips and a cup of coffee and hopped back in his car. He drove west from there, over into Oregon and then North along the winding mountain roads to Astoria.

What a beautiful place, Charlie thought as the tires turned, pulling him closer and closer to the pass.

Charlie rolled down his windows and blasted his music, breathing in the cool breeze of the fresh summer air.

He couldn't remember ever feeling so free.

The pass drew him in closer to his destination, all the while the sun waned in the sky above. He'd left much later than intended. And up in the coastal mountains here, the sun disappeared more quickly than he was used to. Much earlier than he expected, the shadows of night began to creep their way in through and around the trees, enveloping the edges of the highway ahead of him.

Then, without warning, a single raindrop fell from the sky and landed on the windshield. Before he had even had a chance to look up, another drop struck, several inches from the first. And then another.

Huh, Charlie looked out through his windshield at the darkening sky. He hadn't expected rain. It was mid-August – he hadn't even bothered checking the weather report.

A pang of worry shot through him, involuntarily as always, but it settled back down with an immediacy that left him appreciating the calmness of the scene. But it was present just long enough to tug and pull at whatever threads had been sewn and left behind during the attacks of panic in the attic earlier.

A deep drum of thunder echoed off in the distance, catching Charlie's attention. Then, as if someone had merely flipped a switch, the sky seemed to split in two, letting lose all the moisture that had been building behind its protective canopy. Rain like Charlie had never seen before came pounding as if they had been orchestrated bombardments.

"Holy shit," he said to the silence that was accompanying him through the onslaught, his jaw stuck open, showcasing his astonishment. In the wake of surprise, Charlie flipped on the wipers, settled his shoulders, and made to grab the wheel with both hands. There was a lot of water gathering on the surface of the road and, given all the dangers and stories he'd heard about this highway – not to mention the way his father had went – he wasn't about to take any chances with hydroplaning.

Growing up in Portland, August was always a dry month with little to no rain, so this weather came as a big surprise. He'd always spent most of his time during this month with his nose in a book or a writing journal, doing everything he could to steer clear of both his father and the searing hot sun: a combined feat that was very difficult to accomplish.

His thoughts were interrupted by a sudden flash of lightning.

"Holy—Where did that come from?" Charlie was unaware that he was talking to himself. Even the silence had disappeared, lost somewhere on the other side of the rain beating against the hood and top of his car. He watched another branch of lightning burst and split in two before firing across the sky in different directions.

Charlie's back arched forward, his shoulders cocking, and palms readjusting to assume a better grip of the wheel. An uneasiness crept over him. It grew, attempting to occupy whatever space it could in the front of the car. Charlie turned on his wipers to their fullest capacity and ducked his head to see through what was turning out to be quite a large storm. Not used to driving in these conditions, he focused on the road.

Over time, tension built up in his body and mind. Some of it was irrational, he knew, but a good amount was real, tangible pressure. The strain of the day was wearing down on him. It was just a hard rain coming down after all, but given the morning he'd had, the residual echo of his prior panic was not too far off.

For the next hour, the rain was relentless and the strain he had felt had transformed to stress. He should have arrived at his new place by now, but he'd had to slow down to navigate the turns. Charlie was not used to the curvy and blind highway corners that wound their way through the edges and scars of the country hillsides. The longer he drove, the more he was canopied by a mix of shadows and darkness. With the rain, the sun seemed as if it had given up on the day, that it was even considering not coming back out tomorrow either.

His shoulders were shaking and he was showing signs of soreness, both mentally and physically, but still Charlie drove on with as much care as he could. He had to. But he couldn't wait to finally sleep that night.

Frustrated with his lost time, Charlie kicked himself for not leaving earlier. His mother would be worried that he hadn't called already, but he couldn't call her now either. He wouldn't trust his divided attention.

Initially, he intended to drive to his new school for one more quick look before the weekend, but he decided to drive on past it and head straight for his new home; they'd be waiting for him and he wanted to make a good impression. This was causing him quite a bit of stress as well, as he didn't enjoy meeting new people. He was never sure what to say. He was never sure if he could trust them anyway, especially if they were nice right off the bat. *How can people do that?* He always wondered. It normally took Charlie a long time to warm up to things.

The next few weeks were, in certain ways, going to be very difficult for him. He knew that. But that was a part of his purpose here. He would push himself. He would grow. He would, with intention, allow himself the discomfort of what the *newness* brought with it. He would learn to trust people. He needed to.

He arrived at the house a full ninety minutes later than he'd expected. It wasn't quite night yet, and the rain had let up a bit, but the shadowed blanket of the storm lingered still. Charlie peeled his fingers back from the steering wheel, flinching at the rip of the horrible sticky plastic letting go of its grip on him. There were indentation marks on the faux leather where his own grips had been.

Charlie looked up to find the rain still coming down like mortar shells, just a little bit farther apart than before, with each drop exploding upon collision with the ground below.

There's so much water, Charlie thought. Everything was soaked. Charlie imagined everything to be shivering: the houses, the trees, the grass, even the fire hydrant on the corner. He couldn't remember ever seeing so much rain at once before, even after growing up in Portland.

Leaning back from the steering wheel, he stretched his arms outward and pushed his neck up. His shoulders were sore and achy, his lower back tight. His mind, too, was strained from the worry that had been a constant companion with him all day long, most concentrated now on the impression he needed to make momentarily.

Shit. He breathed out and let himself relax as much as he could. He especially disliked talking to people when he was tired or felt stretched thin – mentally or physically. And right now, he was both.

Come on Charlie, you can do this, he said to himself. Maybe some positivity could tip the scales.

Then he changed his tone to be one of dictation rather than a weak plea. *These feelings are completely irrational, Charlie. You're just tired. Just sit for a minute or two and let everything go blank.* He tried to visualize his way through the situation. *I see all the strain and pressure flowing out of me like a river. It's passing and leaving behind peace and calm. The rain is coming down over me, carrying it all away.*

A few moments later, Charlie sensed a *real* weight lift from his shoulders.

Much better.

Looking up at the house again, – an old Victorian, tall and impending in the storm-ridden-out moonlight – Charlie held tight to the hope that was his new life. There were still massive parts of him that felt what he was doing was wrong. Little streaming thoughts and accompanying shifts in his gut were going off, minute warning signs that danger lie ahead. Charlie ignored them and tried to reassure himself again of how often he would feel unsure until he settled in – and who knew how long that was going to take.

Here goes nothing, he told himself, pushing away all those stirring fears and uncertainties. *Lean into the discomfort, Charlie. This is the only way to grow.*

Rain continued to pummel everything in sight. For a moment, Charlie wondered if he should wait for it to slow down or if he should just go for it. Who knew how long that would take? In the end, Charlie decided to just go. It was good practice for him to learn to operate contrary to how he was feeling.

Charlie gathered the few belongings he would need for the night: his suitcase with extra clothes and toiletries, his backpack with his writing journals, the books he was currently reading (*Colorless Tsukuru Tazaki and his Years of Pilgrimage* by Haruki Murakami and a tattered old copy of *Hamlet* — he was hoping to teach it to his honors students in the fall, so he was rereading it to focus his excitement and sketch out a rough plan for their discussions). Everything else could wait until morning.

Charlie readied the car door to open so he could make a run for it. Again realizing there would never be a perfect time to go, he figured he just needed to make the plunge.

Shit, he thought to himself as his nerves were getting the better of him. He had taken several deep breaths when he finally thought, *okay, here goes nothing.*

With that, Charlie shoved open the door and jumped. His foot slammed down into a puddle as he made his way through the elements, the door slamming shut behind him, one step closer to his new life. He had forgotten to lock it, he realized too late, but he figured no one in their right mind would stalk around in that type of rain looking for old cars to break into.

What Charlie had failed to notice as he sat parked for close to twenty minutes gathering his thoughts and as he sprinted his way through the rain was the faded-yellow Chevy truck that had passed by him after he'd stopped. It had driven down the street past several houses until the driver pulled into one of the driveways as if he lived there. The truck sat there idling for a moment before the key was turned over and the engine killed.

The driver could see everything he needed to through his rear-view mirror, and he watched as Charlie's silhouette had gathered its thoughts as well as the few objects needed, all by the sound of the pouring rain.

After several minutes passed, he finally watched the driver's side door open and saw Charlie dash off through the streaming deluge, scampering his way up to the front door of an old Victorian house.

He continued to watch as Charlie rang the doorbell and waited. He saw the front door open and two more people emerge into the light.

The trio of people – Charlie, the man, and his wife – paraded their way through a very cordial scene of smiles and handshakes, Charlie looking very rigid all the while. Then, he watched as Charlie picked up his bag and disappeared into the house behind his hosts.

In the aphotic shadows of that stormy night, the driver stretched and gave a wry but tired smile. Picking up his phone, he clicked on the number he'd called earlier and sent a text: *he's home.*

Without waiting for a response, he tossed the phone back onto the passenger seat and stretched his arm across the top of the seats. He leaned back and prepared himself for what would most likely turn out to be a very long night. In his discomfort, he reminded himself as he always did on these less favorable jobs of the life he had been gifted. Trying to keep a positive frame, he spent some time focusing on what he had been saved from. A smile stretched itself across his face, but not one of arrogance or conceit; it was a smile brought on by appreciation, of gratitude and thankfulness. For such was his response no matter how long he dwelled on what his life could have been. This, he found, was the best way to cultivate contentment.

Charlie's mother, all the while, lay in bed, tossing and twisting, plagued by dreams and memories of a past she was sure she'd outrun. In her mind, she saw Charlie driving through the coastal mountain pass with trees lining both sides of the highway, his car careening around each turn as he pressed forward. Then, out of nowhere, the road itself began to rip apart and the trees began to fade. Everything except Charlie and the car burst into millions of tiny shards of clustered matter and disappeared beyond her vision. With nothing there to hold it up, Charlie's car began to fall through the empty vastness with nothing to catch him. She watched as, with great speed, he grew smaller and smaller until there was no longer any trace of him. And he was gone.

It had been years since she'd experienced a dream so vividly, or fear for that matter. Somehow, she had been so taken by exhaustion, she hadn't even had the chance to consider staying up for Charlie's call. Why would she have? It was ridiculous to think she'd have gone to bed so early.

But there she was, her body writhing, just on the other side of consciousness. Every once in a while, she would call out Charlie's name, but she would not wake from her restless sleep.

All the while, the reach of the crimson glow from underneath her bed grew longer, stretching itself out beyond its veil of shadow.

THREE

Through a stone corridor deep underground, a faint candlelight flickered with the wind that crept in from the top of the stairs. A man walked at a brisk pace despite his age, wearing a stiff woolen suit. His ghost-white hair stood wild atop his head and cast a haunting silhouette upon the walls of slate, his expression equally pale. Devilish.

Up ahead of him sat a single room in which several voices could be heard in a clear, heated discussion. At periodic intervals, their discourse was punctuated by terrible pleading screams.

The man walking down the stone corridor showed no sign of concern for these wailings. His fortitude was shown by the determination in his steps, one in front of the other, on toward the chamber filled with echoing screams.

We're almost there, he thought. *So close!*

His abrupt and seemingly unexpected entrance to the chamber took everyone by surprise. Clearly, he rarely ventured there.

But their attention was stolen back at once by the man strapped to the gurney as he, shaking with terror, gave way to an inhuman howl. This morphed, lowering at first into several stifled and feeble yelps and then settling into a sort of a gurgle – the noises one would expect to hear from a hunted animal, run through with arrows, on the verge of giving up its life altogether. At these few moments of choking torment, everyone turned their attention back to the dying man whose whole body went rigid with convulsions. He would have flopped himself onto the floor if it weren't for the straps holding him down. At once, he gave one last wrenching choke, one last grasp for breath, when the shaking gave an abrupt stop, and he expelled his last breath.

A stale and distant stillness settled over the whole scene.

Everyone looked from the dead man back to the man with the ghost-white hair, whose un-assurance no one ever saw. He made sure of that.

"Mr. Wilkes?" Said the man closest to the door, stumbling backward a pace.

"How are things progressing, Mr. Booth?"

"Um... well, we're moving forward, sir... ma...making progress, but... you see?"

"The same issue?"

The man bowed in agreement. "Yes, sir. The same as before, but—"

"But, with the key *found*?" Mr. Wilkes asserted himself harshly onto all of his men, an adept way of hiding his own worries. "We believe this issue will be corrected?" These weren't actually questions.

"Yes, sir. But there's no way—"

"And *he* will survive? Our man? Not that it really matters, as long as we accomplish our mission."

Nobody came forth to venture an answer.

After several long seconds, Mr. Wilkes asked, "Mr. Booth?"

"Theoretically, sir? Yes. If our theory is correct."

It was Mr. Wilkes' turn to make everyone wait. "Very good. I wanted to come check on things myself. We're too close to make any mistakes now."

"Very well, sir."

All the other men nodded in subservience, the mere presence of the head of their order being enough to keep the air from their lungs.

The white-haired Mr. Wilkes looked back to Mr. Booth and asked, "Is our person in the field on it?"

Mr. Booth didn't hesitate in response to this question.

"Yes, sir. I just had a message from him some thirty minutes ago. I wanted to complete this test before bringing it to you— I was just about to come... up to see you."

Mr. Wilkes stared him down, considering something. "What did he say?"

"He was just pulling through Knappa when he texted. He's followed Charlie in the whole way. Charlie should be at his new place of residence any minute. Then we'll get confirmation."

Mr. Wilkes took this in. His expressions were unreadable. "Very good, Mr. Booth. In the future, regarding this delicate operation, bring me any and all messages right away."

The man lapped in submission. "Of course, Sir. Right away every time."

Mr. Wilkes looked back down at the body and, without looking up, said, "Put this one with the rest. Make sure no one ever finds it."

"Very well, Sir."

With no other acknowledgement, Mr. Wilkes turned and trudged out of the room, back into the shadows of the sparsely lit corridor, leaving his men behind to dispose of the body and allowing himself to feel the anxiety and the weight of this much needed victory.

So close, he told himself once more. Even though they were so close to triumph, still the insipid whispers of the other sects of The Order chirped within him. If he didn't continuously admonish himself forward, the weight of their relentless discouragement would win out. And he, more than anyone else in his sect of The Order, needed to stay focused and keep moving forward.

"Well, here it is, son," said Paul, Charlie's new landlord, as he walked Charlie down the stairs into the basement with his wife, Beverly, in tow.

They reached the final step and Paul fanned them out into the basement as if to take it all in. He flipped on the fluorescent lights, which buzzed, straining to keep themselves on. Charlie winced. There wasn't much to the space: a bed, a chair, some empty shelving for books or whatever someone might put out for show. Everything was worn: the walls, the ceiling, the carpet. Everything. It looked like someone had just been painted over the unwashed grimy walls which would crack and peel open again at any moment. A strong musk hung throughout the room: a stale scent, as if the room had been sealed off for far too long.

Charlie looked around, taking it all in. It would be nice to have his own place. Well, a new place, at least. But the condition of everything seemed to be siding with the parts of Charlie that were telling him this was all a very bad idea. Maybe he was just tired.

You'll feel different in the morning, he told himself, trying to place whatever positive frame he could on things. He was determined to make this work. *It has to.*

"It's great, sir. Thank you." Charlie smiled and reached out his hand enthusiastically to Paul. This was not something he would normally initiate, and it went against everything in him, but he wanted to appear engaging and courageous.

Paul clapped his hand into Charlies with a piercing sting. "Oh, there's no *sirs* around here, please. It's Paul," the man smiled. "And this here's Bets."

Charlie smiled, telling him he understood but also covering up the quick flush of embarrassment that had washed in.

"Well, it's all yours," Paul said. "We've got your check for first and last month's rent. We're not too worried about the deposit to tell the truth. We know it's not normal, but you come recommended from Silas — oh, sorry — Principal Moore, out there at the school, so that's good enough for us." Paul gestured in the direction of Knappa with his thumb.

Charlie was struck again in disbelief at the thought of his *new* job and *new* place. He hadn't even planned for any of this, it just *happened.* Like it *found* him.

Paul took a moment to point out the various aspects of the room, as if it would take more than a glance to notice them. It was a thoughtful but unnecessary gesture and tour. Charlie didn't really mind, though his exhaustion was growing in the tension of social interaction.

"You've got your sleeping area there, your kitchen space with mini fridge there, your private bathroom." He gestured to each amenity as he mentioned them and paused when he was done, as if even he was shocked by how little time it took. "And the rest, well, feel free to do with what you want."

"Thanks again, sir—Excuse me. *Paul.*"

All three of them let out a laugh, though Charlie wondered if his own laugh sounded as stretched and as false as it felt.

"Other than that, make yourself at home. And… oh, yeah," Paul walked over to a door adjacent to Charlie's bed. It opened to a stone staircase that led up into the side yard. "This here is your own *personal* entrance." Paul was very proud he could offer this. "You can use the front door if you want. Actually, we wouldn't mind the company, but we understand people like their privacy, so feel free to come and go as you please."

At the prospect of consistently having to put up a façade, Charlie cringed. But the thought of the side entrance brought him a welcomed relief. He would have to strike a balance there, he knew it. But he didn't want to think about that now.

"Wow, again. This is great," Charlie said, hoping his enthusiasm sounded sincere. He was excited, really, but didn't want to have to explain how he felt to them. "I don't know how to thank you."

"Well, you come highly recommended for your job and seem like an upstanding boy, so, you just be you and we'll be us, and we'll call 'er good. What do you say?" Paul smiled and patted Charlie's shoulder. "Welcome aboard, Charlie West." He laughed. "Welcome aboard."

"It's good to be aboard," Charlie smiled, and found that he meant it. It was good to be taking steps toward something new.

"Well, we'll leave you to get settled then. You don't have too much with you?"

"Oh, I didn't want to carry it all in the rain."

"I won't hold that against you. Better get used to it around here." Paul indicated the storm outside. "Go months without seeing the sun, don't we Bets?"

His wife gave a subservient smile and nodded in agreement; her porcelain facade didn't budge a millimeter.

Charlie took this in. "We'll see if I'm really up to what Astoria throws at me." He winced. It was probably just the tiredness, but something pulled at him like an undertow pulls at the sand beneath your toes. His smile faltered just for a second before it was restored to whatever he figured would meet Paul and Betty's expectations. Neither of them noticed.

Paul looked him up and down. "You look of strong stuff," he said to Charlie. "A real survivor, huh?" He then gave Charlie a wink. It was an attempt at humor, Charlie supposed, but its only effect was to leave Charlie feeling slightly less sure that he had before, which was already considerably low.

Charlie could feel his shoulders turning inward and all of a sudden he had to strain to take deeper breaths. *Oh, shit. Come on, Charlie. Just another minute.*

Paul and Betty were still looking proudly around the room, starved for conversation.

Charlie stayed silent. Maybe he could wait them out and then they'd leave.

In the silence, he tried to talk himself through what the rest of the night would look like. *Okay, Charlie. Any minute, they'll leave and you can unpack. Call mom. Read a bit. Then sleep.* The thought of sleep itself brought a sense of calm.

"Well, shall we leave him be, Bets?"

"Yeah, let's give him some room to breathe, hon." These were the only words she had spoken the entire time.

They said their goodnights respectively, and Paul and Bets made their slow way up the stairs back to the main floor where they settled back onto their living room chairs. Charlie could hear the TV going.

After the basement door closed, Charlie took in a deep breath, holding it in as long as he could before exhaling. He was ready to pass out from the exhausting day.

Picking up his suitcase, he carried it over and set it on the end of the bed, then he pulled out his phone to check the time. Seven-thirty. *Shit.* He knew his mom would be really worried.

I should have called her in Longview. But then he was struck by another thought. If she was worried, she would have called him by now. Why hadn't she? She always called when she was worried. It didn't add up, and Charlie couldn't even entertain the idea that she *wasn't* worried.

He lifted his phone pulled up the recent calls list – it was the only number on the list. It rang. Without even noticing, Charlie held his breath and slowly closed off the path of oxygen to his brain.

It rang another dozen times but still wasn't going to voicemail.

What the hell? Charlie thought. *Where is she?*

Another wave of worry slowly crept over Charlie's shoulders, adding to the hefty weight he was already carrying. Little pinpricks were working their way up the sides of his arms and legs, along the soft, tender tissue that never saw the sun.

His throat went dry. Tension pulsed through him, and his vision began to blur.

Charlie shook his head, trying to brush it all away. He hoped he would be able to stave off what had already come twice that day, so he called her again.

The phone rang and rang, but she still didn't pick up.

Breathing was becoming more difficult by the second.

Come on, Mom, he thought and called her again. *Answer.*

There was nothing.

It was so unlike her, he thought, as panic began to creep further into him. All he needed to know was that she was okay.

Those little voices echoed back through his mind, confirming he'd made the wrong decision in moving.

Shit, he thought, as his whole body was starting to feel gripped, that feeling of being half submerged.

Whatever logic was left in him told him to focus on what he could do in the moment, but he couldn't think of anything. And there was no one else to call. They didn't know anyone.

He imagined something clenching down on his lungs as waves of irrational thoughts swept in through this breach of insecurity.

I should have stayed behind with her; I should have just substitute taught; I should have kept working my part-time job stacking shelves; it would have been better – better for her, better for me – I'm not ready for this! His insides yelled. *I'm not ready for this!*

The world was starting to spin too fast again, and it felt enormous as these thoughts twirled. There wasn't just weight on his shoulders, it was everywhere. His whole body was weighed down and compressed into the ground.

Completely involuntarily, his fingertips began to tap, again, against the ends of his thumbs, four times each – always – before moving onto the next one.

His bed was so inviting, but he knew he wouldn't be able to sleep. Not now. Besides, he still hadn't unpacked or gotten anything ready.

Focusing on trying to get a hold of his mom, another rare lucid thought managed to sneak its way in.

Send her a text.

It was a small and simple idea but it was enough. It worked. It had tipped the scales and somehow had allowed Charlie's body to relax a bit, as if the whole room had somehow been filled with a calming breeze. And, like a warm, inviting blanket, it wrapped itself around him.

Breathing in more deeply then – it was much less of a challenge now – Charlie exhaled slowly, with careful intention, and a string of concrete thoughts came.

I'll send her a text to call me, that way I've done my part; she can call me as soon as she can and I can just wait until I hear from her. I can rest.

Suddenly, Charlie's mind went blank, and he opened his eyes to a new, refreshing atmosphere that he wasn't sure was real or just in his mind. He could think clearly again.

As quickly as he could, Charlie typed out a message to her and pressed send, feeling that whatever remained of the crippling, anxious fog was gone.

All that was left was a thin layer of cold sweat, something he was used to.

He slid his phone back into his pocket, walked to his suitcase, and, without thinking, began meandering through his nightly routine.

Routines had always brought a semblance of calm, even if they were contrived, to Charlie's life. They created consistency, and that consistency always brought peace.

Over the next twenty minutes, Charlie's mind waxed back and forth. He was a car parked in neutral, not going anywhere, but the keys were in the ignition. He stood there in between sleep and wakefulness thinking of as little as possible; it was not mindless though, it was mind*ful*, an intentional stillness — another strategy he'd picked up along the way toward healing. It was part of the rhythm at the end of each day, to reset and cultivate peace before drifting off to sleep. That's where he'd found the real power in his struggles with anxiety.

On autopilot, Charlie brushed his teeth and took his melatonin. He washed his face and set out the clothes he would wear the next day. He tidied up what little mess he'd already made. *A tidy room builds a tidy mind*, he had learned. And he believed it too.

He picked up the photo of he and his mother, the one he'd grabbed from the attic that morning, and he placed in on his nightstand, leaning up against the lamp. He looked at it a long time before turning, thinking that it brought a nice closure to the day.

He would use memories of hope to seed the future he wanted to build.

Then, once Charlie felt good and ready, he grabbed his book and crawled into bed.

Laying back, his head resting on his pillow, Charlie wondered at what the next day would bring. That clichéd 'first day of the rest of his life.' Hope flickered amid the shadows that this day had brought. Still, something in him told him not to trust this hope. He couldn't explain it. Only time would tell which would win out, and he could feel himself getting sucked into the mental debate when he shook his head to clear his mind so he could fall asleep.

Charlie worked hard his whole adult life championing for the hope he'd felt, always pushing for reasons to keep moving forward. Still, the discouraging voices weren't ever very far off to combat him – *it won't be worth it. You might as well give up now. They'll never accept you* – but still he fought on.

He found himself hoping tomorrow would be instrumental in proving those voices wrong, but he didn't dare say anything out loud for fear it would be carried away in the stormy winds. He barely felt comfortable even thinking it.

He had to think about tomorrow in the purest and most logical way possible. Take the emotion out of it.

He would walk into town, grab a cup of coffee, a quick breakfast, and then he would let the sidewalks take him. He would drift with their currents with no agenda. He would check out shops and see what happened. Later in the evening, he would drive out to Knappa and check out his new school, just for a look around. He hadn't been there since his tour when he'd signed his contract. Then he would have dinner at one of the local restaurants. One of the *only* restaurants out there, The Logger — the crown jewel of the town, so Charlie had been told in his interview.

He couldn't help but get excited, but he still didn't want to put too much pressure on it. This was only his first weekend in town, after all. All he wanted to do was get to know his new surroundings.

Charlie glanced over at his phone, his stomach lurching slightly at the thought that his mother still hadn't called him back.

It's only been a few minutes, he told himself, trying to stay within the realm of calm that he had worked so hard to create.

Those same chirping thoughts formed at the edge of his mind, there to disrupt, to invade. He couldn't feel them, but he knew they were there.

He thought about calling his mom again. *Relax, Charlie. She's fine,* he told himself. And, shaking any thoughts from his mind, he turned his attention from his phone to his book. He always lost himself to a story before bed; it was one of the many rituals he'd developed over the year to create calm. That way, when Charlie turned over to sleep, he could leave his thoughts behind next to him within a closed book.

For the next thirty minutes, he meandered his way through Tsukuru Tazaki's journey for wholeness. He loved the story so far. Murakami had a way of transporting whatever it was Charlie was feeling right onto the page.

But no matter how much he read, his mother was never far from his thoughts. It stretched him into differing directions and stole from his rest

Eventually, exhaustion did win out and, even though she never called or texted him back, Charlie slid off into a restless sleep.

FOUR

The next morning, the sun rose steadily in the sky. Its gentle arc cast a soft and inviting light down that coaxed the world awake from its restful slumber. Though it did not fall upon everyone – Charlie's mother was still in bed, much later than was normal for her routine. She was an early riser, but whatever had gripped her had kept her from true rest, and she was unable to fight off the drowsiness which had taken hold.

She twitched and let out periodic moans. At one point, she quickly rolled over and grasped for the nearest pillow, pulling it to her and holding on to it tightly. Her brow furrowed as consciousness expanded within her, letting in whatever thoughts she'd worked so hard the night before to hold back. Thoughts of Charlie, of him driving toward his new life and what she assumed he'd find there. Abrasive thoughts flooded her mind: thoughts of her dreams, of her own past, thoughts of Charlie's father, and even of Charlie himself – images of a looming darkness spreading itself around him.

She let out a frail whimper and tucked herself more tightly into her pillow, looking for any comfort she could find.

She couldn't keep the thoughts from coming. There didn't seem to be any way to turn them off.

Something sharpened within her mind – a hyper-awareness of sorts, a piece of her subconscious operating well above the lucidness of her sleepy mind – as if to monitor the very movements of her thoughts.

This is different, her unconscious-self thought. *Something is different, almost as if some sort of presence...*

It stopped.

It was as if something had infiltrated the room, or her even. Nothing physical, mind you, but something tangible, nonetheless. It flowed and weaved its way through every fleeting feeling that coursed through her, tugging and pulling at whatever seams were holding her together.

Her phone buzzed on the nightstand and she, though still half asleep and barely conscious, shuddered at the alarming sound.

Charlie! Something in her sounded off, triggering in her a reminder that she'd been asleep, that she'd missed his call.

A wave of guilt poured over her, washing away any remnant of peace or rest she had attained.

Charlie's mother clung tighter to the pillow and buried herself deeper into her sheets and comforter. She wanted nothing more than to disappear entirely.

What kind of a mother was she, after all? Something deep within her asked. She had let her child go ill-prepared, and then wasn't even there for him when she said she would be.

Something pressed deeply into these thoughts, these insecurities, and pulled on them.

She pushed even harder against them, trying to will them away from her, leaving her only more entrenched into the trap of avoidance. The last thing she wanted to do anymore was to get out of bed or to pick up the phone.

She needed rest, though. That's what that quiet voice within her whispered to her, anyway.

And so she laid there in bed, crippled by the rising sense of her own inadequacy. Periodically, her phone would vibrate upon the smooth rosewood surface of her nightstand, still indicating that she had missed a call from Charlie. Several calls, actually. For Charlie had called three times the night before, left a text message, and called her twice more this morning after he had woken up. But in her weariness, consciousness just couldn't quite find her. To her, those sounds were merely an annoyance, a distant tapping from within her dreams, a mirage that faded as soon as she would move to grasp at it with any certainty.

She would wake eventually, though, and she would have to face these looming thoughts. But for now, she was exhausted and in deep need of rest. That's what her mind was telling her, anyway. Everything was moving too fast for her to keep up with. So, until that time when she was ready to face it, she would simply try to sleep; she would try to fight away those plaguing thoughts that she'd done wrong by her son.

After showering and getting out of his room, Charlie was able to push his worries aside. He had awoken to see that his mother had still not called or left messages of any kind. Breaking into swift hyper-ventilations was a tough way to start out any day, let alone the first day in what was supposed to be a new season of life. Charlie had followed his steps. He'd done his breathing exercises. He'd reframed his negative thoughts. And he had come up with a dozen perfectly good, rational explanations for why his mother hadn't called yet. *She is fine,* he'd told himself.

She'll call you as soon as she can. Now go live your life, Charlie!

The rest of his day had been filled with wonderful distractions and nuance. The rains had left early that morning, before he woke up, and had showed no sign of returning until much later in the evening. With the clear blue skies came the bright shining rays of the sun and its warm embrace. Still, Charlie had to work hard in order to accept it.

Sunshine in small coastal communities like Astoria always brings out the best in people. It is energy and excitement personified. When it's sunny, people are always easier going and more willing to let things go. Charlie pushed himself to slide right into this excitement and made every attempt, at times with great intention, to allow it to carry him through from one experience to the next. And he tried to keep his worries as far away as possible.

His worry for his mother had never really left, having been planted deeply into the far recesses of his mind.

He had breakfast at a bizarre and wonderful cafe, The Columbian, named after the prominent river Astoria was built on.

He window-shopped around on every street, his eye catching itself on several oddities in the uncharacteristically high number of antique stores downtown held.

He had never seen so many ships steering wheels or nautical clocks in his entire life.

All day, he strolled up and down the river walk, gently being pulled and pushed around by the varying ocean breezes pouring in from all directions of the compass.

To Charlie, the day was happening in slow motion, which was not a bad thing. He loved it. There were moments he had to work for that feeling and work hard. He still had a big problem trusting what he wasn't well acquainted with, which was most everything. But nonetheless, work he did, to embrace it and revel in the freedom of it.

Throughout the day, his mind slowly bent itself back and forth around the idea of what was comfortable. The subtleties of both peace and hope ebbed and flowed around him. He often prayed that one day they would stay for good.

He found two local bookstores too, as eclectic and colorful as the community itself. This did the most for his comfort and allowed him to relax and let down a bit more, even though the workers at both stores were a bit distant and less helpful than he was used to compared to growing up in Portland. He could look past that.

Down the road from where he'd had breakfast, he was even more blown away to find an arcade and comic bookstore. It was filled with nostalgia, bursting with everything developing nerds could ever hope for and populated by people of all ages. He couldn't believe a town this small could field a store like this. There were children, teenagers and adults all playing, reading, and laughing. There was a purity to it.

This clinched it for Charlie. He told himself several times, as if to drive it home, that he was going to like it here.

Some parents looked as if their kids had dragged them in and kept nagging to leave. Likewise, there were kids who looked as if their parents had dragged them in, and they were giving *their* parents that two-minute warning stare. It was great. Charlie spent most of the mid-morning browsing there, through the games, graphic novels, movie memorabilia and posters and toys. They had everything.

Charlie was definitely going to come back.

He'd had lunch at a place recommended to him by all of the locals: The Bowpicker. It was an old fishing boat that sat in a gravel parking lot a block off the river, held up by props and had no indoor seating. Charlie couldn't believe it when he'd heard about it but, upon seeing it, couldn't get the image out of his mind, especially when he saw the line that was two city blocks long. And it went fast. Apparently, the owner was friends with one of the local fishermen who brought in a fresh catch of halibut every morning and the owner of the Bowpicker would pick it up from the docks. Each day, they would fry it up in the boat on land until it was gone. Some days they'd close at noon if that's when they ran out. Other days they'd be open until four or five o'clock. Charlie had lucked out that day and was glad because it was incredible.

The list of places Charlie was going to come back to again kept growing all day long.

After lunch, the rest of Charlie's day was similar to the hours that had preceded it: meandering and aimless wandering.

As the sun sank down in the sky, Charlie checked his phone more and more.

Several times, he contemplated calling his mom and that swirl of guilt would start to spin in his stomach again. But he hadn't justified it yet. *We both need to learn to live apart,* he told himself. *She'll call when she's ready.* Besides, he was just starting to have so much fun. He felt free and he didn't want to think about anything that would undermine that, so he did his best to push it from his mind.

When the sun began to disappear behind the hillsides and the storm clouds rolled in off of a strong ocean breeze, Charlie thought it time to head out toward the school building and then to dinner at The Logger. Then he would get the full *experience* of the community he would be teaching in, which filled him with both excitement and dread.

FIVE

A multitude of colors both warm and serene draped down over the tree line as the faded-yellow truck maintained its close pursuit from Charlie's burgundy Honda, just a few cars back. They were just outside Astoria on the highway headed towards Knappa, and the truck looked tired and haggard. Even though it was later in the evening, he had the disheveled look of just waking up with day-and-a-half-old stubble. This was to be expected, given that he'd slept in the truck. It was all part of the job, though.

He was letting his mind meander wherever it pleased when his phone buzzed. Reaching down, he picked it up.

"Hello. Yeah. Uh-huh. Yeah, he hasn't left my sight all day. Yes, sir. Where is he heading now? From what I overheard, to the school and then The Logger. But I'm on him. Yes. Yeah, I aim to make contact tonight. Yes. Of course. Tell Mr. Wilkes I'll be in touch. Yes."

He ended the call, tossing the phone back onto the seat next to his and taking the wheel with both hands. He was tired but filled with a quiet purpose.

His attention returned to the road when Charlie's car sped just ahead of him – there were two cars in between – as they dropped down one final hill and they climbed their way back up the other side of the last ravine before they came to the first signs of the actual town. Before then, the entire road had been blankets of forests and random

59

gravel driveways, seemingly leading nowhere (at least that's what Charlie thought).

Mist began to sprinkle its way down in little barrages on the windshield and clouds started their slow crawl over the mountains. Knappa, being higher elevated and further inland than Astoria, often catches the clouds of an east wind first.

Charlie blew right past the turn to school.

Must be skipping it for the night, the driver assumed, because The Logger was now in sight, just up on the left.

The clouds were growing in visibility, turning a morose and languid brackish monochrome. A peel of thunder rolled itself across the skyline.

Then, as if a key had been turned to unlock a door, the sky opened and rain cascaded down onto the unsuspecting terrain below.

The driver continued his pursuit as what had previously been a peaceful afternoon was quickly transformed by the shifting winds of an unexpected storm.

As the rain pressed itself down in its full oppressive force, Charlie pulled his car into the first parking spot he could find. It was the one furthest from the door.

Popular place, he thought, his teeth grinding as he turned over the ignition. With nerves firing, he thought of dozens of reasons to simply turn around and go home. But, after several deep breaths, he cracked his car door, pulled his jacket over his head to block the rain and kicked the door shut behind him before running toward the front of the restaurant.

He made it in good time but was still drenched by the time he'd made it inside and the door was shut behind him.

He was shaking the water off his head when he made his grand entrance into the bar, too frazzled to notice all the conversations quieting so everyone could size up the newcomer — the *outsider*. One look around The Logger and it was easy to see that Charlie didn't belong here.

Everyone went back to their conversations as he looked up and walked to the bar. He didn't see how far removed he was from the norm here, but he felt it. He sat down at the bar and waited to order a drink.

When the faded-yellow truck pulled up, Charlie was just walking through the entrance of the restaurant, soaked.

The driver pulled through the full parking lot and around back to a series of spots only the locals knew about – right next to the side door. He parked, killed the engine, and took a look at himself in the mirror.

"Alright," he said, thinking about how easy the job had been so far, "let's go make us a new friend."

Charlie took off his jacket and draped it on the vacant stool next to him, dry side up, and settled down at the bar. He was shaking a bit but not from cold. The phrase 'a deer in headlights' didn't quite capture it; he was more like a scared rabbit standing before the entire blazing enormity of the sun.

Once seated, Charlie looked around the bar to gather himself. He noticed several people staring at him, and everyone he made eye contact with turned away from him quickly to continue their previous conversations or drink like nothing had happened. Each of these broken connections made Charlie feel further and further from home. It wasn't until after this that he thought he felt cold.

He tried to signal the bartender but had no luck with that either.

Shit, he thought to himself. *I shouldn't have come here.* Worry was creeping itself in, taking what ground it had always seemed so entitled to. Charlie felt stupid, there was no way around it. And just when things were starting to point in the right direction. He didn't belong here.

He noticed each person in the bar seemed to be wearing one of three variations of a uniform. Not a real uniform, like for work. They all dressed the same.

The men all wore boot cut jeans, but they *actually* wore boots. Steel-toed and stained with all sorts of substances: glue, paint, oily residues. They wore t-shirts that were either earthy shades or fluorescent with logos Charlie couldn't remember ever seeing before. And every one of them had on a mesh trucker hat. Like the boots though, as opposed to people you would see in Portland, these guys were actually truckers. And they wore them forwards, not backwards.

Charlie had never seen more eagles or American flags in his life, or camouflage for that matter. None of this was bad, he knew, it was just *different*. Even though he was incredibly uncomfortable, Charlie did like that it was *different*. He wanted that to become comfortable.

Right about the same time this was crossing his mind, he noticed several more looks from around the bar. He looked down at his untucked button up shirt, his skinny corduroys, and his navy converse. He wasn't sure if *different* liked him.

The temperature in the room went up a degree or two, and sweat built itself up in his palms, armpits, and around his neck.

He saw the bartender walking by again and tried to signal her once more, but she just kept walking off to help someone else. Someone she knew.

In its own way, Astoria had felt very similar to Portland to him. Certain streets he'd walked down that day gave the impression he was walking down Hawthorne Blvd. or Belmont St. or anywhere else on the east side. Out here, though, this was a whole different world to Charlie, and he was going to have to get used to that.

The women were different too. He was used to girls wearing designer jeans and mountains of make-up, trying to impress wherever they went.

Charlie wasn't sure what to make of the contrast before him.

Like most of the men, they wore hoodies and trucker hats too, but with long hair streaming out of the back. There was less of a separation between men and women. Charlie figured a good number of the women here could have beat the shit out of any guy he knew back in Portland.

Just as he noticed an entire new group of people staring at him, somebody came up and interrupted his thoughts.

"What'll you have?"

"Huh?" Charlie looked up startled. It was the bartender, a woman dressed in jeans, boots, and a collared cowgirl shirt. He stared at her, unaware of what else to do.

"To drink?" Her eyebrows raised indicating her feelings to the situation clearly.

"Oh... ah—"

"Two 3-Ways, Tam," came a voice from behind Charlie.

Charlie swung around, lost and confused.

"Huh?"

A man stared down at him, smiling. "It's a local IPA brewed here in Astoria. They have better stuff – the brewery, I mean – but the local pubs and bars have to stock up on what tourists and travelers might want. It's the curse of a tourist town. You'll have to go to the Fort George and see for yourself. Got some good stuff there."

Charlie was taken aback, a blank stare plastered to his face, founded upon a look that said he didn't trust what was happening.

"The Brewery? Fort George? They made the IPA I just ordered..." The man smiled again. "Can I buy you one? You look like you're not from around here. I wouldn't want to not show you our small-town hospitality."

This interaction garnered quite a commotion. Even more people were looking over at him than before. He didn't like this, not one bit. His first thought was that he wished the man would just go away, that he would stop causing whatever commotion Charlie found himself at the center of, and that maybe he would just disappear altogether. He then noticed the man was just staring at him with his own confused look on his face.

Damnit, Charlie thought, with worry moving through him faster now than before.

"Uh... sure. Yeah... um, sorry." Charlie shook his head and looked away to stave off a bout of shame. After a second, he looked up. "That would be great, thanks."

Tam was relieved when the moment was finally over and disappeared down the bar to get their beers.

"Anytime. I'm Trent, by the way." Trent held out his hand in greeting.

"Charlie," Charlie said. "Charlie West." He reached his hand out as well and shook Trent's, self-conscious the entire time of how sweaty his hand was. "And thank you again for the beer. Sorry for not answering... it's... it's been a long day."

Tam placed two beers in front of them and Charlie noticed they weren't on coasters. Without a word, she walked away.

"You'll get used to Tam," Trent smiled. "She's not much of a talker. And no worries at all," Trent smiled again and held up his beer. "Rough day, huh?"

"Oh, ah, not really. Well... it's been a pretty good day, actually. I just moved to town — Astoria, I mean... last night... and I did a bit of exploring today." Charlie was worried he was rambling, but he didn't stop. "Thought I'd come out here for a drink, you know, see..." he pantomimed to the area around them, cursing his awkward social habits.

"You don't say." Trent took another drink of his beer. "Well, in that case, welcome." He handed Charlie his beer, holding his own up for Charlie to cheers.

Nervously, Charlie grabbed his and held it up, creating a small moment of symmetry between the two.

Their glasses chinked together and they both took a drink.

"Thanks," Charlie fumbled his beer, spilling some but managing to recover with his dignity intact.

"So, why here?" Trent asked.

"Huh?" Charlie gave a worried, concerned look, like he'd done something wrong. He hated meeting new people; he never knew how to react.

Holding his beer up, Trent motioned around the bar. "Plenty of drinking holes in Astoria much nicer than this place," he whispered.

Charlie did his best to act like he wasn't caught off guard.

"Why come here, you know? Twenty minutes out of your way?" Trent asked again.

"Oh, uh... well, I just got a job teaching out here—"

"You're the new English teacher?" Trent shouted out, bringing attention back to them as several more sets of eyes narrowed in.

Charlie lowered his glass. A hint of pride swelled up in him. "Uh, yeah. I am. How'd you know?"

"Small town," said Trent.

"Oh, right. It's my first *real* job out of school, so I'm... uh... really excited to be out here." He hoped his expression matched what he was trying to convey, feeling more panicked than excited. Then, after looking around the bar, he added, "A bit nervous, though."

Trent didn't skip a beat in encouraging him. "Oh, that's normal. Everyone feels nervous for a new job, no matter what it is. I did when I first started mine, and I just cut trees down for a living. But that is pretty dangerous – I can't imagine you losing an arm on your first day because you didn't fasten something in tight enough."

Charlie relaxed a bit, but not completely. He did feel more reassured though.

"So, you're a *logger* then?" Charlie asked. The word felt strange coming out of his mouth, like a misstep.

"Yeah. A regular Paul Bunyan." Trent gave a laugh.

"A who?"

"Who? Paul Bunyan? And the blue ox? You've never heard–" Seeing Charlie's blank look, Trent gave up. "Never mind."

They each looked around and took a sip of beer. It was quiet until Trent finally said, "So, English, huh? I was never much into books. Well... school in general, I guess."

"Oh, yeah? I've always loved literature, um, I mean reading." Charlie felt his confidence making subtle steps forward as they were coming to a topic he was interested in. "It's always been an escape for me. My way of understanding people. Learning about them, you know? Who they are, what they do, why they do it."

Trent took a sip of his beer and just looked at Charlie.

"Sorry. I kinda nerded out there. I..."

"You know you say sorry too much."

"Sorry—"

Trent smiled at this before replying, "The woods."

"The woods?"

"Yeah," Trent said. "The woods are my books, my escape." He stopped. It was now his turn to get lost in his own thoughts. "I guess that's where I've always gone to get away, for the most part."

Charlie was fairly certain that a connection was being made between them, but he didn't want to overthink it. He had trouble reading certain people in real life, and the lack of trust he had made him unable to discern whether or not Trent was just being nice to him or if he genuinely liked talking with him.

"I love the outdoors too," Charlie said. Then, pointing out the nearest window, he continued, "I can't wait to get out there, hike around, explore this place, its vast... the... it's just so..."

Charlie found himself embarrassed again but, to his amazement, Trent showed no sign that Charlie was being weird or strange. He just kept drinking his beer, smiling.

"I'm sorry for..." Charlie's chin dropped. "I just get... excited."

Trent put his beer down. "Charlie, you never have to apologize for getting excited about something. I know exactly what you mean."

"Really?" Charlie looked up.

"Yeah. One thing I've learned, you can never drop your head at something that raises it. At least, that's something someone use to say to me. There's too much in this world that tears it down. I don't think I've ever thought about it too much, but now when I do, when things don't make much sense or if I'm pissed or down, I always go to the woods. I get away from it all."

"Yeah."

"Yeah. I've never really been into reading much, but I can see what you mean, how they'd be the same."

"Yeah..." Charlie made to say something else but found that he didn't have anything else to say. He was more caught off guard by what was happening. Here he was, in a bar, having a drink with someone he didn't know, and even though his internal red flags were going off, he was fine. He was alright. He was pleased with that at least.

This is the exact situation I need to practice getting used to. He thought about his hope to overcome those social anxieties and learn to trust people, especially really nice people who wanted to buy him a beer and welcome him to town.

"You're a good one, Charlie West. Maybe you'll be able to show these kids some things."

Something in Charlie lit up. He didn't show it, of course. He was trying to show as little of himself as possible. But his mind had registered the comment as sincere; there was no reason to think otherwise. Besides, that's exactly who he was hoping to become, someone who would make an impact and better the community around him.

With a mild case of embarrassment, Charlie responded with a, "Wow, thanks. I really appreciate it."

"Yeah. You seem like you care a lot. I sure wish I woulda had a teacher like that."

Charlie let his smile widen a bit more and took another drink from his beer.

Sitting there was starting to feel a little easier for Charlie. It was like breathing with a little less strain.

All of a sudden, Trent slammed his beer down on the bar, and his eyes grew wide and wild. "Say," he straight at Charlie, almost into him, "you're new here. I know the place really well. Why don't I show you around a little bit?"

Charlie choked on a gulp of beer. Flattery and appreciation were two of the emotions swirling around him, along with worry, panic, and terror at spending more concentrated time with someone he didn't know very well. After all, he'd just met this guy. He wasn't used to anyone being so nice to him, let alone someone he'd only known for ten minutes.

Trent must have sensed his caution because he added, "Look, I could take you up into the mountains, see the logging roads, Brownsmead, the hunting fields, creeks. You know, show you the *real* Knappa. Oh, and the jetty! You have to see the jetty! Even though it ain't Knappa."

"Uh…" Charlie didn't know what to say. It had come at him too fast and he was still stuck trying to catch up with the moment.

"Come on. It'll be great. When all those new students come at'cha, trying to push you to see if you got it? You'll be able to tell 'em all about their favorite spots. It'll catch 'em the hell off guard!"

He does make a convincing point, Charlie thought.

All the alarms in him were blaring, *No! Stop! Don't trust this person!* But Charlie worked to push it aside. He needed to start trusting people, and what better time than now? So, he ignored all the voices within himself.

"Yeah. Yeah, that would be great, Trent." Charlie's hand was shaking a little. "That would be amazing!" He was pushing himself to become comfortable with the idea. "You would do that?"

"Sure as shit!" Trent tipped back his beer and drank all that was left in it. "Charlie West, I'll show you some genuine small-town American hospitality!"

Charlie's nerves were firing. Following suit with Trent's gesture, he tipped back his beer as well to chug the rest. Though it was a bit fuller than Trent's, so he struggled a bit. The alcohol worked to keep his embarrassment to a minimum.

And besides, Charlie was making friends. This was new territory for him and with it, just a spark, a glimmer of the future he'd hoped for was starting to appear.

"That'd be great!" Charlie said again.

"It's settled then. Let's get another round," Trent yelled out, banging his empty glass onto the bar top. "For Charlie, the new kid in town with a big future!"

Buzzes settled onto each man, accompanied by contented smiles as they both sat, eager for their next drink.

"Tam! Another round!" Trent yelled.

Tam shook her head and rolled her eyes but walked over nonetheless, grabbed two glasses, filled them up, and set them down in front of Trent and Charlie.

"Cheers, boys."

"Cheers," they said, clinking their glasses together and taking large gulps that would only add to the reverie and weightlessness of the moment.

Charlie felt the slightest tinge of a barrier breaking; something within him, something he'd kept sturdy and fortified all his life. For the shortest of seconds, he wondered if he might be able to live a life with that wall down.

Trent roared and handed Charlie his new beer.

After an hour of drinking, when there were four empty glasses in front of both men, a woman entered the bar. Charlie was too far gone by the night's jovial happenings to have noticed her, but neither did anyone else as she came in. She walked with the learned habit of not being seen, her head down, making no eye contact with anyone, and disappeared as she cut through the scene, making straight for a seat in the back corner. She tucked herself in, completely concealed.

There was an intentional distance in her movements, in the way she walked and carried herself, allowing for her to keep whatever was around her at arm's length, protective in nature.

For a span of twenty minutes, she watched Trent and Charlie's every move, nursing a whiskey double, straight. She watched as Trent taught Charlie the finer points of Jim Beam, as well as other famous names from behind the bar. They drank and laughed, but this mysterious woman seemed grateful to be on the outside.

From time to time, she would look around the bar, take in a deep, well-timed breath, sip her whiskey, and, for the briefest of moments, let the projected security of her exterior falter, just enough to feel herself again.

Before setting her glass back down, she would breathe in deeply once more, then look around the bar to make sure nobody had seen into her world, the one she kept only for herself.

Finish this, she thought. *Finish this and then they might finally let you be free.*

She set her glass back down, her hand still wrapped tightly around it, and kept watching Charlie and Trent. She knew she would have to wait for the perfect moment before making her move.

Maybe it was the alcohol, but Charlie couldn't remember ever feeling so free. He'd drank before, but there was something different about this night, like a grip had been loosened. Trent had also been introducing him to all sorts of people, several of who were parents of his future students.

They were especially eager to meet Charlie and ask him questions about where Charlie had come from and how he'd ended up out here. They thought he was being modest at saying there wasn't much to tell.

The evening was filled with laughter and noise and fun and a lot of drinking.

A person whose name Charlie couldn't remember was in the middle of telling a story, and he excused himself to use the restroom. Standing up from his stool, he let go of the bar with his hand and immediately put it back down to catch his balance. He'd almost fallen over. It took a few moments, but when his vision settled, Charlie gave a slight chuckle and made his way to the toilet.

Plumes of rowdy yelling mixed with laughter continued to rise from the various circles around the bar as he walked toward the hallway where the bathrooms were located.

As Charlie disappeared into the hallway, the woman watching him gave a startled jolt, hands slamming down flat onto the tabletop, sending an echo over the noise. Nobody noticed it. Upon realizing Charlie had left his jacket behind, signaling that he wasn't leaving, she relaxed her arms and settled back into her booth. Both of her hands moved to engulf her whiskey, almost in slow motion.

Charlie found each urinal occupied, and he was a little put off. There were only two of them.

His mind swirled within his confines of his head, as if seeking a way to break free. He was as light and as weightless as a boat on the sea. At least, that's what Charlie assumed the sea would feel like; he'd never actually been out on it. His body teetered there, waiting, seemingly at odds with the idea of standing.

He turned toward the stalls. They were each full too.

"Shit," he whispered to himself and resigned to wait, but he reached out and placed a hand upon the wall for good measure.

Still Charlie waited, contemplating how embarrassing it would be pee himself. Just then a stall door opened up behind him and he jumped at the chance to relieve himself, awkwardly bumping into the man who was walking out. He stared at Charlie, who paid him absolutely no notice whatsoever. He just fumbled into the stall and, without even locking the door behind him, began to undo his zipper.

But then, *something* caught Charlie's eye.

Aaagghhh! He thought to himself while biting his lip. The last thing he wanted to do was attract attention in here. Wincing, he placed his focus back on what had caught his attention.

Carved into the wooden paneling, right above the toilet in front of him, was an image he'd seen only once before. It took him a moment to place it, but when he did his stomach rolled, churning over itself. He felt as if it had landed upside down and was now tugging some invisible strings around his rib cage.

The necklaces from the photo? he wondered. *But... how is it... here too?* He realized he was too drunk to really be considering this too much, but he was sure. The carving in the wall was an exact copy of the medallions he'd seen in the photo in his attic. Probably life-sized, he assumed.

He felt a less-than-gentle breeze slide across his neck, which was impossible because he was indoors. He had the strangest feeling that someone was watching him.

Charlie... he thought he heard someone whisper to him.

"What the—" he spun around only to realize he was still in the bathroom stall and he still hadn't peed.

Come, Charlie... come home...

"What?" he said. But there was nobody there, expect for the people in the stalls next to him. He couldn't imagine anyone in there trying to mess with him like this.

His attention was drawn back to the symbol on the wall. That strange circular top, with its smooth cutting lines hanging down below. What could they be? He wondered.

They're almost like tentacles, he thought.

He wondered why this symbol would mean anything to him.

Why was in my attic? And here too?

Charlie had no connections to the area that he was aware of, and intoxication didn't do well for the speed of synapses. A slight twinge was beginning to expand in the front of his mind. A headache was coming on.

The image called back to him and brought Charlie's thoughts back to the men from the photo in his attic. Their lifeless expressions and fine tailored clothing. The one who looked like his *father*. He must have been an ancestor of Charlie's, someone he'd never heard of.

Maybe there is a connection to me out here, he wondered.

For the shortest of seconds, he considered that life had brought him out here to connect him to his past. Some grand picture of events coming full circle. He could see where he came from and clear the fog of who he really was.

An image of his father passed before him again and Charlie shuddered.

As it passed, he decided that this *fog* might not be worth stirring up.

Waves of prickling discomfort rolled through him from hair to heels. His organs within him seemed to be expanding but at differing intervals, each controlled by some force outside his own. His temperature went up, too.

Shit, Charlie thought, *not now!*

He tried to force the thought of his father from his mind, but it only made him focus on him more.

God damnit! He pushed back. *No!*

But the slow turning of his mind had already begun.

Oh, Charlie. Come on. You can do this.

He looked up and saw the carving in the wall. It was as if it were staring back at him. The spinning picked up speed.

Shit!

He still had to pee, but he couldn't focus. The stall was closing in on him.

Oh, no, no, no, no!

He flipped around, locked the stall door and fell back onto the toilet seat, desperately trying for whatever deep breathes he could.

The room spun faster, the ceiling moving in opposite direction of the walls. He hadn't felt it so far tonight, but often when Charlie drank, he began to feel quite angry, and he was starting to feel angry now. And with it came the creeping panic, building and mounting itself for an attack. It moved, slithered up his legs and past the waist, to his shoulders and then onto his mind. There it swelled. It hadn't even been a minute and Charlie felt he was about to burst. Clenching his fists, Charlie flexed his whole body to fight against the rising emotion. There was *something* rising in him, *something* he'd never felt before. He wasn't used to it, and it was trying to get unlocked.

Just when he felt the whole world would burst around him, Charlie slammed his hands, palms outward, against the walls of the stall and screamed out, "*Stop!*"

All the noise that had filled the space, the levers and clicks, and the faucets and the sniffs, all quieted. All was still. The only thing that could be heard was Charlie's heavy breathing. The rest was silent.

His mind, too, had come to an abrupt halt, left only to consider the reality of whatever social normalcy he'd just destroyed.

"Uh?" came a voice from the stall next to him. "You a'ight in there, buddy?"

Shit, Charlie thought. He realized what he'd just done, what attention he'd just brought to himself. "Ugh... yeah..." He brought his hands back in from the walls and began rubbing them nervously together. "I... ugh... was... I'm... On the phone?" His inflection was strained by how much he was trying to control it. He couldn't let this get any more out of hand. He waited for the response, but none came.

One toilet flushed. Then another. Charlie heard a door open and footsteps make their way to the sink where the faucet was turning on. He heard the paper towel dispenser being used, then another flush.

He would just wait them out. Once everyone who'd been in there had gone, he would be able to leave.

Charlie let out a long exhale, realizing how long he'd been holding his breath, but it brought him no relief. It finally struck him that he still hadn't gone pee. He stood up and turned around only to find the carved image still there, taunting him.

73

In the middle of relieving himself, Charlie's pocket shook and startled him. He was getting a phone call.

Shit, he thought.

Still peeing, he reached into his pocket and pulled out his phone. It was his mother.

"Shit!" he said, out loud this time. *Now she calls!* Charlie felt his anger flare again.

He couldn't talk to her. Not right then, anyway. And besides, in his drunken state, he didn't *want* to talk to her. She'd left him hanging for hours, almost a whole day.

Pulsing sensations began to fire through his brain, from back to front, right down the sides above his temples.

He felt really angry towards her, to a level that surprised even him. It was probably just the alcohol – at least, that's what he would tell himself later as he pleaded with himself to understand his own actions.

There was nothing rational about how he felt though. It was his mother. *On one hand,* he thought, *I should just pick it up, check in and tell her I'm out with friends and that I'll call her in the morning. She could tell me quickly why it had taken her so long to call.* This thought caused his anger to pulse. Then he told himself, *but how could she have done this to me? Does she not know how worried I've been? This is supposed to be about me moving on. This is my weekend! Did she need to take it and make it all about her?*

In the end, he decided upon not picking it up because he was too worried about what he would say or do to her because of how he felt. There was at least some sense of reasoning in that.

The phone just buzzed and buzzed, and Charlie held it out before himself, her name illuminating the screen every time it vibrated, accompanied by her photo.

You should have just picked up when you were supposed to, mom, was the last thought that cross Charlie's mind before the phone gave up its indicating rumble and the photo of Charlie's mother faded to darkness.

The bathroom resumed its normal clamor and the rising fury in him finally began to subside. Where before he could not think clearly, Charlie was starting to realize what had just happened and a dull, warm blanket of guilt seemed to envelop him, wrapping him up tightly to constrict all other thoughts or feelings from being present.

The echoes of everything he'd felt before evaporated, and now he was left with the realization of how worried she must be.

Oh, fuck me, he thought, holding his phone out to himself. The screen was dark. They had missed each other again, but this time it was by choice. Charlie's choice.

His first impulse was to call her back, but he still wasn't in a state to do so.

He sat for several minutes, unsure of what to do. Back and forth he went. *Call her. Don't call her. Call her. Do—*

He didn't want to deal with this right now. All Charlie wanted was to go back out there and live his new life, which was surprising in and of itself.

Before long, Charlie realized how long he'd been in the bathroom and a tinge of panic flashed in him again, leaving him warm and clammy.

What could he do? He couldn't call her now. He had to get back. *She would understand,* he forced himself to say. *After all, she'd waited that long to call him back. It's not like it was his fault.*

Suddenly, he was startled by a knock on the stall.

"Hey, buddy! Come on! They're people waiting out here!"

Charlie jumped, thoroughly embarrassed now. He was sure he'd be known as the guy who panicked and took up too much time in the bathroom now.

"Sorry," he said.

He hurried out of the stall as fast as he could, doing his best to make no eye contact with anyone. He washed his hands and then stumbled his way into the hallway and toward the bar.

He was zigzagging through people when he bumped into someone. To his relief, it was Trent.

"Woah, shit, Charlie. You okay? You were gone a long time."

Charlie stood stunned and shot a quick glance up at Trent, unsure how to explain what just happened. "Yeah. I... uh... my... uh... mom just called.

"Oh, nice. Just checking in on you?"

All the worry in Charlie drained out. He was a bit shocked.

"Uh, yeah. We haven't been able to connect yet. Bad timing, you know?"

Trent looked at him with something close to sympathy.

"That's cool, Charlie. It's nice having people who care."

This left Charlie feeling both thankful and ashamed.

"Yeah," he said.

"Well, my turn to hit the head. I got another drink waiting for you over there."

"Thanks," Charlie said. But, before he'd finished, Trent had lumbered off toward the bathroom.

Charlie made his way back to the bar where a new, nice, cold beer sat waiting for him. He sipped it and tried slowing everything back down again. He could hear all the noise and conversations in the whole room, the shifting stools and chairs, the loud music, all of it. As he waited for Trent to get back, he was working to force it toward the back of his mind when he was started by something even more unexpected. A woman's voice had crept up out of nowhere and disrupted his transition back into calm.

"Can I buy you a drink?" The voice said.

Charlie shot up, dumbfounded.

"Huh?" he said, feeling far too distant to the moment.

The woman's voice echoed, a confused but understanding smile on her face, "A drink?"

"Um... uh... yeah... sure." Charlie tried to shake the look of confusion off his face, as if things like *this* happened all the time.

"You already have a beer," she said, "so how about something with a bit more of a kick. You're new in town, right?"

Charlie, still gripped in a state of shock, was unable to get a read on the woman, not that he had enough time to react to it anyway. Normally, as a person who had grown up with the necessity of being an empath, he could tell what people's intentions really were, or if they were hiding something. In this instance, he failed to notice the lack of anything emanating from her, meaning she was either feeling very little at the moment or was working to suppress what was there. It was a skill that had come in very handy over the years.

But with her standing there over him and Charlie still recovering from what had happened in the bathroom, he was lost.

Instead, he just said, "Okay."

"Two Pendleton's, Tam. Neat," she said.

Charlie marveled at the assurance of which she spoke, the strength she projected.

Charlie's initial estimation was that she knew what she wanted and she knew how to get it. So he saw exactly what she wanted him to see.

Just then, Trent walked back up to the bar.

You could have crossed the Columbia River walking across all the tension between Trent and this newcomer.

"Ellie Stone," said Trent through a frown. "How nice to see you."

"Hi there, Trent." She looked away as she said his name.

Charlie had been looking at Trent when he spoke, so he missed the quick look of uncertainty flash across her face, the grinding of her jaw before she was able to contrive her own smile to match his.

Trent just smiled back at her, as if to stake his claim as the new kid's best friend.

Charlie sat between them on his stool, for some reason feeling as if he'd been the one doing something wrong.

At last, Tam returned, invading their silence, setting two whiskeys down in front of Charlie. She walked away without so much as saying a word, acting as if this whole episode was normal.

Ellie wondered if Charlie could feel that Trent's return had shaken her, not that it would matter. Men normally went for whatever she threw at them.

She was frustrated with herself. She had seen Trent talking to someone else by the bathroom and assumed he would have been away from Charlie for longer, giving her time, a few minutes at least, to sit with him and introduce herself.

"I just bought him a drink to welcome him to town, Trent," Ellie broke first.

"Well," Trent forced a smile. "Why don't you join us then, El?"

She was recovering from Trent's untimely return.

"Oh, I wouldn't want to interrupt *man-time*," she laughed.

Charlie looked away from both of them, shifting awkwardly on his stool.

Ellie cocked her head to the side and gave Trent an even bigger smile, dripping with sarcasm. Then, looking intently back to Charlie, she said, "Welcome to town, Charlie West. It's nice to see a new face around here."

Charlie smiled as Trent growing sterner by the second.

Before leaving, Ellie looked back to Trent and said "And don't call me El, Trent. Ever."

With a quick flicker of a smile, she picked up her drink, made a sharp turn and disappeared through the sea of people in the bar with the same collected strength she had carried upon entering the bar.

Her departure was final.

Charlie got the sense that not many people got the better of her. He had seen exactly what she wanted him to. He also had the sense that she and Trent knew each other from before and that this wasn't the time to bring it up.

All that he really cared about was that the tension was dissipating.

"Sorry for that, Charlie-boy. Now, where were we?" Trent paused for effect. "Oh yeah." He held up his beer and looked down at Charlie's whiskey. "I gotta play catch up now." And, with that, he tipped back the beer and drained it in fewer gulps than Charlie had thought was possible. Once the drink was gone, he slammed the glass down on the bar and signaled Tam for another round. There was a wildness in his eyes, the reckless hues of a tragic sunset.

Tam walked over with their new drinks and set them down. Trent held his up and handed the other to Charlie who did the same. "To the future!" He yelled. "And to whatever trouble we can find this weekend!"

Charlie gave a laugh and, though the battle between fear and connection was still waging in him, he raised his glass and yelled, "Cheers!" Both men drank.

Trent motioned to the whiskeys waiting on the bar top and both men picked up their respective shots. Cheering again, they cocked their heads and threw them back. Trent, with a practiced ease, while Charlie, in contrast, did so with the relish of inexperience and one trying to impress.

"Tam! Another round!" Trent shouted, banging his glass down hard on the bar.

People all around the bar were raising glasses and yelling, both with them and for their own accord. The night felt like a true celebration, a true start to something. What it would be, Charlie wasn't sure yet, but he was glad to be making these first strides.

That night, Charlie got more drunk than he'd ever been in his life, while Ellie just sat and watched. She was merely a shadow on the wall, someone who'd left the real world behind, as if she'd simply stepped backward into a painting and then had faded completely from view.

The night slowly itself toward a natural end as everyone drank and then drank some more. And Ellie sat, an echo in the stillness, sipping her whiskey, watching.

Charlie's mother choked back tears when the call went to voicemail and her mind, stretched and thinned by the mounting strain she'd been wearing, went right to the worst places possible.

She assumed he had already forgotten about her as her thoughts, almost being guided by something else, were being kept just beyond her reach.

Or it's them! she thought. *I knew it! They've found him!* He *has found him at last!*

She burst into shaking tears then, torn between the need to pace her worries away or stand frozen by the desire to keep the world from spinning.

It was her fault. Of course, there was no rational evidence for this, but she was not in a rational place to begin with.

That day, when she'd finally woken to find Charlie's many messages, she had allowed each and every one of them to wrap themselves around her, like damp fabric, and add to the crippling weight she already carried.

She hadn't been there for him when she promised she would be. How different was that from the fear of what she'd always been to him, a burden?

Before, Charlie had always been there to talk these thoughts down, to rebuild her, to calm her rising nerves. But he wasn't there. No one was.

She couldn't remember ever feeling so alone.

So, on the stories spun within her mind, adding to the narrative that she was unable to protect her son. And now that he was gone, that he'd gotten out, he would never return to her.

These thoughts came down upon her with a crushing fury and, in whatever limited capacity her brain was functioning, she wondered what she should do.

She wanted to call back, but she figured he wouldn't pick up. He was probably too busy or angry with her anyway.

She hiccupped at this thought, releasing with it a couple of painful, heaving sobs.

Whatever thought did come to her mind always seemed to be directed to the more negative pathways that occupied her and she, alone, was defenseless against the perpetual onslaught.

I suppose Charlie will call me back when he can? She hoped, but that voice within her told her otherwise. Naturally, she allowed it to erode the little hope she clung to.

This in and of itself was not the way she'd hoped the day would go. After waking late and still so exhausted from her disturbed sleep, it had taken her most of the morning to simply get downstairs.

She'd eaten very little and mostly out of habit and she'd drank even less. At least it was water, though. As well, it had taken her most of the afternoon and evening – and most of her energy – to garner enough strength to call Charlie back. An act that before would have been such a simple task. A non-issue for her, rote and habitual. But the lies had proved too strong for her to reason out that Charlie actually wanted to speak with her. He wanted to connect and check in with her, for her sake as much as for his own.

These thoughts were not able to penetrate the subtle changes taking place within her mind, the growing fear that something terrible was going to happen. And she thought it was all her fault.

She struggled to even think her desperate pleas for her son's forgiveness at this point, so affected had she become by whatever strange force was dictating her thoughts. Her inadvertent sobs were breaking her breathing pattern up into a strange and unnatural cadence.

She sat there in the kitchen, needing her son, but *sure* that he didn't need her. These negative thought patterns dug deep into her and took over.

She needed sleep, but a fear whispered into her that if she went upstairs, she would find no rest there. So, instead, she stood where she was, where she had been standing, caught in the steady path of inaction and unsure what to do, unaware, even, of her inability to complete or manage her rampaging thoughts.

SIX

The next morning came on quick for Charlie, and hard. He's never been much of a drinker, so he wasn't expecting the level of hangover that had been waiting for him. His head pounded with a fierce reckoning, warning him that nights like that should be left very few and far between. It was like several miners, unconcerned of their effect on Charlie, were just chipping away at him in search of wakefulness. Besides the constant banging in his head, the morning had also left Charlie feeling very empty and hollow as he searched his memories in an attempt to put the pieces of the previous night back together.

This, of course, was not too different from how Charlie usually felt in the morning: numb. It was just much more pronounced.

Retracing the night in his head, images flashed before him of Trent and of men and women laughing. There were camo coats and hats, and hoodies, and more boots than he was used to seeing. And there were drinks. Many, many drinks. But before wakefulness had really struck him, an image flashed before him of the woman he'd met, just briefly. *Ella, El-, Ellie? Yes, that was it, Ellie.*

An involuntary smile spread across his face as he considered her presence, her strength, the way she'd carried herself. And she was very pretty, he thought.

Then an image of his phone broke through, the scene of himself in the bathroom. His smile vanished. Worry began to ebb its way back up through him, starting in his gut and working its way up to cut off his breathing, affecting both his lungs and throat.

Mom!

He shot up, awake now.

Tangible waves of guilt flooded over him. They peeled and broke, covering him completely with icy thoughts. It was as if the tide was coming in faster than he could get away.

Charlie reached over and grabbed up his phone, tears amassing themselves behind his eyelids as he tried to recount all the reasons he hadn't picked up her call. He'd settled on the fact that he was trashed.

Mom, I'm so sorry, he kept telling himself. It was then he noticed that she'd left a message. This brought the tiniest shard of hope.

He listened to it.

She sounded exhausted, and little pinpricks of worry began to rise in him, though it was a discomfort he was used to. But still, being so far away from her was crippling.

He pressed the icon to call her and put the phone up to his ear, breathing heavily into the device.

It rang and rang, and with each ring the call drew closer and closer to the conclusion Charlie had hoped against but assumed would happen. She wasn't picking up. And with her voicemail not set up, it just continued to ring.

In annoyance, Charlie hung up.

God damnit, mom! Charlie was frustrated, but he wasn't angry with her this time. Still driven, to a degree, by guilt, he was more worried for her.

He tried her again, but to the same effect.

Charlie couldn't, for the life of him, figure out what was going on. *What's she doing?* He assumed the worst. Had something happened? *No, her tone wasn't panicked in her message.*

He considered calling her again but couldn't see the point. It would just frustrate him more.

Quicker than he'd thought of it yesterday, Charlie decided to leave her a text, reminding her, again, to call him back. He would, once more, have to wait for her to reach out to him.

It was strange, though, and left a very unsettled feeling in his stomach and throat.

I need coffee, he thought to himself as he attempted to take a deep breath and stretch away the strain in his muscles. He needed water too, to rehydrate himself and help his body fight off what he'd done to it the night before.

Charlie thought of the day ahead of him and hoped it would be another day like yesterday, minus the amount of alcohol consumed at the end of it. He thought of how free he'd felt for so much of the day. Not the entire day, but it was a start.

I will recreate that again, he told himself. It was a promise.

With that resolved, he clicked the icon on his phone indicating his mother, typed out a quick message to her, and pressed send. Then, flinging the phone across the bed – creating as much physical distance between himself and it as possible – Charlie stood up from the bed and attempted to shake off whatever residual worry there was in him. To anyone else, it would have been an awkward, uncoordinated shimmy.

He took a few quick steps and found himself in the bathroom where he flipped on the light, turned on the shower and stripped himself down so as to get ready for his day.

Today will be good, he told himself. He would see more of the town and Trent would take him around, too. This brought up a whole slew of other emotions that he wasn't quite ready to deal with; he still didn't know this guy very much, but he'd seemed nice enough. He sure bought Charlie enough beer the night before. There was some warning going off within him, as if it was trying to save him from some coming pain. But given all that was swirling around in his head, who knew what the warning was trying to point out? Charlie decided to push it to the side, as he had been doing with all the warnings the past few days.

Charlie often had to remind himself that how he felt didn't always reflect what was real. This, he told himself, was one of those moments. *You're going to learn to trust people, Charlie West. Everything will be okay.* Today is going to be a good day, he told himself.

The driver of the faded-yellow truck, after a horribly short and extremely uncomfortable night's sleep, had already been awake since dawn. After following Charlie around for all of his exploits the day before, and night, he was now waiting less than patiently for Charlie to emerge from his house. His contentment was wearing thin.

By the time Charlie made his first appearance, the driver already felt in need of a long nap. This feeling would last well into the day.

By midafternoon, Charlie hadn't really accomplished much of anything, and time was dragging.

The driver's contentment by this time was all but shriveled. He felt like a glorified babysitter, but he knew better than to say anything. Hell, he knew better than to think it. So, he did his best to push the thoughts from him whenever they came.

Charlie had managed a good meal for himself – at least, it was good in comparison to the driver's snacks that had to suffice as his meals for the day. He was realizing now that he wasn't as prepared for this as he could have been, and he needed to be able to drop everything and leave to follow Charlie, so he couldn't risk waiting in line at a restaurant or store.

Over the course of the next few hours, he followed Charlie step by step as Charlie merely retraced his steps from the day before. This annoyed the driver to no end. It infuriated him. For a man who was already bored to tears, it was torture. But what could he do but follow orders and continue to shadow Charlie as he aimlessly meandered around the town the driver was painfully familiar with?

At two o'clock in the afternoon, Charlie finally stopped by the food carts for lunch. A late lunch by the driver's standards, who had grown even more annoyed, but was thankful for the chance to alleviate his hunger.

Charlie got in the line for falafel while the driver stood two lines over, hoping for some fresh seafood. It was a longer line, but they went fast.

Five minutes went by and Charlie was already getting ready to pick up his food. The driver hadn't even made it through the line yet and was preparing himself to go without.

He watched Charlie grab his food and turn to walk away when he, Charlie, ran right into someone.

"Oh, shit!" said the driver, and not just in reference to the fact that he was going to have to skip dinner.

Charlie had just run into the girl from the night before, Ellie. It wasn't the end of the world, but the driver crossed his fingers that she would keep walking. It would be more difficult following two people and staying unseen.

She and Charlie seemed to be laughing though, reintroducing themselves and brushing off the fact that they'd almost spilled each other's food. Though, from this angle Charlie looked pretty nervous, like a skittish puppy who'd been underfed. The man had been so focused on Charlie, he hadn't noticed *her* walking by.

Come on, he pleaded to himself. *Don't sit together. Don't sit together,* as if he could will it into being.

Ellie was laughing with Charlie, who was sheepishly following behind her. They were walking off together.

"Fuck me," said the driver, out loud and to the chagrin of several people standing near him. He stalked off without even checking the fact that he was now only second in line for food. He raced to catch up to Ellie and Charlie just as they had turned the next corner.

He caught up to them less than a block later, just as they were entering the river walk. They were heading toward the Maritime Museum, a beautiful place to sit and have dinner, though that was the last thing on the driver's mind. He was frustrated, hungry, and extremely disconcerted at the turn of events. With his hands stuffed in his pockets, he followed behind them with all the distance he could manage while keeping them in sight.

They sat on a bench overlooking the water while they ate, and Charlie was just jogging back after putting their plates and utensils in the trash.

"How about a drink?" Ellie asked, trying to catch Charlie before he was able to catch his breath.

"A drink? It's early afternoon," Charlie said.

It was only after the words had come out that Charlie realized how uncool he sounded, and that he was worried about something being cool or not. As well, he was still hung over from the night before and the thought of alcohol made his stomach lurch.

One of her eyebrows raised but her expression was bare, indicating neither amusement nor judgement. It was sturdy, a consistent construction Charlie was beginning to appreciate. He still found himself unable to penetrate whatever exterior she was projecting; he could empathize with a protective layering through his own experience.

"Yeah. It's Sunday evening," she said. "You don't have to work tomorrow, right? I don't have to work tomorrow. What else do we have to do?"

Charlie could feel himself squirming. She was a very pretty girl, but even just sitting down with her just now had been nerve-racking. But she seemed so sure of herself, and he couldn't think of any good reasons why she was wrong.

This is another good opportunity for you to learn to ignore those annoying voices in your head, Charlie.

He wanted to feel comfortable with this so badly. He checked the time. He was supposed to meet Trent at his place at 7:40 that evening, and it was only 3:27 right now.

But now the inkling was sneaking in that she was annoyed by how long he was taking to consider it. She probably didn't want to go with him anymore.

Shit, he thought. He wasn't even remotely in a place to actually consider what she was thinking.

He had no idea that behind her cold exterior, she was waiting for him to stumble into saying *yes,* to fall into going along with her.

Her look was placid and impending.

"Okay," he told her finally.

"Okay," she said, having known the whole time what he would say.

Without another word, Ellie stood up, turned, and walked off in a different direction. Just as her face moved out of sight, she cracked the slightest of smiles, reveling in the knowledge that she knew he would follow.

Charlie sprinted to catch up to her, and when he did, he asked the question that popped into his mind when she'd mentioned work. He was curious. "Where do you work, exactly? What do you do?"

Ellie's eyes broke away from Charlie, falling to where the edge of the path met the grass. After a moment's pause, she said, "A bit of this and a bit of that." She looked back at him afterwards, revealing a flirtatious smile, which caused Charlie to conveniently forget what he had asked moments before. He shriveled under her gaze and said nothing.

There was a certain peace he found in Ellie, a constancy in her affect that he didn't personally identify with. But it was something he yearned for, even though her spontaneity and assurance brought him a great deal of discomfort.

Before, it was something he would have run from. But now, for some reason or another, he was drawn to it, to her and the fact that he couldn't read her or guess what she was going to do or say next.

It was a stark contrast from the overly prescribed lifestyle that had been his life.

They had walked for fifteen minutes before coming to a place Charlie had only driven by on his way into town. He remembered because it had reminded him of Shakespeare. *The Desdemona.*

"I always felt bad for Desdemona," he said as they walked up.

"Who?" Ellie hadn't been listening. At that moment, she had been occupied with watching him, trying to gauge whether or not her lure was working. Her instincts said he was right where she wanted him to be.

"Desdemona. From *Othello*? Shakespeare? It—Never mind."

She pushed open the door and held it open for him to walk through, her flirtatious smile never faltering and Charlie not thinking for a moment that it was false.

Through the fields of firing nerves that was his stomach, Charlie forced a smile onto his own face, attempting to curb how ill-prepared he felt for what he was about to do.

They stepped into the bar and Ellie let the door fall shut behind her.

Damnit! thought the driver as he watched Ellie and Charlie disappear into the bar. If he went inside after them, there was no way he wasn't going to be seen. Plus, he was still hungry, and now he had to pee.

Looking across the street, he saw the Shell station and tried to convince himself he had enough time to run over and use the bathroom before grabbing some food. He could keep an eye on the door of the bar through the windows.

They just walked in, he reassured himself. *Grabbing a drink, I got at least thirty minutes.*

That had settled it, and the bottom of his boots skidded on the concrete as he made his way across the road, leaving behind little traces of dirt.

The interior of the bar didn't do much for Charlie's mood. Shadows seemed to hang from each wall, as if they were tapestries draped down made up of a stew of some of the regulars' past hurts or discarded memories they'd rather leave alone. Everyone who was already inside seemed to ignore the dinginess, probably accustomed to the stale environment. There was something sour about it all. It was more like walking into a gardening shed and picking up the equipment after it's been stored for a whole winter.

Why did Ellie come to a place like this? Charlie wondered.

"How about here?" She asked him, in an innocent tone.

It derailed whatever thought Charlie had been musing about.

"Oh… um..." Charlie looked down, a little confused, before he realized what she was talking about. "Sure." Each step he'd taken into the bar did very little for his comfort.

Ellie sat down without a word. She looked up to see Charlie still standing, staring around the bar.

"You gonna sit down?" She said, smiling at him to make sure he wasn't too scared.

"Uh. Oh, sure," Charlie fumbled. "Uh, sorry." Then he sat down, looking away as he did so, attempting to hide any embarrassment she might notice.

"It's okay," she smiled again. "You know you say sorry too much?"

Charlie didn't know what to make of her expression, and he looked away, the little self-assurance he'd been maintaining to that point was slowly leaking out of him now.

"So I've been told," he said, trying to force a smirk onto his face to push through the shame. Though, unfortunately, it came out more like a grimace. "Sor—"

"See?" She said.

Shit. He flushed again, his cheeks blossoming into a nice rosy sheen.

"I know, I'm so—oh, fuck." he cut himself off, not being one to swear in front of people often. He figured she didn't care though. She probably hadn't even noticed.

Ellie turned to signal the waitresses, ignoring Charlie's perpetual blundering, and satisfied with how hard Charlie was trying – she almost had him exactly where she wanted him.

Charlie, on the other hand was wracking his brain trying to figure out how he could calm himself down, deeply feeling his painful inadequacy and unsure as to how he'd gotten to this point anyway. He closed his eyes and tried to will his nerves to slow.

You are fine, Charlie. Everything is alright. Just breathe. You are safe. Everything is fine, he told himself.

When he opened them again, he found that Ellie was watching, wearing a quiet smirk.

Shit, he thought again.

"Everything alright?" she asked him, smiling. Despite her best effort, this smile was actually real.

God damnit, he thought as he scrambled to think up an excuse, any excuse. But, finding none, he just said, "Yeah. Everything's fine."

Reading his worry, she knew it was time to come in with a little more finesse.

"*Just* fine?" she said, in a lighter, more playful tone. Then, gesturing to their surroundings, she said in a voice full of well-laid sarcasm, "This isn't sending you over the edge with joy?"

She gave him a big reassuring smile and, at last, something broke in Charlie. He was able to let go of whatever had been holding him back and let out a light chuckle.

"I'm just a bit tired, is all," he told her as he looked away. He told himself not to reveal too much but found, for some reason, he couldn't help it. She seemed to be very open with him. "It's just a big adjustment, you know, coming here. I've only ever lived in Portland. My whole life took place in forty square blocks. I never really left it before." He was surprised even by his own transparency, how it slid right through his lips.

Ellie feigned interest with a natural precision.

For a moment, neither of them said a word. Until, at last, Charlie spoke again, "I'm just tired."

The comment did strike a certain chord in Ellie. To her, Charlie was nothing more than a task she needed to accomplish to bring her closer to the life she hoped to live. She looked up at him and could see the exhaustion sitting in him. After all, he had just moved his entire life over here the day before.

As his eyes meandered around the bar, she found herself wondering: what so important about him? What was it he was needed for? He seemed so inconsequential.

When he finally looked up, he found Ellie still staring at him. Out of discomfort, he quickly looked away again before gathering enough courage to meet her eye to eye. Slowly, he raised his head back up to face her, and he noticed something that he hadn't been able to see before. Beyond her strength, beyond that consistent and placid demeanor, he saw, all too clearly, that same wall he had built so high within himself. Those layers of protection, the artifice, to keep the world from inflicting more pain. In that moment, he saw that, like himself, she was protecting something: herself, her *real* self. That was why she came across so stern, why she exuded such strength. Charlie wondered how exhausted she must feel, keeping that up all the time.

Charlie, his concern falling onto Ellie instead of himself, was completely unaware of how his body had relaxed. He was calmer and able to think more clearly.

"How are you?" He found himself asking, proud that it had been him who had initiated something.

Ellie had been lost in thought, thinking about how tired life had made her, and she was caught off guard by his question. People didn't generally concern themselves with her well-being.

She cleared her throat to answer, but luckily for her, the waitress walked up.

Charlie tried to hide his disappointment, but it only worked because Ellie was too busy ordering her drink.

She ordered a whiskey, neat, the same as the night before, and Charlie ordered a beer. Unused to this lifestyle, he also ordered what he'd had the night before.

"I'll be right back with your drinks," the waitress said.

"Thanks," they both echoed.

The next few minutes were filled with a quiet that Charlie found awkward, but Ellie didn't seem to mind. Charlie thought it looked like she was thinking about something.

"I know how you mean, by the way," Ellie said, with an honesty that surprised even her. "About leaving? About looking for something bigger?"

"Oh, yeah?" he said. "What's that?"

She paused for a second, considering whether this was even worth going into, but she figured *what the hell.*

"We always talk of doing *big* things," she said, "don't we? People, in general."

"Yeah?"

"Well, you mentioned the forty city blocks you lived your whole life in."

"Yeah, I guess I did." Charlie was wondering where this was going.

"But you moved on," she said, her tone lined with a hesitant and questioning admiration. Moving on was all she'd ever wanted to do.

"I… I guess I did," he said, still unsure where this was headed.

"I guess, you know, how many of us really move on? How many of us actually *go*?" Ellie's stomach tensed, and silence hung on that last question. Then she continued, "But you, Charlie West?" She pointed at him. "You *went* for it."

Her tone was still more inquisitive than celebratory, like she was feeling out how real it was and not some story or myth made up that would disappear the harder she held onto it.

Charlie found this spotlight to be a little uncomfortable. "Sort of," he said, shaking his head in a way that neither agreed nor disagreed with her assessment of the situation. "But—"

"Shit, Charlie," Ellie laughed, and her hands fell into her lap. "Growing up around here? Everyone talked about getting out, you know? Everyone wanted to leave or *wants* to leave. I remember whole years where that's all anyone ever talked about. But *did anyone*?" Her voice became shaky, almost frail. "Did *I*?"

She regretted the words as soon as they had left her mouth.

Shit, she thought. Here she was, supposed to get close to this guy, lure him around a bit, but now it was she who couldn't shut up.

She pulled back from him immediately and, clearing her throat, she sat up straight and looked toward the bar to check on their drinks.

Charlie stood in awe, sure that for a few moments, he'd seen the wall come down a bit, a few bricks of it at least. But he'd also felt the hastiness of her retraction. This was not a side, he assumed, that she was used to showing people. Charlie counted himself as lucky and wanted to honor the leap she had taken.

"I see what you mean about getting out, but for me, I almost didn't come. I just felt I couldn't pass up the opportunity."

She looked up at him, knowing how little he knew of *his* opportunity.

"Funny thing is," she said to him, "for you, getting *out* was coming here."

"Why's that funny?"

"A bit backwards from where I'm sitting, coming to the place everyone talks of getting out of. But still, you *went*. Most people never do. They just stay stuck."

Ellie was trying to figure out why she couldn't stop sharing. She needed to change the subject, and soon. The drinks couldn't come fast enough. But before she could say anything, Charlie was already responding to her previous comment.

"I know what you mean," he said, "but I think it varies from person to person, you know? On what you've experienced and what you want."

"How so?" She couldn't help but take the bait.

"Coming here," he told her, "this move, for me? It was huge. For me, it was about taking control. About taking steps for myself. I'd never really done that before." As he spoke, a strange comfort came upon him, telling him he was safe, that it was okay to share. "So much of my life up to now has been dictated by other people, you know? Other circumstances. But now, I'm finally in a place where I can do things for *me*. Make decisions that are best for me. I've always been so... so... so *stuck* before."

Ellie's stomach turned over at each of his declaratives about taking control and, against her better judgement, she asked him: "By what?"

Ellie was finding herself intrigued but him and wanting to know more.

Charlie froze, realizing that he wasn't used to sharing this much with others either. Both his temperature and discomfort were slowly rising.

"It's okay, Charlie," Ellie told him, reaching over and placing her hand on his, a struggle forming in her. She knew she needed him to become more comfortable, comfortable enough to trust her and

94

to share. But deep down, she found that she really did want Charlie to feel okay.

"I wrote the book on being stuck," she told Charlie. "Well, I at least plagiarized it really damn well." This last comment was as much for herself as it was for Charlie. She was beginning to feel a little unsure of what was happening inside her.

But it worked and got Charlie to smile, despite his rising reservations.

It's time to trust, he told himself. Then, letting out a deep and slow sigh, he said, "My... my family. In one way or another, I've never really been able to get past it. Them. I can't seem to move forward."

Ellie let out a laugh that Charlie found to be a bit insensitive. He moved his arms slowly, below the table, and crossed them, an elbow in each hand, a sign of protection.

"I'm sorry, Charlie," she pleaded. "I just... I get that," she assured him, the brevity bringing back a bit more control to her nerves. "Fucking family, right?"

"Yeah, but," Charlie tried to break back in, "they also—"

"I often think of where I'd be if I hadn't been born into the lovely shit storm I was blessed with."

Charlie knew the thought all too well, and the pain.

"Some people are born into luxury," she continued, realizing, "into privilege and big houses. Born into... *love*. While others," Ellie looked away from Charlie as she said this, "well, let's just say not everyone is that lucky, are they?"

Charlie nodded in agreement but didn't speak for several moments. Finally, after considering his words very carefully, he said, "That's what moving out here was for me. It was about starting over, building something new."

This comment struck Ellie in a way she found difficult to ignore. For that's all she had ever wanted, to build something new, to flee, to get away.

A sharp pang prickled the back of her mind as she thought about Charlie being here and her role in making sure he would be exactly where *they* needed him to be at whatever time they appointed later.

Another victim of their *plan,* she thought, as a wave of constraining regret flooded through her. There was something about this that wouldn't settle, something she couldn't quite place. She pushed the thoughts aside as to reengage in their conversation, but they wouldn't allow themselves to be removed from her mind. They lingered on the outskirts and waited until she would once again be forced to deal with them.

"That's pretty cool, Charlie," she said, presenting a well-constructed smile to keep him at ease, an ease she no longer felt.

"I guess," Charlie said, in a way that told Ellie he was downplaying her compliment but, truthfully, Charlie couldn't see the merits of his choices. He'd never looked at himself and seen that much strength before.

"I'm serious, Charlie," said Ellie, unable to keep her tone from one of sincere encouragement. "I mean, most people live their whole lives in fear of... of what? I don't know. I haven't done a thing worthwhile in my whole life. I've never... I just... this is *something,* Charlie. You're *here.* You got out—"

She cut herself off again, realizing that she was, once again, letting herself get too carried away.

"Thanks," he told her. He was very appreciative. "And I'm sorry if—"

"You really don't have to keep apologizing, Charlie. You know you—"

"...say sorry too much," he finished.

They both smiled.

Silence fell between them once more, but this time, it was caught between the strain of both of their struggles to read the other.

Something whispered within each of them not to trust what they were feeling; it didn't help neither was used to being understood.

Ellie sat in silence before him, still in shock at how she'd opened up, rationalizing the fact that it had allowed him to open up to her too. He did seem to trust her now, so she was that much closer to accomplishing her task. That's all he was, after all, she reminded herself.

But still she fed into it. "I just know what you mean all too well," she said. "My life has just been... a bit... discouraging, that's all." Upon her admission, she was even more caught off guard that she found herself holding back tears. Turning her head quickly away, she followed it up with, "I get the idea of being stuck."

"I'm so sorry," Charlie told her. He understood it, after all, that frustration and heartache, that pain, even that strength she had to maintain wherever she went.

He knew he didn't come across with the same level of strength that she did, that fierceness or cold assurance, but he knew the mask. And he knew the burden it was to wear.

For several moments, Ellie stared across the bar, still not entirely sure how the conversation had steered toward these waters, and no matter how hard she tried, she couldn't help but let her strength falter. For a fraction of a second, the real her was laid bare. And Charlie looked up and saw it. He saw her and, to him, she was a sculpture. A perfectly rendered image of longing and sadness. To him, it was beautiful and heartbreaking all at once. And all he wanted to do was to be there for that statue, to catch it if it ever fell. He wanted so much to prevent it from shattering if it ever hit the ground.

She turned back and he turned away so as not to be caught staring.

"It's not your fault," she said to him, her tone returning to that of her forceful strength. "Shit happens, right? So, they say."

And then she was gone, concealed once again behind that protective and well-fortified layering.

Charlie let it be for a long time, and then he reached his hand out toward hers. It was instinctual and so unlike him. He didn't even concern himself with whether it was a good idea. Had he been conscious of it, he would have been more surprised by the fact that there were no alarm bells going off in his head, warning him not to take the chance. At the moment, it was simply the most appropriate reaction to what was happening.

She didn't move her hand closer to his, nor did she pull it away. And just as their drinks were arriving, a hand came down, hard, on

Charlie's shoulder, startling him to the point where he jumped up clear out of his chair. "Shit!" he yelled.

Several people looked over at them from around the bar.

It was Trent.

Charlie tried to laugh it off, his nerves were clearly getting the better of him. Amidst his heaving breaths, he said, "Holy shit, Trent. You scared the crap out of me."

"I know. I couldn't help myself."

Trent's whole body was shaking from laughter.

The only person who seemed not to enjoy the interruption was Ellie, especially when Trent finally zeroed in on her and spoke.

"Well, what's wrong, El? I didn't spoil your fun, did I?"

If Charlie thought Ellie had gone inward moments before for the sake of self-preservation, it was nothing compared to how deeply she'd gone into herself when Trent had arrived. Charlie couldn't even sense her at all anymore. All that was left was an icy cold void.

"Hi, Trent." The speed at which her exterior had shifted had caught Charlie so off guard his own stomach turned over as if he'd been the cause of it. This person was galaxies away from the one he'd just been speaking to.

"What brings you two in here?" asked Trent, seemingly unaware of any shift in the atmosphere.

Ellie lifted up her whiskey then drained what was left of it as a show of force.

Trent's eyes widened as he nodded in faux approval, attempting to appear unfazed.

Charlie was wildly uncomfortable sitting between them. He did his best to remove the feelings from himself, but it was like trying to keep yourself from sweating when it was 90 degrees outside plus humidity.

In a somewhat broken and nervous voice, he interjected, "We... um, we just ran into each other today, Trent... and she was just... she's been showing me around town a little." Charlie hoped he was doing a better job than he felt at hiding his discomfort. "Just grabbing a drink now," he added, forcing a chuckle that came out more like a wheeze.

For a few seconds no one spoke, then finally Trent's voice cut through the silence. "That's great," he said.

"What brings you in here, Trent?" asked Ellie. "Did you come here on behalf of—"

"Same as you, El," he cut her off with a quick burst before she could finish. He forced a laugh only Ellie could have known was contrived and added, "Grabbing a drink, huh?"

Their eyes locked onto each other, and the atmosphere around them settled into silence once more.

Now Charlie understood they had to know each other from before, and that must be the reason for this tension. He wasn't even sure he wanted to know the full story. Worry was starting to trickle up his spine, like a little waterfall in reverse.

And he was caught up in the trance of their glares when they were all brought back to reality by the sudden ringing of Charlie's phone echoing off the lacquered wooden tabletop.

They all three looked down at once, but only Charlie jumped when he saw who it was. It was his mother.

A quick surge of panic flashed through his body, leaving him clammy. He was alert. He fumbled for his phone, moving far too quickly, and was embarrassed even by his own reaction, as well as by his rising temperature and heart rate. No one else seemed to notice, but Charlie didn't know that.

"I gotta take this," he said, his words coming out quicker than his fumbling his hands. He bumped into his chair and the next table over as he excused himself and made his way toward the door.

Ellie and Trent broke their locked stares and watched him leave but turned right back to each other once he was gone.

Charlie bumped into several more objects on his way out, including two people. His journey to the door was no more glamorous than the first walk taken by a newborn giraffe.

Once he'd finally made it outside, he hit the *accept* icon on his phone and put it up to his ear.

"Hi, mom?"

After the awkwardness had become even too much for him, Trent made ready to leave. "Well, see ya around, El." He turned to go.

"Can't wait," She yelled back to him.

Without looking back, he held up his middle finger, the clearest gesture of how he really felt.

Before he'd gotten too far away, Ellie yelled out to him again, "I thought you were getting a drink?"

Trent froze. He turned once more to find her sitting there, a smug smirk written across her, telling him that she *knew* something. He didn't trust her at all.

"I ain't thirsty anymore, on account of the company," he said, thinking that was a pretty good end note. Then he turned and stalked off again, disappearing through the front door where Charlie had gone.

Ellie maintained her smile, assuming herself victorious in their verbal bout. Once Trent was gone, she reached for her whiskey but, to her disappointment, it was already gone. Instead, she reached for Charlie's beer, picked it up and tipped it back, draining half. She then signaled to the bartender for another round.

Charlie's mind was racing.

"Mom? Mom? Are you there?"

"Charlie? Are you—" her voice was coming through scratchy and in waves.

"Mom. Mom! I'm so sorry for last night."

"Charlie, where—" She kept cutting out.

"Mom! Mom?"

"Cha—"

But before he could get in another word, she was gone. Disconnected. After all that time trying to get a hold of one another, he'd finally gotten through, and now she was gone again.

Charlie waited a second before saying, "Mom? Mom? Are you there?"

Only silence made itself known, followed soon after by the blank and singular dial tone that indicated the call was over.

Charlie looked down at his phone in disbelief.

"Fuck!" He was definitely feeling frustrated, angry even, but not at her this time, just with the situation. That made him feel a bit better.

"Everything okay, Charlie?"

Charlie jumped at the unexpected presence of Trent standing there.

"Shit, Trent. You scared the hell outta me again."

"Oh, uh… sorry."

Charlie collected himself as best he could and decided being transparent with Trent would be easier than making something up. After all, he was trying to become more comfortable with Trent. He was someone Charlie could trust. "Sorry, I just haven't been able to get a hold of my mom the past few days. Since getting here, really. She hasn't been picking up the phone, or calling me back, or texting, really, either. It's been really weird. And when she does *finally* call, it gets disconnected."

"Ah, damn. Is everything alright?"

"I don't know. Something just feels… *off*, you know?"

A note of urgency flashed past Trent's eyes, too quick for Charlie to notice, and he replied, "Yeah. Change can bring about all sorts of weird between people, can't it?"

Charlie looked up at him. "I suppose you're right. I'm just really worried about her."

Saying this out loud, Charlie thought that he didn't really *miss* her. It brought about the same turmoil as before within him about whether or not he should have left home.

"That's hard," Trent said. "Nice to have people who care about you, though."

"Huh?" Asked Charlie

"You know," Trent started, "It's gotta be nice to have someone who cares." Trent wasn't sure if it was the right thing to say. He wasn't even sure if he believed it. But he wanted to make Charlie feel better. "And, hey, Charlie?"

"Yeah?"

"I'm sure she's alright, okay?"

After a moment, accompanied by a nod of thanks, Charlie said, "Yeah, okay. You're probably right."

"Hey, so…?" Trent hesitated, looking to shift gears in the conversation but not wanting to seem inconsiderate.

"Yeah?"

"Look, I know you're hanging out with Ellie right now, but…" Trent looked as if he were searching for the right words. "You still want me to… show you around this evening?"

Trent looked away, as if assuming he already knew the answer.

"Of course."

Trent's gaze shot up at Charlie again. "Yeah? Because I just thought you two…"

"Oh, honestly, I just ran into Ellie today. It wasn't planned or anything. Besides, you offered to show me around yesterday, and I can't wait to check out the town and the rest of it."

Trent rubbed his hands together nervously.

"Seriously, I wouldn't miss it," Charlie added. "And, say, what's with you two? Every time I see you guys together, it gets really weird."

Trent cocked his head back and looked as if he were trying to pick the words right out of the sky. "Look, when you've lived in a small town long enough, you'll see. I've known Ellie a long time. You get to know things about people, you know?"

Charlie was shaking his head with understanding. There wasn't much he could say to that.

"How about you text me when you're finished up here," Trent said, indicating toward the bar. "Then I'll come around and pick you up at your place, or wherever you want?"

"Sounds great."

"Great. I'll catch you this evening."

"Awesome. I'll text you."

Trent turned to walk away before pausing for a second. Turning back to face Charlie, he said, "Hey, Charlie?"

"Yeah."

"Ellie."

"Yeah?"

"Be careful, okay?"

"I will, thanks." Charlie wasn't sure where the comment had come from. He had no reason not to trust Trent, but he also didn't feel he had a reason not to trust Ellie. But he would keep this thought with the rest of his mind's warnings, tucked away just in case.

And with that, Trent walked off toward downtown where he disappeared into the crowd of summer tourists.

Charlie's attention was no longer split, and he held out his phone to call his mother back. Worry crept back into him, filling his chest cavity, making it difficult to breathe.

It didn't even ring. It just went straight to a disconnected dial tone.

"Damnit, where are you, mom?" He said, breathing in and out as deeply as he could, trying to be in control of what he was feeling.

Pressure was building, and quick in his chest and throat. His head now felt as if it were doubling in size.

I need that drink, he thought, his palms sweaty, as flashes of heat came and went causing his body to feel like it was on the verge of overheating. Out of nowhere, dizziness had snuck up behind him to the point where even standing was difficult.

Shit, he thought. *Not here. Not now.*

Images began to flash through his mind, of all the different things that could be happening to her. He saw her lying on the floor with a broken leg, unable to go for help. He saw someone breaking in and taking advantage of her withered age and self, scaring her half to death and making off with whatever they wanted. Maybe it was a heart attack, or a stroke, or maybe even an aneurysm. With each thought, his esophagus tightened more and more, closing off his ability to breathe. In every scenario, she was always left helpless and very hurt. The last thing Charlie saw was her lying on the ground, not moving, not breathing.

"F-Fuck!" Charlie stuttered, as he staggered backwards a few steps, colliding with the wall of the bar.

His body was approaching what it had felt like in the attic.

Oh no. Oh, no, no, no, no! His mind was running off now, out of his reach, stretched and pulled in more directions that he could fathom. Any further and Charlie felt it might snap. His stomach lurched and was queasy. He was worried he might throw up.

Oh no, not... not... here...

It was too late. Overburdened, confused, and frail, Charlie's brain had had enough. Given everything that had happened in the past few days, the good and the bad, Charlie couldn't keep up. Rationality and reason had left, and Charlie shook with punctuated tremors. His lungs were about to burst. Leaning against the wall, he slid down the painted brick with his shirt catching against the grains until finally his knees buckled and Charlie fell splat on the cracked and aged concrete sidewalk of this forgotten, sleepy corner of town.

Several people walked by him but paid no notice. They didn't ask about him. They didn't wonder if he was alright. They didn't even look at him. If anything, they worked to look *away* from him. They just walked on minding their own business. Probably assumed he was a drunk and deserved what was happening to him.

It was the cruelest indifference that Charlie had ever experienced, and he would never even remember it.

The next three minutes were hell.

But, as it always did, it ran its course, and when the darkness had finally let go its grip, Charlie's eyes loosened and the world, once more, began to settle

His breathing, though still difficult, became less strained. And his thoughts, though foggy, were finally able to form and take root instead of just slipping through his flailing grasps, searching for reason in an unreasonable situation.

After several long moments, the attack was over. The only remnants left behind, besides the cold sweat that glistened in the sun, were the growing pangs of both shame and emptiness that were settling into his gut.

He knew it would be safe to start counting his breaths again. It would settle him and help him to prepare a story for Ellie so he could explain what had taken him so long.

One... two... three... four... hold. One... two... three... four... slow exhale.

After some time with the salty air being funneled upriver and cooling the sweat that had formed on him, Charlie felt a bit more himself. Just a little more tired than before, but that was also normal.

Using the wall for support, he lifted himself up and straightened out the ruffles in his clothes. He debated whether he should tell Ellie the truth as he stood there in front of the bar.

What would she think? He wondered, trying to prevent his brain from assuming the worst. *That he was weak. A failure. That he couldn't handle life, so why should she waste her time?*

The roots of his shame dug in deeper as he decided to lie to her.

There was a second empty glass next to Ellie's first when he returned, juxtaposed next to the half-full pint that Charlie had left, and a brand-new full pint that hadn't been there previously.

"I took the liberty," Ellie said, pointing to his extra drink. "You need to catch up now." she smiled at him when he saw the empty glass. But her smile faded as she noticed his condition. "Woah, shit, Charlie. Is everything alright?" She sat up a little straighter in her chair in alarm. Even she was unaware of how real her concern was.

"Yeah, I'm okay. Everything's fine," he lied. "Sorry I was gone so long."

"No worries."

Charlie knew she didn't believe him. Something was the matter.

"How's mom?" She said playfully.

"She's good." His stomach lurched as he lied. "She wouldn't shut up, you know. Had to hear about everything."

"Good. You know, you're pretty sweaty, Charlie." She was looking him up and down.

Charlie flushed as the temperature in the whole room seemed to rise a few degrees.

"Uh, yeah." He took a swig of his beer, trying to avoid the remark altogether. "It's hot out there."

She looked him up and down again. Something had changed in him. Shifted. She could tell.

But it wasn't her people, they wouldn't have done that when they knew she was working, and they were sure to know that she was with him. She wondered what could have set him off to put him in this type of state. Then she found herself wondering again what *they* wanted him for. It didn't make any sense. Even she had to admit she was starting to think he was really sweet.

Pushing all of those thoughts aside again, she said to him, "Well, why don't you have a big drink to cool yourself off, *Mr. West.*"

"Huh?"

"Just trying to get you used to your *teacher* name." She smiled at him, this time in half mockery, before taking another drink herself.

He knew she was just trying to be playful, but his worry had led his mind to a more desperate place. He would have to fake it.

He needed to do something to put the attention somewhere else and he was still feeling overheated. Holding up his glass, he drained most of what was left in his beer in one go, and quickly. A rush of coolness traveled through his body, from his hair to his shoes, and his bones to his skin. He would have sworn he could feel droplets of sweat evaporating away in the influx of cold.

"Wow, impressive," Ellie joked. "Welcome back, *Charlie.*"

"Sorry, again, for taking so long." Charlie knew he shouldn't have brought it up again, especially after he'd worked to move their attention away from his absence, and he really needed to stop apologizing for everything.

Ellie ignored it. Now, it seemed more critical than ever to help keep him calm and assured.

"How about you just finish that drink so we can get out of here and see some more of this fine town, huh?"

Her assurance was back, and it drew him in all the closer. He was amazed at the trust that could be built in such a short amount of time, even when he had warning signs going off in his head every few seconds. Charlie put forth a smile and prepared himself to be taken for yet another ride. "Sounds great," he said, before picking up his glass, tipping it back and draining what was left.

Ellie gave another impressed smirk and polished off what remained of her whiskey. She slammed the small tumbler back down onto the tabletop.

"Let's go, Charlie West," she said.

He just smiled at her. He didn't want to let anything prevent him from enjoying the rest of this day.

As they walked out, Charlie found himself thankful for the distraction she was. He knew as they walked around he could lose himself in whatever conversation they might fall into. He had surprised himself with how open he had been and was intrigued to see where it would lead next.

Ellie, on the other hand, was feeling something very different. She was feeling conflict. Whatever task she'd been given before, whatever person she'd been directed to get close to or woo for *them*... she'd never really considered the consequences of what happened to them. After all, she never knew what happened with them and she didn't care. And with Charlie, she still didn't know where any of this was leading, but she did find herself hoping it wouldn't end up too painfully for him.

Charlie's mother was in a dead panic after looking up from her phone and realizing it had been disconnected. Her screen showed nothing, nothing but the signal of a dead battery. In the mess that had been the past two days, she'd forgotten to charge her phone. She was well beyond reason, logic, and even routine.

"Oh, Charlie... I'm..." but whatever thought she'd had was gone, cut off by the solidifying feeling in her, the belief of a sort, that everything that was going wrong, that it was all her fault, and that she was beyond an apology. Something in her, *that* voice, told her she wasn't in a position to placate her guilt away.

"Charlie, I'm... It's all... my—" She tried again, once more before giving up completely.

He wouldn't want to talk to me anyway, she thought. *He's busy, off...* her brain wracked itself to think through what he might be doing. She thought of her dream again, of Charlie being enveloped by darkness.

Her panic began to rise again, but instead of being able to think through what to do, plug in her phone, call Charlie back, just check in, she crumbled.

It's them, Charlie, she thought. *Watch out for... watch out...*

But before she could complete her thought, let alone follow any rational steps towards a solution, Charlie's mother began to pace, back and forth, through the kitchen and dining room at first. She was slowly becoming more and more detached from even herself. As the day progressed, she would find herself making loops around the entire bottom floor of the house, struck in a rut, reciting over and over rambling and incoherent warnings to her son, her dead phone still clutched tightly within her grasp. It would be a long time before she would think to plug it in to charge, if ever.

SEVEN

A lonely flame burned in the massive expanse of the manor's library, casting a silhouette of Mr. Wilkes' wild, ghost-white hair onto the wall of books behind him. He sat in a tall, green, high-backed chair, engrossed in what he was reading, concentrating on not letting his nerves get the better of him. The room he sat in was the size of multiple houses on its own. One could imagine placing a few average family homes side by side next to each other in this space and having room to spare on every side. The candle flame occupied merely a pocket of this space, leaving the rest of the room in cold darkness.

Mr. Wilkes' presence, unlike the candlelight, took up more space than his stature should have allowed. Something he projected with great intent, in a way willing their progress and success.

There were two stately doors, both tall and impending, that acted as the threshold of this venue. And, without warning, one of the two doors opened abruptly, allowing the hallway's light to invade the space. The door's shadow stretched itself out as far as it could, coming just short of Mr. Wilkes.

Through the opening marched Mr. Booth, right hand of the authoritative Mr. Wilkes and a man of importance himself. Yet, his posture and bearing would suggest that he knew his place.

His shoes shuffled across the carpeted flooring.

This intruder, a gentleman, came to a stop several feet in front of Mr. Wilkes, who hadn't allowed his reading to be interrupted. He held up an index finger to Mr. Booth. The message was clear: *wait*. This, of course, was met with obedience.

Several long seconds passed before the silence was finally shattered.

"Mr. Booth. Is everything ready?"

"Yes, sir. Everything is ready now. Ahead of schedule. Preparations are completely finalized — to your exact instruction, in fact. Awaiting your inspection now, sir."

Mr. Wilkes sat up but masked the explosion of glee he felt with a tight and well-practiced restraint. He could never express the relief that flooded through him when he heard the news. It was his responsibility to show unconquerable conviction at all times.

"Very good," Mr. Wilkes said, bringing his hands together, never once pulling his attention away from the fire's subtle ambient bursts. "Very good, indeed." He did allow a smirk to form and for his eyes to grow wide with satisfaction, the flickering fire's flames reflecting in the depth of their unreasoning sights. It gave the impression that something loomed deep within him, an illusion that life could exist outside of his conquest.

"Excellent," he said at last, in a barely discernable whisper.

"When shall I tell them to expect you, sir?"

"Momentarily. I would like to come immediately, but I must finish something quickly."

The man's facade broke for a moment, giving way to nervousness. "Of course, sir," he said, then turned to leave. He had only made it six or seven steps before being suddenly called back.

"Mr. Booth?"

He turned back again. "Yes, sir?"

"I would like to move forward with another matter seeing as we're ahead of schedule. Earlier than originally planned."

"Of course, sir. And that would be?"

"Has our man been given the artifact yet?"

"Sir?" Mr. Booth shifted with both discomfort and alarm.

"The medallion. Has our man been given the medallion?"

"Oh, yes, sir. He picked it up the day before Charlie came to town."

"Very good." He let his hands fall from their clasp and let them down to rest upon the armrests of his chair. "Inform our man of the next phase of the plan and to get on with it, as early as possible. Tonight should be sufficient for him, I would hope. I am eager to see the plan through now. You will give him the message?"

The man, though alarmed, followed through with the painful normalcy of his obedience. Standing even straighter than before, he replied, "Right away, sir."

"Thank you, Mr. Booth. That'll be all." It was the most cheerful Mr. Booth had seen his employer, ever. It was then that Mr. Wilkes waved him away without so much as a glance.

Mr. Booth bowed in acknowledgment to his dismissal from the room. He took several quick steps and crossed back through the threshold of the chamber's door, shutting it tightly behind him. He then disappeared into the other various regions of the house.

Mr. Wilkes sat with one leg crossed over the other. He brought his hands back together and indulged himself, now that he was alone, with a slightly larger smirk. It did not stem from joy or happiness but neither was it ironic; there was an eagerness in it. It drew forth from hunger more than anything. His hunger for the completion of a plan over a century in the making as well as the opportunity, at least for the briefest of moments, to show the other sects of The Order that he wasn't insane for following this path. To show them that *he* had been right after all.

So close, he told himself again. *At last.*

After a time, he too stood up from his chair and, picking up the lone candle, he walked away from where he had been sitting. But he did not walk toward the doors Mr. Booth had used upon entering and leaving. He walked toward the furthest corner of the room from where the light had been. As he drew nearer, the candle flame revealed there to be no door or passageway at all. It was just shelves of books. He came to a stop right in the middle of the last shelf, pulled at the edges of one of the dark pieces of wood paneling, and waited. The wall itself opened slowly, creaking as it swung, revealing a stone

111

archway. And beyond that was a passage that led downward and cut back and forth into the shadowy darkness, a recess of the building reserved only for the initiated.

Once the passageway was completely unblocked, Mr. Wilkes took a step forward past the stone arch and disappeared into the shadows below. His recurrent steps echoed far in front of him, and behind, but when their faint reverberations could be heard no more, the wall of shelves began to close again, as if of its own volition. It creaked with slow intention. A clicking latch could be heard once it was shut tight. And once again the room became still and silent and dark. It was only shadows now – not even the lonely candlelight remained.

Charlie lumbered up the hill to his place, a bit buzzed and a bit more confused. He and Ellie had stopped for one more drink, which was one more than he'd needed. He was, after all, trying to keep up with Ellie's two, which were on top of the two she'd already had. And she hadn't even seemed phased. He wasn't used to drinking this much and was feeling its effects on his body and mind, both of which were very brittle and probably not helping his adjustment, he noted.

On the other hand, his hangover was feeling better and, one step at a time, he made his way up the cracked, worn sidewalk until Irving St. was in sight.

He couldn't tell if it was the sky or his head that was stale. He was tired and felt frail. He worried about not being able to keep up with this regiment but tried to assure himself that things would settle down once school started. He would be able to establish a routine. Then life would even out.

Breathe, Charlie. Just breathe. Everything is fine. He shut his eyes to give them a moment's rest and let his feet carry him up the road and, before he knew it, he was standing before the tall Victorian that was his new home – the basement, at least.

The first order of business for him was to pound two glasses of water. Then he would pee. Finally, he would lay down for a bit and try to get some rest before Trent came to pick him up.

He wondered about cancelling... All he wanted to do was sleep.

No. I have to, he told himself.

Social interaction was very difficult, especially when he was tired. The warning signs were noisier than ever in his current state, but this would be a great chance to keep pushing beyond that, to build actual friendship. These nights would become the foundations of his new life.

It's just an evening, he resigned. *And it won't end up at the bars again, like last night... hopefully.*

Charlie laid himself down on his bed, which wasn't helping convince him to go.

He went back and forth several more times in his head on whether or not to stay or go, when he finally said, and for the last time, *I need to go. I need to do the relational thing. Trust them, Charlie. Trust them.*

The driver of the faded-yellow truck sat waiting just down the street from Charlie's house. He'd been waiting since he overheard them parting ways in front of the bar and he drove on ahead, attempting to avoid any suspicion. After what seemed like hours, Charlie finally made his way, dragging his feet a bit, around the corner and up the sidewalk to his house.

About fucking time, thought the driver.

Now that Charlie was back, the driver's mind hoped for some sort of action. He was growing tired of this assignment. But he knew better. He *knew* what Charlie's plans were, so he knew he would have to wait a while longer before he could leave. He also knew his annoyance was only temporary. After Mr. Wilkes got what he needed from Charlie – as was how it usually went – his life would slide back into one of ease and comfort.

He watched Charlie walk up Irving street, cross over to the other sidewalk and come to the house. Then Charlie stumbled onto the pathway that led to the side yard where Charlie's personal entrance lie. Finally, he watched Charlie descend the stone steps and disappear into his basement room below.

Okay. Now we wait again.

He was startled by the buzzing of his phone. A photo and the name of the caller showed on the screen with each vibration. It read *Booth* in bold letters.

"Shit," he said. "What now?" He felt too tired and worn down for this right now.

He picked up the phone and he brought it to his ear, his brows frustrated and furrowed.

"What?" he spat out.

Then, after pausing to listen to whatever instructions were being given, he said, "Uh-huh. Yeah. Yes. I'm near him right now. He just walked into his place. Yes. Of course I'll see him."

There was another short pause while he seemed to be receiving more instructions.

"Yeah, it's right here with me," he said, an air of frustration infiltrating his words and tone. He switched the phone to his other hand so as to be able to reach under the seat and grab something. Sitting back up straight, he held a small and faded piece of linen in his hand. It was wrapped around something. Moving the phone now between his cheek and shoulder, the driver began to unwrap the linen to reveal the object that had been hidden inside.

"Uh-huh," he said into the phone, his face giving off a perplexed stare as he looked down at what he was holding.

What the fuck is this? He thought. He recognized it, for sure. He seen it dozens of times, worn by men – and men of importance at that – walking through the mansion. People coming and going in and out of meetings with Mr. Wilkes. But *why* did he have it? *What* was it for?

"Um, excuse me, but why do I have this *thing*, I'm—?"

He was stopped short and was given a swift telling off by Mr. Booth was giving him. He nodded his head to show that he understood, even though no one could see him.

"Okay, okay. I get it. I know I don't need to know, it just seems strange to—"

He hated being interrupted and, in his frustration, allowed his chin to fall to his chest and feigned hitting his phone back and forth into his forehead, mouthing several less than appropriate terms directed at Mr. Booth.

He leaned back into his seat again and put his phone back to his ear. "Yes, I understand I don't need to know everything, but—"

Again. Any sense of humor left him, and he began grinding his jaw with a practiced precision.

"Ok—"

He shook his head.

"Alright—" he managed to get in. Then, "So, let me get this straight. I just have to wait until Charlie's asleep or gone or whatever, then sneak in and place this *thing* under his bed, then come back outside, and what? Just watch?"

Again, he nodded in a show of understanding.

"Okay. I got it. It's just weird, you – Okay! I said I got it!"

He pulled the phone away from himself and mouthed a *fuck you* to Mr. Booth before returning it to his ear and waiting for his turn to speak.

"Yes. Okay! Of course, I can get it— Yes, dammit! I'll do it tonight. I said I would get it done, to— No— Look, I'll let you know when it's done, okay?"

To his relief, after another short pause, the driver was able to say, "Goodbye." Then he hung up the phone and flung it back to where it had been sitting before on the empty seat next to him.

"Fuck me," he said. Sometimes he just wanted Mr. Wilkes to call him himself instead of using his lackey to give the orders.

Amid his frustration, he let his gaze fall to the mysterious object in hand. He'd seen it many times before, but never up close like this. It was always something he'd seen off in the distance, worn by the great men who visited the mansion as they walked to and from their ancient rites and rituals, those of which he had never been allowed to attend.

On the more rounded end, a great crimson jewel was embedded. This piece sat atop the lower chunk, more rectangular but not exact in its measurements, broken up by etched lines that always reminded Trent of tentacles, though he didn't know why.

It was a made of a heavy bronze and was much larger than he'd expected, but its shine was greatly diminished in the shadowy confines of the truck's cab.

Dangling from its top was a matching chain. It hung over his hand, as if reaching toward the cab floor, willing itself to get away.

He had often wondered at their purpose, these medallions. They'd never seemed anything but decorative to him before but, given his instructions, there must be more to them.

Memories swirled through his mind of Mr. Wilkes and those high and mighty members of The Order disappearing into those lesser-known chambers of the property, shrouded in their cloaks. He'd always found their chanting eerie. Haunting.

It was after he'd first heard it that he began to question his involvement with Wilkes and The Order. But, even after, he'd never really felt a reason to leave, no matter what feeling festered in his gut. No guilty thought had yet outweighed his need for Mr. Wilkes' assistance, so there had never been any reason to act on them.

Holding the Medallion now, he realized that there were certain aspects of his job that didn't make any sense to him. But they did put his current task into a better context.

Wow, this kid must be really important, he thought, staring back down at the medallion.

He had never been that in tune with his own intuition; he'd never had reason to be before, so it was quite normal that he simply ignored the rising levels of discomfort in his body, his fluctuating body heat, the minute and subtle shifts within his stomach. He took it for nothing more than the fact that he was exhausted and just needed a good night's sleep. It never occurred to him that there was a part of him that disagreed with his actions, that there was a part of him that wanted freedom from his responsibilities. Those thoughts came at odds with the more rational parts of his brain, and he'd always shoved them aside, falling back onto the reminder of the life he could be living versus the life he was living.

All of these thoughts, though, this internal dialogue, he wasn't even aware was taking place.

Okay, let's see what this thing does later, he focused himself back, sensing nothing more than a slight ping of worry rising in him.

He did find himself at odds with not liking the fact that this assignment had something to do with *those* more obscure people from within the organization and all the fuss that had been taking at the manor these past few weeks. The many visitors, most of whom he didn't recognize whatsoever.

But recognizing people wasn't his job, he reminded himself. Nor was having an opinion about the functions he was asked to perform. His job was to follow orders and follow them he would.

His mind wandered back to Charlie.

What the hell does this *thing have to do with this kid?*

After watching Charlie these past couple days, he couldn't even begin to fathom why they were remotely interested in him.

But a job's a job, he told himself, pushing to keep his curiosity at bay. But, no matter what he did, something nagged at him, something he couldn't explain. Something he feared would unravel the very foundations of the life he'd managed to build for himself – or the one Mr. Wilkes had allowed for him to build – if he pulled on the thread. Terror came with this thought, so he shoved it aside as quickly as it came.

Putting it all far from his mind, he neatly wrapped the medallion back into the linen coverings and placed it back under the front passenger seat of his truck before picking up his phone to make another call.

Ellie decided to walk along the river path for a bit after parting ways with Charlie.

Just past the piers and pubs, she saw kids playing with their friends and families. All around there were people who, in her mind, had lived far more innocent lives than she had.

She had never really had reason to question what she was doing before, about any job or task she'd been given, regardless of what it was. Everything, to her, had always about coming closer to what they had promised her. That one day, she would pay off her debt and she would be free to go, free to build whatever life she wanted. Until then, she would be stuck living whatever life they told her to.

Her steps propelled her forward – at least in terms of her pace, for forward was never a direction she'd felt her life ever moved toward.

Who are you, Charlie West? She found herself wondering again, much more freely now that she wasn't with him trying to keep him engaged.

She wondered again what they might want him for. Why he was so important? The buzz surrounding the conversations she'd overheard about what was being planned was unlike anything she'd ever heard before. And that part of the job had rarely concerned her so, like every time before, she'd kept out of it.

Now, pacing up the river path, passing person after person who lived what she would term a *normal life*, she found herself kicking herself for not going out of her way to find out more.

And he's so sweet, she kept thinking, her hands stuffed into her pockets, as if they needed saving from the warm summer breeze.

It was a beautiful evening. The trees and the grass swayed in the currents of the air. The sun seemed perched right in between two peaks of the coastal range, and the sky was lit up with so many varying hues of fire.

It was breathtaking and Ellie saw none of it.

She'd always been stuck, but as she'd never felt trapped before.

Fuck me! She thought, as she made an abrupt stop in the middle of the walking path, almost causing a wreck between two bicyclists – though she was barely aware of this.

Something in her, something she couldn't quite explain, told her something bad was coming, that this wasn't going to end well.

But what did she care? She would counter. Who was Charlie to her? And what did it matter what *they* did as long as she got what was promised? As long as her slate was cleared and she became free? She'd lived far too long under the debts her father had left behind when he passed. But that was the way of the system, wasn't it? Born indentured until you worked your way out of it. But what was Charlie to her debt? It had never mattered before, but there was something different about this. Something in her had changed or was changing.

A very thin, subtle stream of guilt and shame seeped in at the thought.

Fuck! She thought again, almost laughing at the fact that she might be growing a conscience right then of all times.

Then she shifted gears.

But why could I not stop telling him my life story? She wondered. *He just seemed to care so damn much... why?*

She couldn't figure him out and it was killing her.

Out of nowhere, something in her urged her to tell him what was happening to him, that he didn't have the control of his life he thought he did.

But what was happening to him? She didn't know. All she knew is that she was to contact him, get to know him, gain his trust, and be ready for further directions.

Just then the other side of her consciousness swung in.

You don't even know if anything bad is going to happen to him, it said.

This was true enough, she thought, as she stood there on the cusp of another summer storm.

Things could still end up okay, she thought. *Why am I so worried about this?*

Feeling no further along in understanding how she felt than she had at the beginning of her walk, Ellie decided the best course of action would be to do what she'd always done. She would simply carry on. She would just see where things lead.

Charlie was meeting up with Trent in a little bit, for some plan Trent had put together – she couldn't worry about that – but she was going to meet him after that. That was a good sign, and part of her was even looking forward to it.

Something in her settled.

That's it then, she said to herself. *Just roll with it and see where it goes.*

She figured if anything happened that gave credence to these whims and feelings, there would always be time to act on them later. But for now, it was too early to tell.

What possible harm could come of it? She wondered as she turned and once again began to follow the path that was laid out before her. *Everything might end up fine.*

EIGHT

Charlie was half asleep when his phone buzzed, startling him. He knew it was a text because it only buzzed once. He let out a slight moan but made no attempt to pick it up.

After a minute, he finally opened an eye and reached over to see who had messaged him. It was Trent. *Be there in 5,* the message said.

That only left Charlie a few minutes to get ready. He groaned and looked around the room to see if there was anything he might need, only to realize that he didn't know what he might need. Then he looked outside to check the weather. It was raining.

Charlie stood up from the bed, grabbed his raincoat from off his chair and walked toward the back door. He opened it while simultaneously sliding his arms into the sleeves of his jacket and shut the door with his foot as he stumbled his way out into the summer rain.

When Charlie reached the street, Trent was standing there to welcome him. His arms were crossed and he was leaning backwards onto the hood of an old, faded-yellow truck, the paint peeling badly.

He greeted Charlie with an eager smile. "Hey-o Charlie. How goes it?"

"I'm a bit tired but ready to go." Charlie rubbed his eyes

"Let's do this," said Trent, clapping his hands together. Before getting into the truck, Trent turned to peer up through the weak rainfall. He pointed out to the dark clouds emerging out by the horizon. "It's gonna be a good one tonight, Charlie. You're in for a real treat!"

Trent's smile was sincere. To him, Charlie was merely another assignment, but that wouldn't stop him from enjoying his time anyway. He was going to make the most of it.

Charlie thought of his bed and how comfortable he'd just been. He wasn't sure he was ready for anything, to the point where he was almost ready to agree with the quiet voices in his head telling him to stay home and not try anything new.

Charlie merely smiled at Trent in way of response.

"Tonight is going to be sort of an initiation," Trent coaxed him with a wicked grin.

Charlie said nothing in return but stopped and looked up at his friend. He raised his brows to indicate a comical level of fear, one that he wouldn't admit to Trent was all too real.

They hopped into the truck. Charlie buckled and noticed that Trent did not. Then Trent turned over the ignition. Almost as if connected in the depth of something unseen, as the truck roared to life so was something awakened in Charlie, triggered, as if it had been injected into him. He felt it swirling and moving about, making him more alert, more aware. The more he focused on it, the more it seemed that some specter was reaching its hand out and was gripping his heart and squeezing.

Charlie looked all around the cab but saw nothing strange.

He had to be imagining it, but it felt so *real*, so tangible.

Something was coming on, and fast.

Oh shit oh shit oh shit oh shit, he thought, trying to breathe out ever so slowly and not gather Trent's attention.

Trent, meanwhile, didn't notice anything. He just hit the gas and off they sped – Charlie at the mercy of Trent's volition – in this case, to the South Jetty, the mouth of the Columbia River. In some respects, one of the many edges of the world. A place where violent, thrashing waves came to crash and assert their power. A place where mankind made its attempt to reach out its arm and tame the wilds of nature.

Charlie sat there frozen by a growing fear. He was starting to sweat again and realized he was holding onto the seat with one hand and the handle atop the door with his other

A strange, looming dread filled the cab, but every time Charlie looked over, it seemed that Trent was completely unaware of it. He was just sitting there whistling along to the low volume on the radio.

The truck pulled its way down the road and, with every revolution of its tires, Charlie's worries wound up tighter and tighter.

What the fuck is going on? He wondered. He thought about how he'd felt in the attic the other day before he'd left. This was starting to feel just like that. Unbridled worry and anxiousness, all the while accompanied by varying waves and overtones of anger and dormant frustration.

Charlie wasn't aware that he was holding his breath again, just as before. He was involuntarily taking in and letting out tiny breaths, the least his body could do to keep him conscious.

Shit, what the hell– He was already to the point where he couldn't even finish his thoughts, and his whole body was tense. What would Trent say if he looked over and saw him? It had to be obvious that something was wrong. What would he say? What *could* he say? He was reeling and couldn't think at all.

He stole another glance over at Trent, who was still smiling. Charlie looked out the window, away from his companion. He tried to focus on something else, anything else. He started listing things off he could focus on. The trees, the river, birds flying overhead, the sky, the sunset. It was a beautiful sunset, but Charlie thought he could *feel* it. He could merely acknowledge that it was there, but there was *something* getting in the way of him experiencing anything.

He tried to consider what all this could mean but, instead, his thoughts were thrown off course by a quickly rising flare of fury. He flexed his entire torso, sucked his breath in and held to keep himself form screaming out. He had to stay calm. He needed to not attract Trent's attention to this. But how long would *it* last? What was *it*? He still didn't know. Twice now this strange mania had overtaken him, but he didn't know why.

He tried to place his attention back onto the scenery and moved to control his breathing once more. He focused in on the details. The colors and textures. Anything but the growing feeling of terror within him.

Still, the truck made its way along the country road toward the edge of the world.

Charlie steadied his breathing the best he could, still trying to appear that everything was normal, even though everything was *far* from normal. He tried starting his breathing exercises several times but found he couldn't focus long enough to get any traction with them.

What the fuck! What the fuck! What the fuck? His thoughts could only stream in a repetitive, linear fashion.

The level of hyperawareness he was experiencing brought his attention to his awkward posture, his tensing back and muscles, the painfully regimented breathing — only through his nose as to not bring attention to himself, but he felt it was still loud — he was starting to sweat and, worst of all, the lights from the street, other cars, businesses, and all were tracing as his vision wasn't able to focus itself to work properly. One thought over every other was recurrent in his mind, that Trent was weirded out by Charlie's behavior and couldn't wait to get Charlie out of his truck. He kept looking up at Trent to see if he was noticing anything, and Trent seemed contently focused on the road. Charlie's inability to see *Truth* at that moment left him lost and confused.

It was one thing going through this in the attic by himself, but this — with Trent — was way worse.

Outside, the summer storm continued to bellow and was beginning to crash down hard. The turgid skies had shifted and broke open above them, crowning the sky with a torrential inconsistency.

Still, the truck carried them forward toward their destination.

Breathe, Charlie. Just fucking breathe, he told himself, the panicking getting the better of him.

124

His lips rounded themselves into a sort of funnel as he tried for a release of several long exhaling breaths. He wondered if he looked as ridiculous as he felt. Normally if he was able to slow his breathing down, his heart rate would follow, and he would then be able to calm down. But just as before in the attic, the hurricane within him continued to no avail. He felt utterly powerless. His heart rate continued to race. His overstuffed mind stayed bloated, as if it had been expanded and filled with so many thoughts they would weigh him down and drown him. And maybe worst of all, given that it could give him away to Trent, his body wouldn't untense. He was stuck, rigid like a statue.

To Charlie, the trip seemed to already have taken days, even though, in reality, they'd only been driving for a few minutes.

Unbeknownst to Charlie, Trent drove the truck completely unaware of all that was taking place in Charlie's mind. He had either become too good at hiding his feelings over the years, or Trent was too caught up in whatever song was lulling him over the radio. On the road took them, Trent's thoughts lost to avenues of his own worries, and Charlie to his own acute panic.

They drove through the neighboring town of Warrenton and landscape shifted, though it went unnoticed by Charlie. It went from rich coastal mountain soil and thick deciduous brush to the sandy-rooted spruce tree forests that lined the ocean dunes.

The storm began to stir itself up and flags whipped themselves atop their poles. People held onto their hats and bags as they ran from store fronts or their homes on to their cars. The electricity in the air whispered of a preternatural past. It hummed through the open sky with energy building, as if storing up for some unknown yet looming event. Off in the distance, thunder invaded with pangs peeling themselves across the skyline, drawing everything into the quiet center of the assault.

Charlie wasn't aware that he was grinding his teeth, but his jaw was sure to be sore in the morning. The muscles over his temples were twitching and he had once again began tapping his thumb onto his fingertips. He was in complete default mode now. Not *out* of control, but he surely not *in* control of himself either. He was surviving. He pursed his lips and began breathing through his nose again, hoping that Trent wouldn't hear or notice him.

Like the storm converging outside, Charlie could feel the swells of anger gathering within him, crawling its way to the surface from the deeper and darker caverns of the shadows within.

He managed a glance at Trent once more. He looked so much more self-assured than Charlie felt, even when he wasn't falling to pieces. In his state, Charlie made the false assumption that Trent probably hadn't been shattered by his own life experiences as Charlie had. Like so many others, he had forgotten that each person carries their scars in their own way. Charlie didn't know Trent's scars yet, nor how he carried them.

A blast of sharp pain struck Charlie in the upper part of his mind, just at the top of his skull. He winced but found he couldn't turn much further away from Trent to keep from being found out.

Trent drove with a rote ease that spoke of how often he'd driven these roads. It was second nature, as if they were etched into his very heritage.

Charlie's fists were clenched and he worked to maintain a slow and steady breathing pattern, but still the anger burned and grew. His grip was so tight, the creases around his knuckles were going a pale white.

Just as his anger was beginning to outweigh his anxiousness, the road widened, and they pulled into what appeared to a large parking lot. About a hundred car lengths long and forty lengths wide. There was a sign that read: *Welcome to the South Jetty*. On the left, down the whole length of the lot, was a strip of grass thirty feet wide that stretched to the edge of the jetty itself, the 6.6 miles long rock wall that men stacked fifteen feet high in 1895. It was an awesome feat of man's ingenuity, especially in its attempt to tame the wilds of nature.

The truck pulled up to a wooden structure that stood level to the top of the jetty wall. It had a stairwell built into its middle to reach the top. Trent turned over the ignition and the truck wound down, its rickety hum lost to the rambles of the winds.

They raged and were anything but gentle.

Without looking over at Charlie, Trent asked if he was ready.

126

"For what?" Charlie asked with as much control over his voice as he could manage. His hands were sweaty and fidgeting. The sides of his head were swelling with paralyzing pain and all he could think about was receding inward and ignoring the world.

In a contrived and over-dramatic voice, an attempt at humor, Trent lifted his arms above his head and yelled, "To face true power, Charlie." He lowered his arms back down and looked over at Charlie for the first time since the drive started. "Woah, shit. You okay, Charlie?"

Even he didn't realize the depth of his concern.

Charlie flinched and looked down. It was obvious that something was very wrong. He looked like hell.

"I'm fine," he lied. Then, desperate to escape the moment, he mumbled, "Let's go," and went to open his door and get out of the truck. All he could think about was *getting out*.

"Are you sure?" Trent said, caught off guard. "We could, we could do this another time."

Charlie paused for a second. He couldn't focus or think straight. He needed air. "No. Let's... let's go."

Trent looked for a moment to be considering something, mulling something over, and his glance fell, slowly, toward the floor beneath the seats where he'd placed the medallion. He found himself wondering if there was a connection, still taking the shifting in his gut to mean nothing more than an effect of his exhaustion.

No, it couldn't be, he assured himself and, brushing it aside, he readied himself for what they were about to do.

The wind was screaming outside the truck, tearing its way through the lower atmosphere. Whole puddles of standing water were being pushed across the parking lot as if one singular lake of asphalt was retreating from the storm, heading for the cover of the trees.

"Alright, Charlie. Let's go! And don't worry about how you feel. *This* tends to have quite an impact on people."

Charlie shook his head that he understood, though he was lost to the powers of something much greater than himself.

127

"Come on, Charlie. You'll feel true power out here. Trust me. You'll be thankful afterwards."

The rain was pounding the windshield, but it was the wind that ruled the night, sweeping through in screeching bursts, ripping at the centimeter-thick glass that was protecting them.

Charlie turned to Trent. "Let's go."

The corners of Trent's mouth turned up. "Alright, Charlie-boy!"

With that, Trent's door swung open and he was gone. The door slammed shut behind him. At first, the only thing that registered to Charlie was the pronounced rise in the noise level from the storm reaching in through the open door. Charlie, as well, pressed his door open against the wind. He had to push hard, as his side of the truck was facing its oncoming direction. Once he was out amidst the elements, he let go of the door and it slammed shut completely on its own.

The skies were in full assault. Each massive drop of rain was like a bomb carried to its target on the back of peeling wind, and each exploded with force enough to make one reconsider moving forward.

Charlie kept moving forward though. Unable to see a thing, he reached out in front of him and grasped at whatever he could. But there was nothing there. He yelled out for Trent, "Trent? Where are we going?"

A voice called out from the darkness. "Just follow me!"

Charlie continued. It was a matter of trust now. Assurance that Trent would lead him in and out of the storm. There seemed to be just as much chaotic turmoil churning within Charlie as was happening around him. As had become his norm, he worked to let it all go and ignore the pangs of worry and warning.

He kept moving forward and, like a lost child, kept calling out for Trent every few seconds, trying to keep in contact.

After several times calling out and not hearing anything, he started moving more quickly through the blasts of rain and wind. He called out once more, loudly, but he heard no response and then *bam*!

"Shit!" He said. Charlie had hit his head on something large and wooden. "What the hell?" He rubbed his head and stood there in the rain, dumbfounded, and looked up to see a towering wooden platform blocking the rain and Trent laughing.

"This is the viewing platform!" Trent yelled.

"For what?"

"For that!" Trent pointed over a gigantic rock wall.

"For what?"

Just then, a massive tumult of water came crashing down over what Charlie could barely make out as the jetty wall. A spray of salty, ice cold water, like several fire hoses pumping out to sea, splashed down onto Trent and Charlie, leaving them soaked to the very marrow of their bones.

Trent howled back at the wildness of the scene. He looked at Charlie and saw the fear in his eyes, the fear that exists right on the other side of feeling fully alive. At least that's what he thought.

"What... the... fuck..." Charlie stood frozen with shock.

Trent let out an unrestrained laugh and yelled out to the night, a primal howl that shook even Charlie. "This, Charlie," Trent's voice carried over the waves, "is the Jetty!" He pointed to the rock structure beyond the platform. "Let me be the first to introduce you to the Pacific Ocean!"

Looking up, Charlie saw the huge pylons that held up the structure he was standing under. He understood the shelter it brought. Directly in front of him was the massive wall constructed with the largest stones Charlie had ever seen. It looked ancient, something laid out by the gods. Each stone in and of itself was a gigantic chunk of basalt, several feet tall and several feet wide, and there were thousands of them, each asymmetrical to the others, laid out stretching in both directions for a length Charlie couldn't fathom. But he could see the top of the wall. About twelve to fifteen feet high, depending on the spot. Easy enough to climb on a pleasant day, and probably made for a nice view too, but it would have been suicide to climb up at the time. This was the wall built to curb nature, to hold the water back. On the other side was the Pacific Ocean, one of the unruliest beasts in existence. Wonderfully dangerous and beautiful.

The ocean, Charlie thought, could calm you with its serene lulls just as soon as it could kill you with hidden power. Power enough to pull you down to an unmarked grave. Power that spelled doom to those who dared to face it without a certain meekness.

Charlie was shaking he was so scared. It wasn't the panic he was used to, this was deeper. Something much older. It came more as a sign of respect.

"People come out to the platform to see the ocean! It's size! It's danger!" Trent yelled out.

Charlie felt the growing excitement and fear building within him.

"But we're not going to do that!" Trent yelled out again.

"What?"

"I said we're not going to do that!" From Charlie's vantage point, Trent looked insane. "Follow me, Charlie!"

"W-Why?"

Trent didn't answer. He just smiled.

Without waiting, Trent was off. He ran from underneath the platform and scrambled his way up the wall of basalt stones, almost jumping from one to the other. To Charlie's amazement, he somehow navigated his way through unrelenting blast after unrelenting blast of wind and water that was shaking the world around him.

Charlie had never been more terrified in his life. He was completely unsure of what to do.

But he was finally able to think again and only one thought permeated up through the scattering noises of all the other warnings: *why else am I here?*

The ocean called out to him. Its anger, its fury, its rage.

Fuck it! Was the last thing that ran through his conscious mind before he broke out from under the shelter and struggled to follow Trent's path up the slippery rock. The thunder welcomed him with the bellowing pounding of its drums.

Before he knew it, Charlie was clinging to the rock, eye-level with the platform, a dozen feet above the sand. The storm cracked at what seemed mere feet above his head. Another tremendous wave of water came crashing down over the wall and pounded down, knocking both Trent and Charlie backward. Trent screamed and ducked down so he didn't fall off and Charlie just clung for life, fear ruling every inch of him.

Charlie was frozen in fear, which might have saved his life as it kept him calm and still while the water poured over him. His mind was a blank canvas which, for him, was actually quite nice. There was a looseness in it. A way of *being* he was unused to.

Trent continued his joyous screaming.

Charlie became conscious of his frailty. It solidified in him, the fact that at any moment it could all be over. Not just here, though. Anywhere. Anytime. Life was a tiny, fragile thing, insistent in its reach and its need to move forward. Charlie stood there, powerless, an obvious *who,* or *what,* was in control.

"Come on!" Trent raised his arms up, yelling, and he leaned forward into the wind. Charlie thought he was going fall as he kept leaning forward but something miraculous happened… Somehow, it propped him up and held him in the air.

Charlie had never seen anything like it. *That's trust,* he thought, as he clung, shaking and wet, to the rock.

"Here we are!" Trent continued to scream out into the darkness.

Charlie took several deep breaths and, somewhat lucidly, told himself, *this is defining. Just one step, Charlie. Come on, just one more step.* Charlie investigated himself for anything he could use. Everything he found told him to go back down. To go home. To stop. He ignored it all. *No,* he said to the more demeaning corners of his mind. *No. I can do this!* But now he was thinking too much. *That's it!* He thought. *Thinking. Stop thinking, Charlie, and just* do *something for once.*

Trent was still screaming next to him. Charlie watched from the rock below him.

Without turning to face Charlie, Trent yelled out, "Charlie! Come on! Just close your eyes and lift your arms! Lean forward and *feel* it!"

"This is fucking crazy!"

"I know!" Trent yelled, laughing away whatever fear remained in him. He felt charged and alive.

Any other day, any other moment, it would have seemed an absurd suggestion to Charlie. There was a more rational part of his brain that told him he was about to die. That part of him was sure of it.

But he was *here*, and something in him or around him beckoned. *It* called out him to take those steps outside himself. To be *more* than *what* he was.

Still shaking, Charlie managed a look at Trent, still leaning into the wind. Charlie noticed something: Trent wasn't fearless. He actually looked terrified, but he was *leaning* into it. He had completely let go despite the fact he was seconds away from imminent doom.

What the hell! Charlie thought as another cannonade of water washed over them and thrashed down on the rocks.

This is totally crazy! Charlie said to himself. *Totally-fucking-crazy!*

Eyes and fists clenched shut, Charlie actively shut his mind down. Slowly, he pulled himself over the edge so he was now on the top of the wall but still hugging the rocks for dear life. He then pushed with his hands and went to pull his feet underneath him when another wave crashed down on him, pushing him back down to the rocks. He would not be put off, though, and again pushed down on his hands and slowly began to raise himself up on the jetty. He pushed himself up to his feet. Then, from a crouch, he went to raise his arms up from where they were tucked in at his sides. It was difficult to remove them from their tucked position but slowly, moment by moment, he was able to reach them up, higher and higher. The wind pushed against him. He'd never felt such power before. He was surprised to find that it made him feel so much more alive. Soaking wet, fear fought to gain its dominance over him. It wasn't too far off from winning. Yet, somehow, in these conditions, the electricity in the air, the vibrant thrashings of life, Charlie kept going. Somehow, he was able to turn down the inner voice of doubt and he stood up a little taller, lifting his arms at first to shoulder height. Then he was startled by Trent screaming out into the void again.

Fury continued to explode all around them.

After the last crash of waves and water, Charlie's eyes still clenched shut, he stood taller and leaned forward into the wind. He raised his arms in defiance of everything that had ever held him back. All the worry and panic and shame. And everything that had created it. Right then, nothing would get in the way. From this moment onward, his life would be defined by a new set of terms, not by fear. That was a thing of the past. His new life would be defined by reaching out and taking chances. He might fall flat on his face but that wouldn't matter. He wouldn't be sitting there watching anymore.

Another strong burst of winds came through and somehow Charlie knew it was time. All the voices within him quieted. He was standing on the jetty, wide open and unprotected by whatever the elements threw at him. He might as well be a sacrifice to the ancient gods for a good harvest.

Now, he told himself. Up to this point, he'd been bracing himself against the wind. Not anymore. Charlie opened one eye, momentarily, just to sneak a look at Trent, who was still leaning, half-floating in the air, hollering with the wilds of nature. *Yeah,* Charlie thought, with a new sense of rousing courage flowing through him. *It's time.*

He did it. Charlie kept his eyes shut. Stretched his arms away from him and gave himself to the winds. He *let go.* He leaned forward until he was sure he would fall flat on his face but just before he started to *fall,* the winds caught him. There he was, with Trent during the wildest storm he'd ever experienced, being carried by the wind.

Charlie had never felt freer in his entire life.

He found breathing to be quite an easy feat in this state. He took in the air deeply and released it smoothly back out into the atmosphere. Surreal didn't begin to capture how Charlie felt. His mind was clear.

Charlie opened his eyes just a crack. He wanted to witness the chaos. He saw millions of drops of rain being carried this way and that by the wind. Whole hills of air moved about in the sky. There were bursts of thunder that boomed across the sky. The rains and winds were so thick it was as if there were full, deep rivers moving through the air, pushing against him. With him. He was a part of this primal system. He was connected to it. Its power bled into him and filled him with a certainty he'd never known before.

He heard Trent scream again but blocked it out. He blocked everything out. His thoughts were only focused on his exact present. The winds. The pounding thunder. The damp rocks beneath his feet. Every individual drop of rain. There was a strange beauty and madness to how little control he felt over any of it.

He knew he wasn't in control. Where that would have left him feeling dread before, now only brought upon feelings of warmth and comfort. He felt safe.

Charlie followed Trent's example and let loose the loudest yell he could. It was primeval. Primitive. An echo of the past before the mind had become so cluttered with modern worries. He didn't know it was in there. It was a scream of liberation, filled with defiance. It caught even Trent off guard, almost forcing him to deal with the rising level of admiration he was feeling toward Charlie; Charlie had followed him out here and was proving himself to be much stronger than Trent had originally supposed.

Charlie had never felt so alive. That night, he was baptized by the rushing waters. He would never be the same.

His conscious mind was clear. There was no room for negative thoughts or attachments. It was as if out *there*, he knew what he wanted. He knew he was meant to be free. And he was learning *how* to be free. Right then and there, he determined to himself never to be forced into a cage again. His father had built his first cage, and after he was gone, unbeknownst to Charlie, he and his mother gladly kept living within it. No more. Never again would he allow his life to be manipulated or directed by other people.

He welled up with thankfulness. This was one of the first moments he could consciously remember where he was without worry. And just then, Charlie West started to cry. Not tears of sadness or loss. Tears of abundance. Of joy. Tears hard fought for and well-deserved.

Charlie was thankful for the danger and the power of the storm. It brought with it release and freedom. For the first time in his life, Charlie felt powerful. *He felt himself.*

NINE

"You did what?" Ellie burst out, her look and tone proving her astonishment. Even she couldn't perceive how much Charlie was growing on her or that she was becoming quite taken by his subtle shift in strength, who she subconsciously believed him to really be.

"I know, I know." Charlie was backpedaling with each syllable. "It was crazy, and really, really dumb. I know. I didn't even want—" he stopped talking and caved under the wicked glare she was giving him. "Yeah, looking back, it was a bit insane. And stupid. But," he stopped and grinned, "you should have felt it!"

"Charlie," she couldn't help but laugh, "people die, like, every year doing that!"

He tried to shrug her comment off casually by taking a sip of his beer, but deep down he was proud of the risk he'd taken. He was proud of how he felt in general. He wasn't conscious of it, but at that moment, the battle within him for peace, which dictated the majority of the choices he made, was the quietest it had been in a long time. He was free to choose, and to simply be. And with that, he smiled at Ellie and took another drink from his beer.

There had been the ride back from the Jetty in Trent's truck. Some of those feelings had come back but seemed less persistent. He was more annoyed and angered than anxious or fearful. But he'd been so excited and so filled with adrenaline that he'd barely noticed.

Ellie watched him, nursing her whiskey. "Seriously, though," she said, "It's normally tourists or drunk teenagers who pull that shit on some dumb fucking dare and they end up getting washed out to sea. A few times it's taken the Coast Guard weeks to find their bodies." She wasn't getting through to him, she knew. There was nothing that could wipe that smirk off his face. But still she tried a different tactic. Besides, even as she was berating him, deep down, she was impressed. The more she got to know Charlie, the more she took him for someone worth knowing. "Or some newbie-townie-wannabe who moves out here to find himself and wants nothing more than to desperately prove himself in some pissing contest with his new, super insecure friend."

Charlie put his beer down and looked up at her. His mind moved quickly over everything she's just said. It was all true.

They both laughed and lifted their glasses up for a drink.

The ease of this conversation had settled in right from the beginning for both of them. They had each opened up in their own way and, whether either of them would admit it or not, they were each becoming a space of comfort and trust for the other.

It would have been the hardest for Ellie to admit. She hadn't even tried starting the conversation from a place of secured distance. Part of her had silently been looking forward to being able to be herself. That's what Charlie brought to her, mission or not: a brief peek at the future she hoped to build. The freedom to be herself.

"Look," Charlie told her. "I understand it was stupid. You couldn't get me to do it again if I were standing there right now. I normally wouldn't have done it in the first place, but," he paused, "the truth is, I'm glad I did. It did something. It cleared something out in me."

"Ugh," Ellie grunted at him and rolled her eyes in a melodramatic fashion. "Grandiose-macho-male bullshit?" She couldn't hide her smile even from herself.

Charlie looked at her, holding his glass. "Something like that." He took another swig. No one had ever called him macho before, even as a joke. "Just a nice, macho pissing contest between friends."

"I know Trent's compensating for something, so what's your excuse, huh?"

She found in Charlie's newfound freedom an opportunity for herself to step forward. Nevertheless, she couldn't let Charlie grow too confident, she thought playfully. And Ellie reached down to pick up her glass and threw it back with a well-practiced rhythm. Charlie would have been impressed but, after the past two days of drinking with her, he'd just become accustomed.

"Bartender!" Ellie yelled out, "I need a refill!"

"This ain't that kinda place, Ellie. Ya know that," grumbled the bartender, a grizzly old man living at the latter half of an unkindly life.

She and Charlie were the only two people in the bar.

"Bullshit and you know it!" Ellie broke into laughter then stood up and looked over to Charlie. "Next round's on me, but I have to go get them because this isn't *that kind of place*." Ellie nailed her impression of the raspy, broken voice of the bartender.

As she walked away Charlie finished his beer in preparation for the next drink.

As she made her way to the bar and back, that conflict gravitated back into her, reminding her not to get too close, that she was taking things too far. She looked over to Charlie, who sat there so unsuspecting of what was to come. But again, she didn't even know what was coming. She found herself musing what she would do if she knew. Would she tell him? How would he respond? Surely that would break whatever trust they were building now.

Shuddering at the thoughts, she pushed them away and made her way back to the table with their drinks.

Upon returning, two whiskies in hand, she found Charlie looking around the bar. As she set down the new drink in front of him, he asked her, "What kind of place is this, anyway?"

Looking from one grungy wall to the next, Ellie said, "Charlie West, this is the Portway." She stood again and raised her hand in mock salute and added, "Welcome aboard!"

Both of them broke out into low chuckles, but when it faded, Ellie's joyful façade faltered and she let slip, in a determined and all too truthful tone, "Where the forgotten go to forget."

Her smile dissolved and she clenched her jaw in a manner that Charlie knew all too well. He could see that she was holding back tears.

Ellie, contrary to all her assumed strength, when she was with Charlie, found it difficult to keep hope away. Over the last couple days, she found herself thinking through, and overthinking more, the situation she found herself in. The debts she needed to pay, and the life it had forced her to live. She wanted out.

Charlie watched as her countenance fell, wanting nothing more than to catch it. It hit him, again, the reasons for her sharp and caustic demeanor, for that wealth of protective layering, the fortifications. He knew she'd been hurt, and bad, and wondered when she'd trust him enough to tell him her story. That would be big.

He thought he was witnessing something happening in her tonight, something shifting. Even since he had seen her earlier. He felt it in her humor. Her lightness. And he felt it in the quick turn of her last comment.

Charlie felt, even if for only the briefest of moments, she was letting him glimpse her true self, in all its weary shame. He looked up at her, wanting nothing more than for her to see that he was there.

She looked away, feeling stupid for not being able to maintain her normal composure.

Come on, Ellie, she told herself. *Keep it together.* Deep down, she also knew that this would only help bring Charlie closer. This was also a thought that brought her less and less comfort.

Charlie recognized the look of embarrassment on her face, one he knew all too well. It was something she was probably not used to.

He put his hand out toward hers and she made a quick motion to pull hers away. For a moment, it sat hovering above the table.

Looking up at Charlie, she set it back down on the table, and he placed his hand on top of hers and curled his fingers underneath. She gently squeezed her own hand in his, as if to test if the moment were real. Neither one pulled themselves away from the other.

Ellie gave him a faint smile, fearful of how real it felt.

Charlie returned it with a brightness that can only shine from one so used to being shattered.

"It's okay," he told her.

"No, it's not, Charlie," she said, overcome by an urge to tell him everything. It disappeared as quickly as it came.

"What's wrong?"

She looked at him for a long time before answering. "Ask me again soon, okay? But not now. For now, can we just keep this *this*?"

Charlie didn't understand but, out of respect for her, he said, "Okay." He didn't want to push it. He knew what it was like to need that space. He just never thought he'd ever find another person that he felt he could share his space with. *Each other's* space, that is.

This only made her stomach turn over even more, and she picked up her new glass and said, "Bottoms up, Charlie West." And, raising the glass as if offering last rites to the indifferent gods above, she tossed it back and drained it in one gulp.

Charlie had managed a few sips before she did this and choked whiskey out of his mouth in astonishment. *Holy shit,* he thought.

"Wasn't that a double?" He asked her.

"Yes, it was," she said. "Yes, it was."

He smiled at her and she forced one back, feeling even more trapped by her newfound desire to be free. The longer she sat in it, the harder it became to simply be.

The room was filled with a mixture of happiness and stale pain.

Charlie was looking over at Ellie when she stood up and walked over to the bar again to order another round.

When Charlie asked Trent to drop him off to meet Ellie at the bar, Trent found himself very annoyed. But, given that it was the perfect way to get Charlie out of the house so he could hide the medallion, he caved. Trent obliged him.

What the medallion was or what it did, he had no idea. He was intrigued to know, however, especially after seeing the change that had come over Charlie in his truck.

Was that the medallion? he found himself wondering again. *Or was that just Charlie being tired?*

It was an emerging concern that had snuck up on Trent, even as he sat there in his truck. He was growing worried for Charlie and for what *they* wanted him for.

Something had begun to dawn on him as they were driving back from the Jetty. He was actually starting to like Charlie. And a suspicion was growing in him, beginning to emerge, that Charlie was being involved in something sinister and it wouldn't end well for him. As well, Trent was the one leading him through the winding maze.

It irked him then, how contrary he felt to what he was about to do. How wrong it seemed. He'd never experienced that type of moral opposition before, and he wasn't really sure what to do about it.

He was stuck.

For the briefest of moments, he considered not following through with his task, but as a flush of worry fired through him, the thought vanished immediately.

Part of him wondered how he could have even considered it. For he owed Mr. Wilkes everything and, as a result, he would give everything.

He had dropped Charlie off at the bar and was now standing just at the edge of the path that led down to Charlie's room.

Sorry bud, he'd thought as he made his way toward the door to plant the medallion, unaware of the endearing term he'd used in reference to Charlie.

He managed to get into Charlie's room quite easily and knew he would go undetected. Then, he removed his boots to ensure he would leave no prints behind.

Upon entering Charlie's room, the stone in his gut started acting up. Guilt and shame fell upon him like a bitter fog in a way he hadn't experienced since he was a child.

That's exactly how he felt right then, like a child who had broken the trust of a loved one – having done something that would take years to make up, maybe even a lifetime. He was not used to these feelings.

He struggled for a breath but found the task difficult.

Woah, shit, Trent thought to himself. *This is… I…*

His thoughts were confused now, at odds, and he found, right there, that it was only obligation moving him forward.

This only proved to increase the rising discomfort within him.

Fuck! he thought. It was strange being there without Charlie. It felt weird and wrong.

Unused to grappling with any sort of moral opposition, he leaned back toward the cold voice of reason and justification in his mind that had driven his life since being gifted his second chance.

Just get the job done, he heard his own voice reassuring himself. He thought of Mr. Wilkes and what he would say if Trent failed. A fear gripped him, the weight of which he could not withstand.

Shit, he thought to himself. *Shit, shit, shit. Just get it done and get out!*

He placed the medallion underneath Charlie's bed, exactly where Mr. Booth had expressly directed him to put it, where it would be in constant proximity to Charlie, but where he would be unaware of its presence.

Then, shaking a bit from the nuances of this agitation, he slid his boots back on and struggled his way through lacing them up. Once he made sure there was no sign of his entry or presence, he left.

Okay, he said, trying to calm himself by breathing in the cool, night air. *Now we wait.*

With the words, a dread fell onto him, crushing and seeming irrationally final. He was caught between the crashing of two waves: his old way of thinking, of seeing the world – blind obedience – and this new rising and unfamiliar conviction. He was glad nobody was there to see him in the midst of it.

Now that Charlie knew his truck, he parked it a little way down the road so as to not be seen. And there he waited for Charlie to return, hopefully without Ellie.

Then, he would watch. More of him than his cold reason was comfortable with was hoping that his observations would come to nothing, that he would simply watch Charlie come home, ready himself for bed, and fall slowly into a deep sleep. Then Trent could rest too. But something within him told him not to hold too tightly to these hopes. For they were false, it said. It whispered warnings of preparation to him, for the coming of something unnatural and wicked, for a fallout he could not predict nor prevent.

He thought of how Charlie had changed and reacted in the truck. *Could that have been the medallion?* he wondered. Then, he remembered that Charlie had seemed fine afterwards, relatively, and wondered if that was an indication of what he was about to witness. All he could do was wait. So, Trent sat in his truck and waited for Charlie to return, a worry growing in him like he had never experienced before, the comforts of his life fleeting in the wake of the slow burning realization that Trent didn't really have a choice.

Two short bursts of laughter and the sound of an empty can hitting the pavement shook Trent back awake. Startled, he had to look around and remind himself to why he was parked in his truck at the end of that cul-de-sac.

He remembered that he was supposed to be watching Charlie and his stomach sank.

Looking up, he saw that it was Charlie *and* Ellie

Fuck! Why is she here? He didn't like how she kept over-complicating things.

Ellie and Charlie stumbled their way down the sidewalk towards the back door, while Trent watched them giggle with every step. They were drunk.

Great, he thought. *That's just perfect.* He already wasn't in the best of moods.

The two disappeared behind the house, making their way down the stone stairwell to Charlie's room. A few seconds later, a dim light flickered inside and spilled onto the grass.

Okay. Here goes nothing, Trent thought.

Gently, he opened the door, stepped out into the cool of night, and hid behind the bushes next to the stairwell. He had a clear view of the entire room but was certain that no one would notice him.

Through a series of badly unchoreographed and awkward, drunken stumbles, Ellie and Charlie made their way over to his bed. It was the only place in the room they could both sit comfortably.

Earlier that evening, only a few drinks in, Ellie had all but accepted the blurred line between entrapping Charlie and letting herself enjoy the process. So she laid down on the comforter and scooted herself back, her head coming to rest upon the pillows, before signaling for Charlie to follow suit.

He did as he was directed.

As they lay, shoulders up against each other, Ellie slid her foot over so it rested next to his.

He didn't notice it. As soon as he'd entered the room, he was distracted by the strangest sensation that the walls were closing in. It was slight but present, nonetheless. Upon making contact with the bed, it was as if something invisible was tugging on a thread that had been woven through his mind. He tried to push it away and focus on what was before him.

To Charlie, the evening had been bliss. His time on the jetty had unlocked something in him, and the time with Ellie afterwards had been weightless and free.

She looked up at him, contented by the fact that she was actually letting herself enjoy a moment. She already knew she had him where she needed him, so she stopped paying attention to the small minutia of his feelings. If she had been paying close attention, she might have been able to feel the rising pressure within him.

But as they lay there, Charlie noticed more and more the tiny shifts within his body. *Something* was trying to creep back in. He tried to shake it off, but his mind was becoming increasingly preoccupied by whatever it was.

A few minutes in and that *something* was starting to pick up speed. It was like oxygen being released back onto a newly put out fire. He felt he could feel the sparks reigniting and beginning to flare. How long would it be before it was in full flame again?

Shit! Thought Charlie. *Not here. Not now!*

Worry was slowly seeping its way back into the lesser-guarded recesses of his mind, all those left over the cracks in the foundation, of which there were many.

He shook his head, trying to wave the shadowed thoughts away.

"Are you okay?" Ellie asked with a legitimate concern. She couldn't help but pull away, just slightly, so she could get a better look at him, but also because her trust was still very frail.

"Uh… yeah." He lied to her again, his tone sharp and piercing. It carried the sort of weight one would normally reserve for the words you used to create distance instead of closeness.

Ellie read something in his voice. It flagged something in her she couldn't quite explain, and she pulled back even further from him. She could feel herself going inward again, as the involuntary walls rose to protect her from whatever perceived danger she felt.

Her shift in proximity this time was pronounced, and Charlie froze, looking up at her from where he sat. Not *at* her exactly, just near her, near enough to calculate where she'd gone.

His anger flared as he saw this going in the wrong direction, a feeling that caught him off guard at first. It was soon lost in the continued rise of his unchained emotion.

Charlie, with his head starting to pound, tried to force a laugh to ease the moment.

"Yeah, look. I don't know what came over me." This was true. He had no idea what was happening to him. "I'm just tired is all."

He watched as the shadow of concern grew in her. She took another small step backward. That was the moment his worry spiked.

He sat up and, in a sort of rambling yell, said, "Seriously, Ellie, I'm… I'm great."

She took another step back, pulling herself away from him in a calculated and protective fear. There was a familiarity to the situation where instinct kicked in. Her only surprise was that it had come from Charlie. Her mind was in conflict again, wondering if she had misjudged Charlie. Something didn't add up.

"Yeah?" she said at last, making no attempt to move closer. "Are you?"

"Ellie? What's wrong?"

Charlie found himself hoping she couldn't see the anger growing in him. He wanted to explain what was going on, but even he wasn't sure.

Ellie, though desperate to say something, felt equally trapped, but in terms of feeling stupid for opening up. It wasn't until then that she'd realized how much she had trusted Charlie.

Charlie asked her again, "Ellie? Ellie, seriously, come on. What's the matter?" His tone grew shorter and colder with every word.

After several more nudges, she finally said, "It's... nothing, Charlie. Really." But, still, she stayed away.

Charlie felt pressure from both inside and outside of himself. He didn't know which was worse. But he felt the strain of their teamwork as he was finding even breathing to be a chore again. It didn't seem like nothing to him. Something was the matter.

Is it me? He wondered. He thought about how he felt, how it must look. *It must be me making her feel this way...* Normally, that thought would have crippled him with thoughts of inadequacy and lack of worth. But now it only fueled how he felt. The fires were growing hotter, burning more steadily.

"Seriously, Ellie. What's up?" He tried forcing out a chuckle to ease the growing tension. It backfired and she leaned away. Charlie made to reach his hand out. "Ellie, what's wrong? Tell me!" These last two words came out in an angry burst.

Ellie stepped back again, still saying nothing, but visibly shaken. *There's something different about this*, she told herself, unsure if it was just what she wanted to believe.

Charlie reached out with what he could feel, though his emotions were flailing. She had cut him off. He felt it. He was shut out. Having kept his own walls shut most of his life, he knew the feeling all too well. He felt her fear as well, and he registered that she was afraid of *him* for some reason.

What the hell, he thought, but again, all of this only came together to spurn his anger on all the more.

"Ellie? Come on—" He yelled this time and stopped himself in his tracks. He couldn't control it.

Ellie took two quick steps back, further away from the bed, and Charlie slid across the bed, reaching out to take her hand.

She pulled away from his grasp even quicker than before, narrowly escaping him with a practiced efficiency.

"Dammit Ellie!" Charlie burst out, standing up from the bed. "What the hell is going on?"

She leapt around to the end of the bed, ensuring there was something between them and that she was close to the door. She wasn't thinking anymore; her mind had slid into a protective state. But, deep down, something told her that this wasn't Charlie. That there was something more at work here, but that didn't mean she could trust it.

Charlie was shaking, now, fists clenched at his sides.

"Ellie—" he started to say, gritting his teeth.

"Charlie, what—"

"Why are you backing away?" he screamed.

Ellie backed up against the wall with alarm. She didn't know what to think. *Where the hell had this come from?* She wondered. She didn't know what to say to him or what to do. This was a completely different person than the one she'd just spent an evening with. The only thing going through her mind now was that she needed to get out.

For a moment, something broke through. Maybe it was the look of terror in her eyes or some kink in his ballooning anger that allowed some semblance of a normal thought through, but Charlie looked up and, through his own eyes, saw Ellie, frozen and shaking, leaning against the basement wall.

"Ellie... Ellie?" he whimpered, rubber-banding to the other side of the emotional spectrum, now broken by grief. "I'm... I'm so sorry." He slowly reached out his hand to hers. "I don't know—"

"Don't come near me!" she yelled at him with that same protective force she'd showed before.

"Ellie?" He went to take a step towards her.

"Stop! Stop it! Don't move!"

He stayed still but reached his hand out.

"Charlie! Stop!"

He stopped, but right away his frustration began to boil over again. He was trying to keep it down, but the pressure was too immense. He was going to burst.

"Ellie! God damnit! Just talk to me!"

She flinched at his outburst.

"Charlie, what... what the hell's going on?"

Her eyes pleaded with him, but they went unseen.

"What do you mean—" he said. "You're no—" He was unable to complete a thought. He was being overtaken. Everything was becoming fuzzy, so he couldn't think straight.

As he attempted to gather himself, the whole room seemed to take a very necessary yet difficult-to-come-by breath.

Ellie stood, hands against the wall, ready for anything, and Charlie exploded. He jumped at her and reached his arms out to grab her.

Ellie shrieked and spun away. She whipped her body back and forth, her elbow connecting with Charlie's jaw.

He gave a yell and stumbled backwards to the floor. Instinctually, he brought his hand up to where the blow had caught him and looked around searchingly. The veins in his neck and forehead were bulging. His chest heaved in and out, showing how hard his heart was working to sustain his outbursts.

He yelled and turned to throw himself at her again, but when he looked up, she was gone.

The back door was wide open, and the evening air was rushing in to fill the space.

He could feel her absence, but he was too agitated to recognize the regret he would feel later. He just stood there, firsts still clenched, and screamed out into the darkness, "Ellie!"

Only the wind whispered back in response. It could just be heard over the heavy sounds of Charlie's breathing.

Trent had heard the door burst open before he saw her. Then he watched Ellie tear her way up the stone steps, and down the side path before she made it to the street. Then she was gone. He had jumped out of the way at the last second, behind a bush, and had just barely escaped being caught. Even if he hadn't moved though, she might not have noticed him in her frantic state.

He wondered what he had just witnessed, how Charlie could have turned that quickly, how he had changed.

Horrorstruck, Trent grappled with where the docile and meek Charlie had gone.

That explosion, that anger, that level of rage, Trent thought. He never would have thought Charlie capable of it.

For a moment, he considered the only variable difference in the room... the medallion.

No way! he thought, gripped then by a sudden panic, *That's crazy.*

The conversation he'd with Mr. Booth came back to him. *Plant the medallion, and report back on* whatever *changes you see in the boy.*

He'd followed the directions exactly, as he always did, and this time against his rising judgement.

His mind was racing, and he considered Charlie's behavior in the truck to and from the jetty.

Oh. Trent's stomach nearly fell out from beneath him. His mind was doing somersaults within his skull. Part of him didn't want to accept the reality that it was *he* – there was no escaping it – who had placed the medallion in Charlie's room, thus causing this violent shift in him. It was *he* who had had it in his truck when Charlie had initially started acting a little weird. It was *his* fault, Trent knew. *He* had done this to Charlie, a person he was having trouble fathoming why he cared about at all. The weight he felt in that moment was immeasurable and crushing.

Even Ellie, Trent found himself thinking, who he didn't remotely care for in the least: *She didn't deserve that*, he reasoned, wondering how a simple artifact could hold so much power over a person. After all, it had been in Trent's truck all day and it had no effect whatsoever on him.

Everything within him tightened and sank deep down into the pit of his gut. It was like the hull of a ship ripped open, being pulled down through the depths of the sea, well beyond the light of day.

I… I'm sorry, Charlie, Trent found himself thinking. The recognition of the statement only leaving him feeling worse.

His mind spun and reeled. He couldn't think clearly anymore.

Shame spread over him like water on a dry, flat surface, spilling and reaching out to envelop everything. It showered down like cold rain. He couldn't remember ever feeling this low in his life, even in his more reckless days.

This is wrong, he thought. But now he was a part of it. He was partially responsible.

But what could he do?

Something in him told him to just run in there and grab Charlie and tell him everything. Just blow the whole lid off everything.

But then he'd have to tell Charlie what he'd done, what he'd been a part of.

What would Mr. Wilkes say? Trent shuddered. The mere thought of Mr. Wilkes restructured his thoughts for him.

Everything could still end up alright, he reasoned his way over to the other side of the spectrum. *Who's to say this won't work out for Charlie in the end?*

Then Trent looked back down into the room, at Charlie. His heart sank as he watched Charlie lying there, curled up on the edge of his bed, weeping wild and ugly tears.

His stomach tightened itself into a little painful ball again and twisted.

Trent watched him for the next several minutes as his body contorted and reeled itself back and forth between states of being limp or gripped by strained flexes. There was so much emotion pumping through him, so much pain. It seemed that thousands of tiny, little needles were poking and prodding into him. Into each of his many wounds, both physical and emotional. He was lost to the chaotic recesses deep within himself.

Trent sat there, still overcome by the urge to run down, grab the medallion and throw it away – into the ocean maybe – and simply be done with it all. Why he didn't was beyond him.

But always, his thoughts were drawn back to Mr. Wilkes and his generous hand. Trent him owed everything and hadn't the strength to throw it away.

Dammit! His mind strained in from mental tug-o-war.

In the end, he did nothing. He just stood by and watched as Charlie struggled.

Charlie convulsed and shook. Every minute or so he erupted once more into a bout of angry tears.

Trent crept closer and closer to the window, still well hidden behind the bushes, leveled by his hellish shame. As a sort of misguided and tortured penance to his responsibility, he felt the need to keep watching.

Then, ever so faintly, he heard a knock at the basement door, and a voice calling from off in the distance. Trent took another cautious step back, careful not to let himself be seen by anyone.

"Charlie?" The voice came down the stairwell. It was muffled by the closed door at the top of the stairs and Trent could barely hear it through the open back door. "Is everything okay down there?" It was Charlie's landlord. He must have woken them up with his outburst.

Trent watched Charlie freeze before he heard the soft knock come again and Paul's words, "Charlie? Are you okay?"

Trent watched as Charlie grew frantic.

Charlie's own mind was a cloudy mess.

What should I do? He wondered. *What will they think? Will they want me out? How will I find a new place? What will the school think? Oh, shit. I'm going to lose my job!*

He fought for focus but couldn't seem to clear his head. He managed a strained, "Yes?" and was able to suppress that burning frustration in him just enough that he hoped Paul would let it go. "Everything's okay, thanks," Charlie said again, after another pause. "Just watching a movie with a friend, and I—" he scurried to think up a lie, but his mind was as blank as a night with no stars. "Sorry about the noise. I... I didn't realize it was so loud. Sorry. I... uh... my friend just left," he threw out at the last second. It wasn't completely untrue.

No one in their right mind would believe this, he thought. *I'm done. You're done, Charlie. Done. Pack it up now. Fuck! Fuck! Fuck!*

"Are you sure?" Came the soft voice again. Charlie stopped berating himself and looked up. "I thought I heard yelling."

He continued to reel and squirm. The overloaded emotion looked to escape from him through each and every pore of his body. He fought hard to keep control of the tone in his voice. "Uh, no, no. Really, it's all fine. Sorry again. I'll keep it down."

Charlie waited.

"I heard someone say your name, though."

"Uh – yeah, but... I'm sorry, Paul. Look, it won't happen again. I promise." He needed Paul to leave. The last thing Charlie needed was for him to come into the room.

After several more excruciating seconds, Paul finally gave in. "Okay, well, let us know if you need anything?"

He was so thoughtful. If only Charlie had been in a place to have noticed, he would have been thankful. But instead, Charlie was ruled by this unknown triggering fury that flowed through every ounce of him.

"Will do. Thanks, Paul. Good night," Charlie said through pushy exhales. When he'd finished speaking, he held his breath and waited. After a few more stretched out seconds, there was no response and Charlie, slowly, let out an extended exhale, making him a bit lightheaded.

The room started to spin around him, slowly, with objects and images flashing themselves in front of him.

Fuck! He cursed himself. *What the fuck is going on?*

Charlie tried letting go of everything. He tried to breathe, but the strained tension held to him tightly. Its grip was strong and wouldn't let go, like was a captive to his own mind and body – exhausted to the state of flex.

Normally, after an episode, letting go would bring about a release of emotion, a cathartic purge. Charlie would feel himself *lowering*. And, normally, it would happen quickly. But just as had happened in the attic, as Charlie went to let go, nothing lowered. No purging came. Everything just clung to him tighter, and held harder, like dead weight.

If he didn't do something soon, he would seize up like an engine on the verge of complete collapse.

He tried picture Ellie's face, from when they were at the Portway earlier. It was a stark contrast to the Ellie he'd just seen, the one filled with fear. Fear that Charlie had caused, no less.

Fuck her! He screamed internally. The anger was like the air pressure that had built up within a capped bottle; with nowhere to go, it had built and built and built until it could be released. He wanted to release it but couldn't seem to be able to find the cap.

He couldn't stop thinking of Ellie and the perceived slight she'd given him. There was no remembrance at all now of what Charlie had done.

Who does she think she is? Does she think she can get away with that? The frustration was mounting again.

Images flooded into his mind, and they were many. First, they were just images from the night. The ups and the downs. He and Trent standing on the Jetty, screaming. He and Ellie having drinks at the Portway before walking home. But then they shifted to remembrances of his life. Images of hurts and pains. His anger burned and the world was growing fuzzy. Dizziness was beginning to overwhelm him, and he was losing whatever clarity his conversation with Paul had brought him.

Through sheer strength of will, he was attempting to reason out what was going on, but it was no use.

Stop it! He yelled at himself. *Focus!* He began hitting himself on the side of his head with his palms, over and over. *Focus! Dammit!*

Nothing.

Charlie flung himself onto his bed and buried his face deep into a pillow so as to let loose muffled and violent scream.

It was *all* too much. The pressure. The pain. His mounting anger.

Tension only grew in him, cinching tighter and tighter, as if it were trying to close off his chest and esophagus. He could barely breathe, and the pigment in his face was bordering on the color of a second-degree burn.

The human body can only take so much, and after so much strain, so much struggle, Charlie West finally began to sob. It wasn't the same as his angry tears from earlier. These were much more subtle. They were softer and seemed to show that something was working its way through him.

It started out as a single whimper that was punctuated by several gasps for breath, followed by a lonely tear that clung to his cheek, as if holding on for life. Like Charlie, it feared the fall. Several more tears followed and found themselves spilling out. The rest came en masse.

Within minutes, Charlie was a waterfall of salty tears, but he still looked as if he would burst. There was no release from the pressure. He took turns between heaving breaths and hyperventilating. He still had no control.

He wept for forty minutes straight until, eventually, his whole body simply gave out.

Too exhausted to keep going, Charlie West fell off into a tortured and restless sleep. One that no calm or peace could penetrate.

From outside, Trent watched in horror as Charlie, his *friend*, continued to suffer.

He too felt the turmoil – granted, not as much as Charlie. That much he knew. And definitely not as much as the guilt was telling him he deserved.

He felt nothing but that ache.

What have I done?

But it was no matter. Looking down at the unconscious Charlie, it was as if something had made the decision for him, to continue on his forward path.

"I'm sorry, Charlie," he said, in a whisper so delicate it might have shattered in the gentle wind.

He pulled his phone out of his pocket and began to make his way back to his truck.

Still at odds at what to do, the cold reason of his experience told him to call Mr. Booth and complete his task. This was the only course of action.

The night was cold and the wind was just beginning to stir once more. That day's storm had dissipated some time long before, but tomorrow's, Trent felt, was already brewing.

Here, in this part of the world, the next storm was always just around the corner.

Trent stood there, his cell phone to his ear, when Mr. Booth finally picked up.

"Trent? Is that you?" Mr. Booth asked. "Tell me everything!"

Trent stood there, caught in the ocean's rising tide, helpless against its unstoppable current and power. He wanted anything but to be there in that moment but, like everything else, that was out of his hands. He knew, deep down, that he was going to tell them everything they wanted to know.

Charlie's mother was a vehicle moving forward without a driver now, pacing through her house, doing lap after lap after lap. She hadn't eaten. She was barely sleeping. She could barely focus. But when focus did come, she thought only of Charlie. They were not happy thoughts, though. They were thoughts plagued and weighed down by the loss of her connection to her son. When lucid, they were tainted by a subtle recognition of her assumed maternal failures – nothing that Charlie had ever accused her of before, of course. These were weights and slanders she had devised all by herself over the years. But they had grown in his absence and metastasized within the supple and unguarded soil of her mind.

Without a prayer of knowing what was happening to her, let alone how to fight it, Charlie's mother was slowly disappearing from the world. Not just from Charlie, but from herself too.

TEN

The doors to Mr. Wilkes' office were hand-carved and high-arched. They burst open, an echoing reverberation carried through the room, seeming to shake the very air that had, just moments before, hung there motionless. The iron handle clicked back into resting position as Mr. Booth released his grip and entered the room. He stopped just in front of Mr. Wilkes' desk, the antiquated centerpiece of this well-appointed space.

Never in his most remote speculations would Mr. Booth have ever considered the level of worry that was streaming through his superior at the time, the weight he carried in pushing them toward the culmination of their plan.

Positioned prominently behind this desk, Mr. Wilkes sat, his ghost-white hair protruding in all directions, reading over a set of time-worn papers by lamplight, doing everything he could to keep himself steady.

Mr. Booth played the obedient hound well and waited until spoken to before revealing why he was there. His patience was practiced and expectant.

Mr. Wilkes, who was all too aware of the man, continued to read through the papers before him until finding a satisfactory stopping point. This was just one of the many ways he projected his dominance over his men. After several silent moments, he asked without looking up, "So, are we moving forward?"

"Yes, sir."

"Very good. And what is the latest update?"

"I've just heard back, sir, and the results were — how should I say — very favorable."

"Indeed?" Mr. Wilkes said, looking up. His tone shifting closer to one of a hesitant excitement, but he could never let on to just how excited the news made him. He lay the papers down on the table to give the news more attention.

"Yes, sir. It appears that our suspicions were correct."

Leaning forward, his chair squeaking from the strain, his eyes lit up like two candles hovering in a dark and forgotten corridor. Mr. Wilkes was eager to know more. The foundations of his restraint were showing signs of weakness. Something was shifting in him, something even he couldn't quite explain.

A pregnant silence filled the room as he seemed to be considering a great many things.

The subservient gentlemen waited, once more, to be acknowledged

"Mr. Booth?"

"Yes, sir?"

"I want to move the timetable up again."

"Sir?"

"The timetable. I would like to move everything forward, ahead of the appointed schedule."

"But sir?"

"Are the tests not completed?"

"Yes, sir."

"Do we not have sufficient belief in the success of the coming ceremony?"

"Well, yes, sir—"

"Then what is the problem, *Mr. Booth?*" said Mr. Wilkes, thinking he needed to reassert his strength and his dominance. He hated feeling like he was losing control of his men.

A hint of worry crept into Mr. Booth's expression, betraying his steady hand. For just a moment, the man's consistent demeanor was broken, but he immediately recomposed himself into the expected repose. "Of course, sir."

"Thank you, *Mr. Booth.* I believe we should go and make ready for our guest now, shouldn't you say?" Mr. Wilkes once again looked back down toward the papers he'd been reading. "Say, for tomorrow?"

Mr. Booth said nothing but fidgeted.

"Is that going to be a *problem*?"

"Uh... no. No, sir. I'll make all the necessary arrangements."

"Very good," Mr. Wilkes said. "And don't fret about the brothers. I already have them on stand-by. You just need to worry yourself about contacting our players in the field." A wide and grim smile spread itself out on Mr. Wilkes' face like wings unfolding, about to take flight. In the candlelight, he looked as wild as a neatly carved, deranged jack-o-lantern, set about to scare any who passed. "The final stage is finally upon us," he smiled.

"Yes, sir. Right away, sir." Then Mr. Booth gave a practiced bow, not rising until released.

Mr. Wilkes hung onto that moment a few moments longer than even he thought was necessary before saying, "Very well. That will be all."

"Thank you, sir." Standing up, Mr. Booth turned to leave. But, as he was crossing the room again, he was called back.

"Mr. Booth?"

"Yes, sir?" He stopped and turned once more.

"Ensure that our man keeps an extra close eye on young Charlie over the next thirty hours. Everything must be *exact*."

"Of course, sir. As you wish."

Mr. Wilkes waved him away and returned his attention once again to the papers in front of him, but he couldn't read a word. His focus was gone. All that remained was the fury of excitement at what was to come. He knew not to show anything until he was completely alone.

Mr. Booth turned again and took his final steps through the room, grasped the door's iron handle, and scurried his way back through the high-arched doors, closing them as gently and quietly as he could once he was through to the other side.

Alone at last, Mr. Wilkes broke frame from his statuesque self, the fire lighting in his dark and impassioned eyes. His smile widened underneath the wicked shadows cast by the candlelight.

The following morning brought with it the worst summer storm the town had seen in decades. It was a nonstop barrage of explosive, deafening wind, seventy plus miles per hour, and continuous mighty walls of rain. The entire county was steeped in cloud cover of a silvery, deep steel grey. It was as if some malevolent and ancient god had placed towering, sheer mountain cliffs on each side of the town, blockading it from the rest of the natural world. Any natural light that found itself able to creep its way through was, by the end of its journey, sickly and dim.

Charlie was kept half-awake most of the night, trapped between states of alarm and restlessness. In the winds, a large branch next to his bedroom had snapped from a tree and was hanging down by the wiry threads of its bark. It dangled, reaching its long arm downward where it scraped endlessly back and forth against a window over his bed. It clawed at his thoughts, keeping him from his already unsteady, turgid sleep, and assisted in populating his already grim dreams with a heightened sense of unease and disquiet.

The inconsistent clamor even kept him from falling back asleep after he'd woken early to use the bathroom at around four in the morning. After a time, he finally resolved to turn and check the time. It read 7:37 am.

Goddammit.

Charlie was in rough shape – far worse than even he knew. As far as he felt, he might as well have stayed up all night. He couldn't even remember falling asleep, just the frustration and mounting pressure in his body. Thoughts flashed back to him of his mind ballooning, outgrowing the space available in his skull. The sharp tweaks of pain he'd felt, the exhaustion and the numbing remnant lingered still. Even as he lay there, his heart rate and awareness couldn't drop below a level he was certain was beyond normal, even for him. It strained itself within him and, just like Charlie, it longed for its own escape. Instead of swirling him into an early despair, these restless thoughts and feelings proved only to rekindle, to reawaken, it seemed, the anger within him that also ached for escape.

As his thoughts fell upon it, he felt it spike.

Fuck! He covered his face with the nearest pillow as if to stave off whatever yell might explode out of him.

The more he focused on it, the more it grew.

He was so lost and confused as to what was happening and why. Charlie had spent a lot of years in his life cracked and overwhelmed by his flailing, unbridled emotions, but not like this. He'd never experienced anything like this.

The more awake he became, the more difficult it became to sort out his thoughts or to keep up with them.

They turned, almost against his will, to Ellie. At first, he saw them, he and Ellie, walking downtown and having lunch, then going to the bar together. It was pleasant, but something still burned beneath it. Then he remembered running into Trent and the phone call with his mom.

At this, Charlie's anger exploded, pushing him closer towards the irrational.

Charlie, calm—Calm do—

But he'd lost focus again.

He remembered the jetty, how he'd felt in the truck, the discomfort. It had been similar to how he was feeling now, but this was much, much more pronounced. More acute.

His thoughts carried him along back to the Portway the night before. He and Ellie were laughing, enjoying themselves. Some of that joy attempted to penetrate his thoughts as he lay there in bed, but it was not allowed in.

Then something crashed within him and his mind went blank.

Shit, he thought. *What—*

Something flashed, an image. He couldn't quite make it out. But he heard the screams. His screams. The fires in him began to burn brighter again, and he saw who he was screaming at. It was Ellie. A flash of heat flared, flooding his whole body.

No...no!

But he felt no sympathy or even guilt. All he felt was the boiling fury towards all the people who had ever hurt him. His body stiffened and he protectively pulled the blankets up to cover himself.

An image of his mother flashed in front of him, unconscious and laying on the floor.

Another flash of heat burst forth and Charlie shook. His body was twitching and he found himself caught in a state of flex, unaware that he was, yet again, holding his breath, depriving himself of much needed oxygen.

Images of the waves crashing over the jetty, having drinks with Ellie, laughing, yelling with Trent out at the vast canopy of stars over their heads, careening in his truck only moments before. He saw his mother again, panic stricken and worried, then Ellie screaming – his anger, all the while, rising to the surface within him. A bubble about to explode. He couldn't hold it in.

Then, without warning, a scene materialized in his mind that took place a week before Charlie's father had died – a scene of his father coming at him with those cold, precise, glazed-over eyes. That look of premeditated intent. Pain. Charlie heard his childhood-self scream and then he himself let out a strained yelp as he was unable to curb the mounting pressure from within. With an almost violent twist, he turned over and buried himself deep into the pillows and cushions that would bring no comfort, shaking and afraid.

In his truck, several houses down the street from Charlie's, Trent also attempted to sleep. It was not going well by any stretch of the imagination. Better than Charlie, but he didn't know that. His conscience kept him from traveling too deep into the realm where he could experience real rest. Every so often, he would twitch or shake, and his brow would furrow at his growing discomfort. His lips would warp as they were tugged on by the streams of worry that flowed through his mind.

He lay there, his head propped up on the driver's side window, with a camouflage sweatshirt for his pillow and his arms crossed over himself for warmth. There was half a week's stubble on his face and, as of then, it had been two whole days since he'd had a shower.

Trent was haggard and worn. Not even he could have told you if he were more tired physically or emotionally. He was unused to the weight he was carrying and paralyzed by the inability to act upon his own convictions.

His phone buzzed once, a text message. But he didn't hear it. He didn't budge. He was so tired that his conscious-self stayed put as he slept, just on the other side of being able to recognize such waking sounds.

Like the rest of the world, the message would have to wait.

Though it counted for very little, it at least was a break from carrying the strain of what he should do. Either way, he needed rest. He yearned for a deeper sleep but realized that, unless he acted, it might never come again.

As the morning began to emerge, his face and shoulders would periodically twitch, his jaw giving way to a subtle tremble. Whatever thoughts were hiding behind his eyelids, they were not pleasant. For his expression was filled with a deep anguish and the growing lines upon his face alluded to the mounting burden that Trent feared would slowly consume him.

At the rundown rental house where Ellie lived, she sat on the single chair that made up her living room, gazing out the front window, lost to thoughts of Charlie and the night before. She had barely slept and had spent so much time trying to figure out what had happened. She held a mug of strong but bitter coffee and wore a thin, distant stare.

What had caused Charlie to go off the rails like that? She wondered. *Was that hiding in him the whole time? Was what I had seen before just a façade?*

She thought of his sweet disposition, how much he had seemed to care before. She thought of the hope she had been filled with when spending time with him. And she wracked her mind trying to figure out what *they* wanted him for. Even after his burst, despite the fear she had felt, she wanted – all the more – to keep him from harm.

She had hoped so much before that this job might lead to her freedom, but now she felt more imprisoned than ever before. Trapped by the debt that she owed. Trapped by her inability to do anything about it. She wanted to help Charlie. Obviously, something was going on, something that he was completely unaware of. But what could she do? And how? She was powerless, that much was clear.

So, she sat there, sipping her bitter coffee, which had long been cold and only brought about the illusion of warmth, when her phone rang, startling her.

Ellie looked at the time.

Fuck, she thought, *only* they *would call me at this time.*

Her stomach turned over before it seemed to reach up, morphing into a mucky cement, infecting her entirely.

The phone rang again.

Oh, shit… oh shit… oh shit, she thought, holding her breath, unsure what to do. The last thing she wanted to do was answer it, but she knew what would happen if she didn't.

Her hands trembled as her whole self-caved under the pressure of those practiced, well-defined expectations.

"Goddammit," she said under her breath as she reached up and rubbed a few tears away.

Then, she set down her coffee and stood up from the chair, her phone in her hand.

She knew they were in complete control.

Maybe after this is all over, she thought. *Maybe…*

Then, closing her eyes, she hit the answer button and placed the phone to her ear.

"Yeah?" She said, her tone timid and very restrained. "Uh-huh. Yes." She started chewing her thumbnail nervously and, as she spoke, wells of tears flooded forward, ready to spill out of her. "Yes?" her voice cracked so she cleared her throat to better prepare what she would say next. "Yeah. Yes, I'm here alone. No, of course —really—but Char—no... are you—okay. Okay. I'm sorry. I'll be here, waiting."

Before she could say anything more, they had hung up, leaving her waiting there, even more alone than she was before. She hadn't found out anything new, but maybe as she went along, she could.

Something in her told her to call Charlie, to check on him, or even to tell him to run away. But she knew she wouldn't. She knew she would do what she always did, which was to cave and comply.

She turned off the phone and, holding it with both hands, rested it right above her heart. She fell back into her chair by the window and steam continued to rise out of her coffee mug. For a while, it was the only thing that moved until Ellie let out a tremble. And with it, any poise and strength she had left crumbled. It disintegrated into wails of inconsolable tears. And Ellie Stone sat there, wondering if she would ever be free.

By midday, the rain had not let up and the winds were doing everything they could to remind everyone that the storm was still there. What was normally the brightest part of the day was masked by a slate-hued sky, still trapping everyone underneath it in a shadowing prison. It wasn't helping Charlie's mood.

He lay, still in bed, fatigued and exhausted.

He had rolled over several times, a maneuver that left him feeling taxed and tired, and would reach out to check the time.

There were no missed calls or messages, a fact that left him both relieved and agitated. He didn't want to talk to anybody but, at the same time, something in him told him that he shouldn't be alone in this state.

But who would come be with me now? This thought sunk its teeth in deeper than most. It stayed with him, swirling up the ebbing unrest that had taken over.

He still couldn't focus and found that he was still foggy, feeling as though he were trying to run through water in an attempt to keep up with his own thoughts. They were somehow able to keep just ahead of him, just out of reach.

Any time he tried to focus, memories of the night before would flash intermittently before him, again triggering an irrational response.

At one point, he flung his phone across the room and buried himself back into his pillows with the blankets pulled tightly over his head, perpetually on the verge of bursting into angry tears. He felt that the whole world was out to hurt him. Everyone. There was no one he could trust.

Hours passed with no change. Charlie was stuck. Trapped. There existed no conscious way for him to pull himself out of this prison. And as the day pressed forward, he grew more tired and faint. He hadn't eaten and his growing hunger was only working to increase his agitation.

He was a smoldering fire awaiting the fuel it needed to burst back to life.

After his lack of awareness had let another chunk of time slip past him, his phone rang.

Charlie jumped but didn't reach for it right away. He needed to make sure it was real.

It rang twice more.

Surprisingly, he found himself hoping that it was Ellie, but then shook the thought away.

No, she wouldn't call me.

He took a deep breath, an attempt at calm himself before seeing who had called, and he got up to go grab his phone that still lay on the floor across the room.

"Shit," he said as a blast of frustration rang through him. It was as if a lightning bolt had struck the bottom of his spine and wrung the whole way up until it had exited through his brain.

All the anger he'd felt was reawakened now.

It was his mother.

He thought of all the messages he had left, all the calls he had made. He tried to think of what she could have been doing that was so important she had failed to call him back.

He even considered not answering it, of letting her dangle on edge for a while. These thoughts blew fresh air on the kindling coals within him.

On the verge of not picking up the phone, given his state, Charlie thought of all the things he'd *never* said to his mom, of all the times he'd had to be there for *her*, of his whole life as she'd been there but not really *been* there. She'd been nothing more than a ghost, hovering around his presence, searching for life.

Though these thoughts might've been filled with half-truths, he'd never been so blinded by rage in his life.

Fuck it, he said, and he answered the phone.

"Hi, mom." His tone was restrained and filled with what he was holding back.

"Charlie!" She said in a panic. "Charlie! Is that you?"

"Yeah, Mom—where the hell have you been?" Charlie let it loose, seeing no more reason to hold anything back. He exploded.

"Charlie, I've— It's been— I need—"

"Mom. What the hell happened the other day? I've been trying to get—" All traces of empathy were gone, having been burned right out of him.

"I know. I know, honey. I just—" But she started to cry.

Goddammit. Here we go again, Charlie thought. He was completely unaware of how not-himself he was being.

"Mom? Mom! For fuck's sake!"

Her crying stopped for a second before erupting into higher wails and hyperventilated panic.

"Goddammit, Mom! I need to *talk* to you!"

"I'm so— Charlie, I'm sorry—"

"This is how it always fucking is," he yelled. "How it's always fucking been."

"Wh—"

"No! Dammit, Mom." Charlie plowed right through. "I *needed* you!" Now, Charlie started to cry angry, warm tears, entirely bereft of sadness. "I've... I've always *needed* you... and you've never been there... for me!"

Charlie had had these sorts of thoughts before, for a good portion of his adult life, but they were always cushioned by understanding, by the knowledge that she too had been shattered and had never done less than the best she could. That understanding was nowhere to be seen now. Before this moment, he never would have said anything. He'd always tried to protect her. But now, Charlie wanted *justice* for his life. Now, he wanted retribution.

A dark and brooding quiet entered the space between them when Charlie had finished his last burst, where only the heaviness of each other's breathing could be heard.

Something was happening in him. Something neither of them could understand. But all the same, she lacked the means or understanding to explain that something had been happening to her too. And with his unreasonable explosions, how could she even attempt to share it with him?

Charlie flung himself back into his tirade. "I've always had to be there for you! For *you*! Goddammit! I've always had to put *my* life on hold! For *you*! Put *my* dreams away! And for what? Huh? For what? For fucking what?"

His voice was hoarse and, after yelling for such a sustained amount of time, he was left gasping for breath.

Charlie's mother, having been reduced to inconsolable sobs, gave no response or defense. She knew that some of what he was saying was true. She'd always known it. It was what had kept her awake so often over the years. Her one reprieve from these demeaning thoughts were that Charlie had chosen to love her anyway, to endure with her, to heal together. But everything he was saying was right. His explosion had been her worst fear realized. The complete and utter failure of her ability to be there for her child.

Charlie's tone slipped into a controlled plea. "Mom, I've *barely existed*."

She gave no response to this. All that could be heard on her end were muffled sobs.

Even now, he thought, wrongly, *even now she's only thinking of herself!*

"And *you*! You were never..." he started, "never more than a vapor, a ghost of what I needed you to be."

"Cha—"

"No!" He exploded again. "And Dad? You never did anything about him! An– Why, Mom? Why? What the—"

Charlie hadn't planned on taking their conversation to his father, but when it came to Charlie thinking about his life, the whys and hows of how he'd developed into what he had become, things tended to gravitate there — to the mark his father had left on them both.

Before this strange episode, Charlie had always associated both he and his mother as the victims. But *now*, by some block, some inability to see beyond his own pain, something had changed in him. A feeling. A belief. Something had *shifted*, and anything save for his singular experience simply did not exist. His mother's experiences, for that matter, all of her pain had been erased.

Memories poured into him after that, speeding by faster and faster. Mostly of his father, and the weight and pain he had carried, the prison it had created.

He paused long enough from his tirade for his mother to stumble through a few words before trailing off once more into distant sobs. "Charlie, I'm so s—"

Her voice triggered him back into full force.

"No! Fuck your apology! You don't get to be sorry! Not anymore! Never again!" With a deafening finality, he screamed, "Leave me the fuck alone! Don't call! Don't text! No more! Cut me off! Leave me the fuck alone!" And he hung up.

The immediate silence of the room was disrupted only by the quick and consistent hyperventilation of his breathing. The veins in his neck and temples were pulsing, ready to burst, and his skin looked as if it had been bathed in crimson dye.

Just as the night before, he wasn't coming down from this. He let out a scream at the top of his lungs, with no thought this time of Paul or Betty, and ran into the bathroom, where he slammed the door shut behind him as he entered. From within his room, all that could be heard were the echoing sobs of uncontrollable tears.

Charlie turned on the faucet, hoping to wash away some of the burn he felt, as well as the tarnished feelings that had attached themselves to him when his phone buzzed.

He picked up a hand towel and quickly dried off his face before checking who it was.

It was Ellie.

"Holy shit," he said as a mixture of frustration and relief battled its way through him.

He fumbled with the phone in his hands as he turned off the water and went to read the text she'd sent.

He was shaking, right on the edge of collapsing again, but hurried to read what she'd sent him.

Sorry about last night. Emergency! Something's come up! I need you to come quick!

What? He was confused and re-read the message several more times to make sure he was getting it right.

"What the hell?" he thought aloud. "What could have—I don't even know where she lives…" he realized.

Unsure of what else to do, he called her. No one picked up.

He tried again. It rang and rang and rang, but still there was no answer.

Charlie felt his anger sharpening, as if consolidating to a singular purpose. Any thought he'd had of his mother vanished, as if that conversation hadn't even taken place.

In his state, it was difficult to follow his thoughts, but he wracked his brain trying to think of what to do with no luck.

170

Just when he felt ready to let loose another burst of screams, his phone rang again. This time it was Trent.

"What the hell is—" Charlie was caught off guard, but too off-balance to make any real connections.

He picked up the phone and cut off whatever it was Trent was going to say with the utmost urgency.

"Trent! Do you know where Ellie lives?"

"Huh? What? Yeah. Wait. Why? Charlie, what's the matter?"

"Can you get me to Ellie's place, right now?"

"Jeez, Charlie, yeah, but what—"

"I need you to come pick me up, like, right now. Okay? Right now!"

"Okay, but Char—"

"Trent! It's an emergency! Something's happened."

Trent paused, taking this in.

"Okay, Charlie, but—"

"Ellie's in trouble!"

"Okay, okay. I'll be there in fifteen."

"Be here in five."

There was another pause while Trent seemed to be thinking things over. Then he said, "I'll see what I can do."

Charlie hung up before he acknowledged what Trent had just said. He threw his phone onto the bed and began to frantically get dressed, pulling on whatever he could find near him. His heart was about to rip right out of his chest, he was breathing so quickly. But it wasn't moving as fast as his mind was, trying to figure out what exactly was going on.

The *last* thing on Charlie's mind at that moment was his mother and what he had just done to her. There was no guilt or shame. All that mattered then was the immediate problem at hand: Ellie. He couldn't even focus on whether or not he was angry with her anymore. He needed to know what was going on, what had happened to her. His anger now was providing him with a strange focus, and he knew he would do whatever it took to find her.

Charlie's mother was shaking uncontrollably when she'd loosened her grip on the phone and let it fall from her hands. It landed with a keen sense for gravity onto the floor below and there it sat, still and silent, no longer the connection she'd hoped it could be.

She'd spent the better part of the last several hours pacing around her home in a deranged fog. She'd barely slept in days. But what rational part of her brain was left had been proud of the fact that some routine in her remained. Once her agitation had somewhat calmed from the day before, she had managed to plug her phone into charge, at least so that if Charlie called, she could be ready.

When he hadn't, in her own daze and confusion, she was unable to quench her need to hear from him any longer, so she had decided to call him again – to her own devastation.

It was her worst fears realized, the proof that all the voices in her mind hadn't been lying all along.

Suddenly, she grew faint and collapsed on the kitchen floor, knocking a chair over and a box of crackers off the tabletop as she fell.

On the floor, she lay. Not limp or easy, but rigid, as if still very much caught in the grip of some unknown force.

She wanted to speak, to reach out, to Charlie mostly. She wanted to make things right and apologize. She wanted to make sure he understood. But instead, she took his words to be the truth. She had lost him. That much she believed.

So, instead, she allowed his words to reinforce her own insecurities, and the last thought that crossed her mind before she slipped into an exhausted unconscious sleep, was that of her own failure to protect her son.

ELEVEN

Charlie paced on the sidewalk outside his house, waiting for Trent. Worry was now outweighing the frustration within him. As soon as he left his room and walked up the stone stairwell, he felt the strain and tension that had held him so tightly loosen as if, given time, they would melt away entirely. He breathed again, not quite with ease, but he relished in the fullness of it.

It didn't make any sense. He'd even found the rain coming down to be a welcome change to the atmosphere. He stood for a moment, trying to consider all that had happened in the past twenty-four hours.

To his surprise, he found that he could think quite clearly and in smooth, simple patterns. But with that came the realizations of what had taken place. He thought of Ellie, and of his mother.

What have I done? He thought, horrified. Just as quickly as he had been released from the grip of his anger, he was now held captive by the bonds of shame and the stench of his own guilt.

He didn't know what to do. He thought of calling his mom back, but would she pick up? How could he face her ever again after what he'd done?

Just then Trent's truck, with its faded, peeling, yellow paint, practically drifted its way around the corner, pulling up right in front of Charlie.

"What the fuck's going on?" he said, half out of the truck before Charlie motioned for him to stop and opened the passenger door to get in. He paused when he saw Charlie. Trent thought he looked like absolute hell but didn't dare bring himself to comment on it on account that he didn't trust himself to hide the fact that he'd witnessed the whole scene. It was hard enough playing dumb as it was.

"I don't know. I just—" Charlie spat, trying to catch his breath.

"It's okay, just get in. Why are we going to Ellie's?"

"Look," Charlie said, exasperated. "I don't know what's going on. I got this message from Ellie that said there was an emergency and that she needed help, like now."

Trent's expression, for the most subtle of seconds, gave way to the fact that he did know more than he could let on. But he also wasn't entirely sure what *was* happening, so the look of concern than Charlie did see was very real.

Charlie, in turn, sat down, buckled his seat belt, and positioned himself to face whatever it was they were about to do.

"So, to Ellie's?" Trent asked.

"Yes! GO—" Charlie yelled. "Sorry... I... let's go!"

Trent said nothing, nor had he shown himself to be put off by Charlie's frantic burst. He merely turned over the keys so the engine roared to life and tore off down the road.

"It's gonna be okay, Charlie. You'll see," Trent lied. He didn't know completely what was going on but figured he had a pretty good idea and understood the underlying story.

It didn't matter. Charlie wasn't listening anyway.

Trent's mind kept reverting back to images of the night before. Every so often he'd steal a glance over to Charlie, who still looked like hell, and Trent's stomach turned over again, compressing itself inward like a damp towel someone was trying to wring the guilt out of.

After driving for several minutes, they found themselves on the outskirts of town between Astoria and Knappa. It was thick with forest. Charlie impatiently asked, "How long until we're there?"

"Not far, Charlie. She lives just past Knappa-Market. A few more minutes, tops."

"Can you drive faster?" Charlie asked, leaning forward in his seat, tapping his fingertips systematically against the end of his right thumb.

Moved mostly by guilt, Trent obliged him and pressed down hard on the gas pedal, pushing the old truck on as close to her limit as he could. He figured he owed Charlie that much, at least. They rattled their way down the highway, through the winding forest roads.

Trent found himself thankful for the tense immediacy of the moment. Despite the continued sinking feeling in his gut, being so engaged in the necessity of getting to Ellie allowed for his mind not to dwell on the reality of the situation.

Minutes later, Trent slowed down, taking a right at the old gas station. It had been abandoned for close to a year and was fenced off. They veered their way back and forth around a few turns and came to a four-way stop with Knappa-Market at one corner, a house on another, and the local grange on the third. The last corner was just an empty gravel lot used by the locals for parking.

Charlie saw the market and began tapping both hands on his lap.

"Come on, come on, come on…" he said to no one in particular.

"It's just up ahead, Charlie."

At the four-way, Trent turned right and puttered another hundred yards or so down the road before slowing down, almost to a complete stop, to where it looked as if a set of tire tracks led right into a small break in the trees.

"Trent? When—"

"It's right here, Charlie. Look." He pointed up at the opening. "Right there."

It didn't look like a driveway to Charlie. It wasn't, really. But Trent followed the dirt ruts into a little clearing on the other side, where stood a lonely and desolate house, mistreated by the cruel and intolerable years.

Trent pulled up to the front of the house, but before he could even come to a stop, Charlie had opened the passenger door and jumped out.

"Charlie, wait!"

Trent made to reach over and grab him, but he was already gone, off sprinting toward the house. Trent slammed on the breaks, killed the engine, and ran to catch up.

By the time Trent reached the front door, Charlie was already inside. He stopped before crossing the threshold of the house, noticing the door itself hanging at a slightly awkward angle. The top hinge had been ripped entirely out of the frame.

He found Charlie in the living room, standing amidst an eerie, restless quiet. The house was in disarray. It didn't contain much in the way of furniture, but what was there was everywhere, thrashed and thrown about. There were picture frames smashed and tossed on the ground. A full-body mirror had been wrenched from the wall and lay shattered on the floor, revealing three gaping holes in the wall where it had before been bolted to the frame. Glass shards cracked and crunched with each of their steps.

"What the hell happened here?" Charlie asked. Bewildered, he looked up at Trent in a desperate hope for answers. "How? No... *who* could have done this?"

"I...I'm not sure..." Trent lied again, struggling to swallow the expanding knot in his throat. He didn't have the complete picture of what was going on, but he knew exactly *who* did this, and he had a pretty good idea of *how*. He realized as well, when he looked back at Charlie, that he also knew *why*.

The battle raged on in Trent for whether or not to tell Charlie everything. So much of him wanted to; he wanted to be free of this burden. He wanted to breathe in the fresh and weightless air that now seemed so far out of reach.

And standing there, right then with Charlie, he yearned for nothing more than the peace of absolution.

But Mr. Wilkes' strength and influence were swift and strong and returned to counter Trent's wayward thoughts.

But how would Charlie react to this? He wondered, upbraiding himself. *At this point, would it even make any difference to him or to any of it?*

He was torn but, in the end, he knew what it was that he would do. Deep down, he had always known.

They moved through the house looking for any sign for Charlie to figure out what happened but found nothing.

The longer they were there, the more unsure Charlie grew, the more agitated. He didn't know what he was doing, or why. How could he help Ellie? He wondered despairingly. Even if he found her, what could he do then? What could he say to her? He was sliding back into the secure comforts of his former powerless self, falling deeper and further into insecurity.

"Trent," Charlie's voice was shaking as he struggled to compose himself. He was desperate. "What do we do? She... needs our help... she needs *my* help!"

Trent looked up at Charlie, at the devastation that littered the floors before him. This wasn't even the full extent of Mr. Wilkes' hand extended, Trent knew.

This will never end unless... Trent had begun. He knew there was no other way out.

Then, weighed down by the guilt he wore, even though there was so much of him that just wanted to grab Charlie and run – just go – he knew what needed to be done. He also knew what he *wanted* to do but, with no uncertain reasoning, he became painfully aware of what he *would* do.

There was a time, as Trent looked back, where he still could have gotten Charlie out of this. Not himself, though. He was in too deep. But he also knew that Charlie wouldn't leave now, not with Ellie involved.

Shit! Trent thought, realizing how far along the game had played out. A thought struck him too. He found himself wondering exactly when it was in the past few days that he'd started to hope that he and Charlie would shake hands after this and maybe walk away as friends. It was laughable – for, in Trent's position, he hadn't the luxury of friends.

Trent tried to take a deep breath but found no relief in it. And his thoughts were interrupted by Charlie's pleas for help.

"Trent? Trent, if you know anything, anything at all. Please. Please help me now. We have to do something!"

Could we still leave? Trent thought. *Get away?*

"Trent? Trent please!" Charlie's words were soft and pleading, barely a whisper.

No, it's no use, he thought, as he resigned himself to what he truly believed.

"Trent… Trent, please?"

Trent's decision had been made. One he was sure would seal the fate of them all. When he finally looked up at Charlie, sure that he would never know peace again, his heart sank.

"Charlie?"

"Yeah!"

"There's a house."

"Yeah? What house? Where? Where do we go?"

"There's a man, Charlie. A very powerful man."

"Yeah. Yeah. Where Trent?"

"If something like this were to happen," he looked away from as he spoke, unable to bare the pleading stare, "he would be the man behind something like this, or he would at least know who was."

"Let's go, Trent! What are we waiting for? Where… where do we go?"

Trent's heart cracked in two and he found himself wondering if Charlie would have been so eager if he'd known everything.

"Take me there now, Trent. Please?"

Trent let his eyes fall shut and his head slip into a droop. His insides were splintering. From this single act, he knew he would be changed forever. It would become his greatest regret. But even knowing this, he could not step from its course. He just couldn't. Even as those parts of his mind tried to sway him, the ingrained voice of Mr. Wilkes stepped in and silenced them.

He would find us, Trent knew. *It wouldn't make the slightest difference.*

Without answering, Trent turned and began to make his way back towards the truck, walking right past Charlie. At the front door he stopped and said over his shoulder, "Come on, Charlie. I'll show you."

Charlie followed him without question, like a curious yet frightened Labrador – trusting, but showing signs of nervousness.

Charlie felt an onrush of the old familiar crippling strains within his mind. His chest was beginning to tighten itself, making breathing difficult again. These feelings weren't anything he wasn't used to but, as they came on, he found himself defaulting back to his motor memory, where he would go on a sort of autopilot to conserve himself. In doing so, he consciously decided that he would let Trent lead him to where he needed to go, despite the fact that every single facet of his internal alarm system was blaring. In this moment, he was choosing to trust Trent, this man whom he had no reason, he thought, not to trust. So he ran to catch up.

"Trent, where are we going? How long will it take to get there?"

Trent just kept walking.

"Trent? Are you sure Ellie will be there?"

"Just get in the truck, Charlie."

"But where? Where are we—" but Charlie stopped himself when they got to the truck. He'd noticed that Trent too had stopped before climbing in. He stood there holding open his door with a heavy weight and burden upon his shoulders.

"Trent?"

"You'll see, Charlie." With that, Trent climbed into the truck, followed obediently by Charlie, and the doors slammed shut behind them.

"Trent?" Charlie couldn't help but ask again. "Where—"

Trent stopped himself again at Charlie's question, the keys in the ignition, waiting. "We're going to where this was always going to end, Charlie."

"Wait—what?"

And he turned over the keys so that the engine roared to life. Placing his arm across the top of the seats, he turned to make sure there was nothing behind him, sure to not make eye contact with Charlie, and said, "Just be patient, okay. It'll all make sense soon."

Charlie was silent, trying to take it all in, as Trent backed the truck up and swung around to face the exit. He hit the gas and they took off back out onto the road. Neither of them was wearing their seatbelt. Given the situation, it hadn't even crossed their minds.

As they drove, the truck retraced its steps back through the four-way stop and to the highway. But this time, instead of turning and heading back toward Astoria, they crossed over and began making their way down a small turn off that Charlie had never noticed before. It led them deep into the deep woods, towards the backroads that wound their way around the river.

"Trent?"

"It's not far now, Charlie. Just a few more minutes."

There was a frightening assurance in Trent's tone that left Charlie feeling increasingly more anxious and unsettled. He, as well, noted the strange hint of reluctance. But with nothing else to do, he let both Trent and the truck carry him onward through the twisting turns of this unknown land.

Unknown to himself, he'd begun his finger tapping routine once again, but to little avail for his nerves.

He kept quiet as Trent drove them deeper and deeper into what appeared to be an older part of the forest, much less touched by mankind. Less interfered with.

Trent felt something solidify in him. What had before been a churning sea of squalls and raging battlements was then settling into a silent and placid surface, still as glass. Colorless and utterly without. A slight fear crept up in him, but infinitesimally. He wanted to weep, to purge whatever emotion was left in him, or had been there, but something intrinsically told him he wouldn't be able to. That there was nothing left in him to expunge. That was his penance, which was all the more reason to cry.

A few moments later, they came to the point where the road went from pavement to gravel, and soon after from gravel to dirt. The shadows continued to pull them toward their destination, sliding a bit from time to time as the ground had been softened by the unexpected summer storms, and the road narrowed, becoming more of a path with random tufts and patches of grass cropping up every several feet. It would surely have been a cause for worry for smaller or less capable vehicles.

"Not much longer now," Trent said, still not looking up at Charlie, though he could feel his rising apprehension.

As they drove, darkness and its gathering shadows closed themselves around the truck, blanketing its vision with a canopy of twisting and crooked branches. Together, they formed what looked to be an impermeable roof. The landscape here, Charlie thought, seemed specially designed to keep out the light. Maybe it was that that brought on a quick bout of shivers as his head tingled and grew foggy for a moment, as if he were on the verge of passing out. Or maybe it was his growing worry as his brain overworked itself, trying to figure out what he was about to walk into. Either way, it passed and the world seemed to refocus itself around him.

Just as his thoughts began to clear, the truck rumbled over a series of potholes too consistent to be natural and trees opened up into an expansive clearing where, at the other end, sat a house of colossal size, especially for the geography, tucked neatly away from the light of day. It was an impressive structure but dilapidated and worn with time. It was more of a mansion, a manor, Victorian in style – like most of Astoria's historic homes, though this was not Astoria, not really – and included several buttressed towers and aggressively stretched out architecture and woodworking. It was striking.

Trent, familiar with the property, seemed unaffected by its imposing presence, but Charlie seemed to cave even further under its looming stature, and he sank even further into his already quivering self.

Trent pulled up near the front entryway and killed the engine.

"Here we are, Charlie," said Trent, numb to everything around him now. Even his regret was growing less pronounced.

"What is this place, Trent?"

"This is where it all started, Charlie."

"What? Where *what* started?"

"You'll see." And with that, Trent opened his door and stepped out. "Come on inside, Charlie. Everyone's waiting."

Charlie's expression gave way to his confusion as his eyebrows lifted in wonder. There were too many questions on his mind so, in the confusion, he stuck to what seemed most pressing to him, though he was feeling much less confident than before.

"Is Ellie here, Trent?"

Trent didn't respond; he merely lumbered up the front steps.

"Trent! Is Ellie in there?"

Finally, Trent looked back to Charlie. He was crushed by the worrying look on Charlie's face. "I'm not really sure, Charlie. But... they'll know what happened."

"How do you know—"

But Trent turned and walked off, a guilty man to the gallows — someone who *knew* his fate and knew that it was just.

Charlie stared at him but didn't move, unsure of what to think or say. He watched Trent walk up to the front door and turn the handle. He did so with a practiced consistency, as if he knew he'd be welcome. Charlie couldn't believe it. The door opened, and Trent disappeared into the darkness beyond.

Charlie didn't know what to do. Again, his mind was ringing with the thought of leaving.

Just turn around, something in him said. *Get out! Go! Leave now!*

But something else in him told him he couldn't leave. He couldn't leave Ellie. And what would Trent say? Why was he being so weird? He was growing dizzy with all the conflicting thoughts as they swirled through him. His stomach cinched and he pushed back against whatever was constricting his breath.

Damnit, he thought as he slammed the truck door shut and, against all rational, judgement sprinted up the path to the house, then the stairs, up to the door and followed Trent into the darkness through the open doorway. All the while, his body was shaking with minute tremors.

Outside, the winds grew more and more blustery. They could be heard cutting through the trees, in and out of interlocking branches which, in their fashion, created an atmosphere of claustrophobic co-dependence. The violent rustle of late-fallen leaves could be heard being dragged across jagged rocks and fallen brush in the yard. Like most things that stumbled upon this fell land, they never left.

Upon entering the house, Charlie was dumbstruck to find a finely dressed man waiting for them at the entrance. The man wore a suit of thick, black wool, a three piece with matching waistcoat and bowtie and the strangest, most congenial smile Charlie could have imagined at the moment.

Everything about the scene caught Charlie off guard.

Charlie half noticed – it was difficult to keep focused in his agitated state – that the man wore a strangely familiar bronze chain. It hung about his neck and disappeared beneath his waistcoat. He thought he recognized it but couldn't remember why.

He could feel his mounting panic settling, shifting almost, and an assured bold flame rekindled somewhere within.

The man took a step forward, giving Charlie a slight bow, and Trent broke in to make introductions. "Charlie, this is Mr. Booth. Mr. Booth, Charlie West."

The finely dressed man reached out his hand as if to offer a gesture of good will. "A pleasure, Mr. West, I assure you, to *finally* meet you face to face."

Charlie drew a step further away from the man and, without reaching out his hand, he asked, "Who… are you? What the hell is going on here?"

"Your frustration is entirely understandable, Mr. West, but—"

"No! Cut that shit!" The anger was rising in him again. "Where is Ellie? Tell me. Now!" his voice grew louder and more confident with every syllable. His focusing was returning to him.

"I can assure you, Mr.—"

"Stop calling me mister, goddammit!"

"As you wish, Mis— I can assure you that Miss Ellie is perfectly safe, for now."

"For *now*?"

"Yes, *for now*. You will have a chance to see her soon, but first things first."

"What *things*? What the hell are you talking about?" Charlie's thoughts began to burn. He didn't know it, but his fists were clenched at his sides and he was standing up a little taller.

Trent stood, noticing again the changes he was seeing. *Holy shit,* he thought, and actively took several tiny steps backwards, avoiding eye-contact to all parties involved.

"Right this way, sir. You are expected."

"Expected—what? How?" Charlie looked over to Trent, who was busy burying his own view deep into the floorboards.

But before Charlie could say anything else, Mr. Booth turned and began to march toward a lofty and grandiose doorway that led them into another wing of the house.

Charlie was growing more confused with each passing moment, but that only proved to fuel his growing frustration. He wanted answers and he was determining himself to find them. He would find Ellie and figure out what the precise fuck was going on. Knowing the answers would lie on the other side of the door Mr. Booth was leading them, he supposed the best course of action was to follow.

He looked at Trent once more to try to get a read off of him, but Trent was already gone, stolen off in the direction of the veiled room, his countenance collapsed, propped up only by whatever necessities still remained for Mr. Wilkes.

"Trent?" Charlie called to him, jogging to catch up. He grabbed Trent's shoulder and pulled him around. "What the hell is going on?"

Charlie's voice was sharp and lacked any of the meekness that Trent had come to expect from it.

Trent stepped back, still trying to avoid any and all eye contact with Charlie, shocked and surprised at Charlie's change.

Even as Trent continued to grow numb as they progressed further and further along this road, seeing Charlie like this tugged at him. His pain and regret resurfacing, he said to Charlie, "Look. I'm sorry, man. Alright? But everything…" he stopped as he looked up and saw the wild look in Charlie's eyes, "…everything will make sense in a few minutes. Just know…"

"*Know* what?"

"Just…" He felt as if he might implode from Charlie's glare, the callous exterior still unable to hold itself up in front of the man he'd betrayed. "Just know that I'm sorry, okay, Charlie? Please?" His eyes were pleading, filled with a dying hope, in want of a forgiveness they were certain to never find. "No matter what happens through these doors?"

Charlie said nothing. He just looked at the man who he thought was his friend, while his eyes lined themselves with distrust.

Trent was certain now that he'd chosen wrong. Not just today with Charlie, but in general. He wondered at what chance he'd ever had to choose something different though. Any other life had seemed so far removed from him.

Was it always going to lead to this? He wondered. *Or something like it?* He turned then and followed Mr. Booth through the doors and into a large room that flickered with candlelight.

Charlie followed.

Upon entering the room, Charlie froze, struck by the forced quiet and strain exuding by those who watched him enter. Dozens of eyes from every shadowy corner zeroed in on him. A fire roared in the hearth and crackled, shedding some light throughout one side of the room, while other regions and nooks were illuminated merely by a series of small candle flames. This effect left the entire scene feeling lopsided, thus increasing how off-balanced Charlie felt.

Just as the silence was growing to be unbearable, it was shattered by an authoritative and chilling voice.

"Charlie West. At last we meet in the *flesh.*"

It's force and power boomed and echoed throughout the room, reverberating off the walls imbued with a soft but failing candlelight. The man who had spoken stood at the dead center of the room, and the sprawling shadow of his ghost-white, wild hair cast itself onto the drapes behind him, making it seem as if the vast tentacles of the leviathan were readying themselves to strike down upon them. As if it hoped to bring their breathless bodies down into the crushing depths below.

Charlie looked around at those who stood by, servient even in their posture, as the man had spoken. All of them were of a generous age and were dressed in similar fine and expensive looking black suits; they each wore the same chain of bronze around their necks like the doorman, but these, Charlie could see, held the same strange and intricately carved medallion upon their breast.

Charlie shuttered as his mind stretched forth, reaching. Searching through the bank of his memories.

Like the photo, he thought. *What the—*

Charlie looked back to the man at the center.

"Welcome, Charlie. My name, as you may not know, is John T. Wilkes. I— No... *we* have been *dying* to meet you," the man said, a contrived smile plastered to him. He seemed to Charlie, for one brief and undistracted moment, to be putting on somewhat of a show.

Wilkes! Charlie's mind connected the dots suddenly.

"What—what is all this?" Charlie asked, feeling sturdier by the minute.

"*This*, Charlie," Mr. Wilkes paused, "is a little homecoming, one might say."

"Homecoming—what do you mean?"

"All in good time, Charlie, my boy. All in good time. The question, Charlie, is how are you?"

"Me? Why would you care about how *I* am? I'm just..."

"It's all a bit confusing, isn't it, Charlie?" Mr. Wilkes feigned a look of concern, of sympathy. He was also having a much more difficult time than usual of holding back the giddy excitement that

186

pulsed through him. He hadn't abandoned himself to it yet, but he was much looser than he normally was around his men. "That's why we've been keeping such a close eye on you, Charlie," he said, and his gaze fell on Trent as he spoke who, at the time, was working very hard to disappear within the shadows of the room.

Charlie's head whipped around, almost involuntarily, to catch a glimpse of where Trent had slid off to. A mixture of confusion and anger swirled in him. His mind was racing to catch up.

"What? What the hell are you talking about? What's going on here?" he screamed, the anger growing in him, pulsing.

"Now, that's the spirit!" Mr. Wilkes laughed, clapping his hands together. "That's what we need, Charlie! That fire!" He seemed to be savoring every single moment of this. To him, their triumph was already at hand. The completion of their task and the vindication it would bring, even if only temporarily.

"What—why?" Charlie's anger continued to mount. With every moment that passed, he disappeared further and further into it. "Would somebody tell me what the fuck is going on?"

"Charlie, my boy," Mr. Wilkes calmed himself on the outside once again, but his hands shook with assured joy. "I apologize for keeping you so in the dark, and I promise soon you will know everything."

"Everything about *what*?" Charlie yelled again.

"All you need to know right now, Charlie, is that we need you."

Charlie stopped, stood up a little straighter, and stared up at the man in shock while pointing to himself.

"We've been searching for *you*, Charlie, for years."

Charlie stood frozen on the spot, his mind working to catch up.

"And *now*," said Mr. Wilkes in an enthusiastic burst, "here you are, Charlie! You're back! Exactly where you need to be! Exactly where we intended!"

Charlie shuddered at the statement.

Back? He wondered. His hands begin to shake. The walls appeared to be closing in around him. With every inch lost, his frustration and fear built.

"Back?" Charlie said. "What? Why? Why... *me*? I don't understand..." he trailed off.

Mr. Wilkes chuckled.

"As to be expected, Charlie. So full of questions, aren't you? So much fervor." Mr. Wilkes turned to the man next to him before continuing. "Isn't he just perfect?" And, without waiting for a response, he turned his attention back to Charlie. "Charlie, we figured you wouldn't know much. That's why you were moved away, after all. To escape us. To escape this." Mr. Wilkes motioned his hands to showcase the surrounding room. "How much, Charlie, do you know about *The Order*?"

"The *what*?"

"*The Brotherhood*? The *Nameless*? Anything?"

Charlie shook his head in mad confusion.

Mr. Wilkes gave a wide smile. "Again, that is as suspected."

"Look, I don't know what they fuck you're talking about, okay? I'm just here for Ellie. Where the fuck is Ellie?"

"Ah, yes. Of course. The girl. In time, Charlie. All in good time. Really though? You know nothing of us? That *is* very interesting. We weren't entirely sure how much you would know. We figured it wouldn't have been much, given the circumstances of your family's departure, but we figured some, hence our somewhat dramatic means of procuring you."

Charlie felt lost at sea without the slightest chance of being found. In his growing confusion, a few questions managed to bubble their way to the surface.

"Why... why would I know about you?" he asked. "You said homecoming? What... what are you talking about? I grew up in—"

"Portland, yes. But you're not *from* there, Charlie." Mr. Wilkes gestured again to the surroundings of the room. "These halls, Charlie West, are the birthright of your heritage. And with them, our mission. And you are so important, Charlie, to our mission. The sort of *key* to our success, if you will."

Charlie gave a look that indicated he still had no idea what Mr. Wilkes was talking about.

"Charlie, you were born here. In this very house, actually. I was there." Mr. Wilkes tried to conjure what warmth he could into his smile, but it wasn't his strong suit, especially in the wake of his maniacal determination. "And with your birth… your *father*…" Mr. Wilkes paused at the mention of Charlie's father, noticing the definite rise in Charlie's agitation. "Well, you see, we rather failed with your father, Charlie. Or *he* failed us, more to the point. Your mother convinced him, somehow, to leave this place. His home. *Your* home. She harbored a desire for you to live a life free of the burden we carry." A cold chill seeped into Wilkes as he spoke.

Charlie stared back, barely following what was being said to him.

How… how could this…

The rage building in him derailed his thoughts.

"And somehow – your father was very careful – we lost track of you. All three of you."

Charlie thought of the father he'd known. *Could that man have really made a decision to help me? Had he really wanted what was best for me?* His mind split with the dissidence of these seemingly contradictory realities. It went against the entire experience of living with his father. The revelations, true or not, were dizzying.

"No matter what painful lengths we went through to pursue you, all of you, it was as if you'd somehow just disappeared." Mr. Wilkes was less able to restrain his excitement with every second. As he was walking Charlie through the process of finding him, his hands were waving about, almost flittering, until he would notice the excess motion and bring them back to his sides to rest.

"After years of sifting through paper trails," he continued, "your father had been smart about this – all official documents had been signed under aliases, buried in bureaucratic trails, filled with holes – we'd almost given up hope. He had somehow built a new life for himself and for *you*. But in the end, he slipped up and we found him. You should know that Highway 30 is one of the most dangerous roads in Oregon, the most fatality accidents every year. It was perfect, wasn't it? And in the end, we found *you*."

Charlie shook as the conflict flowed through him, both pulling and pushing at his every thought. Like everything else he'd just heard, this revelation came with its own numb and overwhelming crash.

Just as Mr. Wilkes' placid mask was being peeled off, Charlie's was slowly being built up to protect and cover himself from the growing uncertainty.

"We figured it was always going to come down to *you*, Charlie. That made him disposable."

Confusingly enough, Charlie's stomach turned over again at the continued mention of his father's demise.

"We only needed one of you, in the end, and he'd made his choice." And then, Mr. Wilkes' tone grew much cheerier as he said, "And we've learned much since then, Charlie. So much! We've nearly perfected the science of it and figured, with that, we could try a different tactic with you. You see, with your father, we tried to make him understand. He was raised in *The Order,* after all. We had no other reason than to take him to be a *willing* member. We know better now. After years and years of research and testing, we've realized that *willingness* is irrelevant."

"Willingness?" Charlie's said, his tone lined with cautious frustration, but to his own shock was free of fear.

"You see, Charlie. You are a legacy of sorts in The Order." Mr. Wilkes walked over to the mantle and picked up a photograph, the strength he'd always strived to project becoming more real in this moment, more authentic. Right then, he felt there was no force in existence that could have stopped them, or *him,* more like it.

He brought the photograph back over to show Charlie, who recognized it immediately.

"More to the point, Charlie," Mr. Wilkes continued, "*we*, you and I, are part of a legacy."

Mr. Wilkes handed the photograph to Charlie, who took it. He was tiring of the number of somersaults his stomach was doing.

"Where did you get this?" He said, his determination for answers was piercing.

"Recognize it, do you?" Taunted Mr. Wilkes, his excitement and energy still rising.

Charlie shook his head indicating that he had.

"Good." Mr. Wilkes smiled, taking the photograph back.

"I know it's confusing, Charlie, but—"

"Where did you get that photograph from?"

"Did you ever stop to wonder why you'd never seen that photograph before, Charlie? Or any of the other contents of that box that miraculously *appeared* before you moved?"

Charlie's stomach clenched and he took a step back, faltering ever so slightly. He had wondered about that. He felt sick.

"You see," Mr. Wilkes continued, "when your father left *our* world behind, he left behind certain items that would normally have harbored a sort of familial and sentimental value. So, as timing allowed – and, in the end dictated – *we* saw fit to return them to you."

"Wait, what?" Charlie's confusion again sharpened itself into a cold anger, burning even hotter than before. "You've been in my house? *You* put—what? What the fuck!" Charlie screamed out. He was unable to hold it back.

"Yes! Yes, Charlie! That's the spirit! Let it out! Let it all out! We will need that!"

Charlie's mind swelled. He was sure his skull would rupture any second. Each breath grew more and more difficult to attain; he was on the verge of hyperventilating.

"*Why*?" Charlie asked, through gritted teeth.

Mr. Wilkes looked at him and, letting his smile grow wider, he said, again in a falsely protective voice, "It's okay, Charlie. *Everything* will all be alright, in a way. You'll see."

Charlie's head dropped as he fought for a whole breath. In a barely discernible whisper, he asked again, "Why... why do you need... *us*... or *me*?"

"Come again, Charlie?" Mr. Wilkes played with him. "I didn't quite catch that."

Charlie said again, though it was more of a strained growl, "I don't understand. *Why?* What do you want?"

Mr. Wilkes pointed down at the picture, and said, "It's all right here, Charlie. And don't worry, all will be explained."

Charlie looked down at the photo again, desperate, caught between a growing rage and despair.

"That is your great-grandfather, Lester. And that man," Mr. Wilkes pointed to the man next to him. "That man was my grandfather. They were partners, you see. And together, they had a plan. A vision. But for reasons unknown to us, that vision faltered. Things went... wrong." Mr. Wilkes lowered his voice into a mulling droll. Even what silence remained in the room seemed to lean itself in to hear him. "Together, Charlie, you and I will correct this failure. We *will* fulfill their vision and bring about the finality of their plan! We will *unmake* what has, to this point, been made." A cryptic smile crept across Mr. Wilkes' face at this last comment.

"What plan? Unmake what...? What the fu—"

Ignoring Charlie's question altogether, Mr. Wilkes turned to the other men who had thus far simply stood there listening. "What do you think, gentlemen? Shall we bring young Charlie here, and go finalize our preparations for this culmination we've worked so hard to achieve?"

Everyone in the room, save Trent and Charlie, gave yells and cheers.

Trent was still busy burying himself as deeply out of the way as possible. He knew this was all wrong. He'd never had reason to question it before, but now, standing there watching Charlie struggling helpless before Mr. Wilkes, Trent's would-be *savior*, Trent was filled with more regret, more shame than he ever knew possible. It was all his fault. He was the one who had brought Charlie to them. He was the one who had merely followed orders. Even when he'd felt the burden to act otherwise, he'd ignored it. His comforts and apathy had always won out.

I'm so sorry, Charlie, he thought from the corner of the room, as far out of sight as possible, just watching as Mr. Wilkes took one step closer to Charlie.

Mr. Wilkes stared at Charlie. His smile faltered some, revealing to Charlie, ever so briefly, of what resided behind the façade, the mad determination of a man who would stop at nothing to accomplish his goals.

With everything that was flooding through Charlie – the rage, the confusion and pain – something in him told him he couldn't give in, that he must fight, that he must push back against this force.

For a moment, they both stared into each other, eyes already locked in a piercing and fiery battle. Mr. Wilkes, satisfied, gave in first and cracked a smile before turning to walk away.

The whole room began to shift as each man followed suit and started to move about the room.

Charlie's frustration had about reached its max and he yelled out, "Wait! What are you—"

But just then, Mr. Wilkes turned and spoke again.

"Momentarily, Charlie. Your questions will all be answered momentarily." Then turning to two men next to him, he said to them, "Bring him," and he strode off through the small sea of men, who parted as he passed. He was like Moses, leading them off to their coming salvation through the red sea. Right then, he was more the man he'd always aimed to be than ever before. Deep down, he knew everything was coming together. They had Charlie. Nothing stood in their way.

Everyone else followed behind him, and two men grabbed Charlie by the shoulders and dragged him along with the flow. It was like being swept up in a current when you lacked the strength to swim away.

The mob made its way through the room, but not toward the main doors. They marched over to the opposite corner of the large room, to where the furthest section of bookshelves stood, and Mr. Wilkes reached up his arm and twisted an unlit candle fixture. The entire shelf, from ceiling to floor, opened up to reveal a stone passageway, much older than the house itself. Behind it was a stairwell that snaked downwards, disappearing into a shadowy and stagnant darkness below.

Mr. Wilkes reached into the corridor and grabbed a lit torch from off the stone wall. Without turning to face the men, he said, "Come gentlemen. It's time to go remake the world."

TWELVE

The stairwell spiraled down further than Charlie would have imagined. It took ages for them to reach the bottom. Likewise, once they reached the end, the corridor that followed stretched on well beyond what they could see even by torch light. The men marched in silence, but an agitated and nervous energy hung in the musty air, each breath bringing with it the heavy scents of earth and decay.

There were torches placed every fifty feet along the walkway. Just as you would begin to lose your vision in the dying light, the next hints of illumination were there to catch you and guide you on.

Mr. Wilkes set a vigorous pace that everyone worked to keep. The corridor echoed with muffled breaths as the men worked to keep down their growing apprehension at what was to come.

Time was lost on Charlie now. The very construct of it seemed irrelevant. Yet, eventually, he saw the end coming, and they arrived at what looked to be a single slab of stone, massive and ancient, set into the tunnel. Within it a fabricated steel rested with a torch burning in perfect symmetry on either side.

As they approached, the door opened to reveal the mysteries of what lay beyond. Charlie looked up, astonished more by the fact that he didn't think anything could quite surprise him anymore.

He followed as the men poured into a strange circular chamber – roughly a hemisphere, domed ceiling and all, a hundred feet in diameter. Its walls arched themselves upward, carved, it seemed, out of time, to an odd contraption that hung down from the room's apex.

It was filled with all sorts of scientific equipment, some of which seemed identifiable to Charlie, but other objects seemed to him to be beyond description and were more akin to medieval torture devices than objects of study. Shelves were scattered around at the edge of the room, filled with books and beakers and other tools. Switches and wires hung from the wall and from built-in rafters that hung from the stone ceiling. It was a room that, to Charlie, came right out of a nightmare.

Charlie looked up at what protruded down from the room's center: a conic chunk of iron, sort of like a man-made stalagmite, with wires going from every which direction and running into its base. The object itself looked to be a conduit of sorts and pointed down, ominously, to a gurney that stood directly beneath it with thick leather straps, broken and worn with age, meant to hold someone down.

Probably against their will, Charlie thought. His heartbeat faster as he entered the room. There was a sense of worry in him now but, somehow, it was kept at a distance. He was more overwhelmed by a growing and foreboding dull ache that was yet again keeping him from thinking straight. Besides, from where he stood, there was nowhere else to go. Nothing else he could do. He focused on the best he could on the gurney's straps and noticed scratch marks that had been cut across them. Still, any fear within him was mysteriously held at bay.

On the far side of the room, Charlie noticed, though barely, a single, much smaller, iron door. It matched the entrance they'd come through, and he found himself wondering what they kept in there.

"Welcome, Charlie," Mr. Wilkes' voice boomed, "to where we've strived for so long for our discoveries!" He indicated for Charlie to look around the room. "This is where the future of existence as we know it was dictated." A confident and wry smile crept into his expression, deepening the growing pit in Charlie's stomach – Trent's too, though that might have surprised Charlie had he the mental capacity to consider it.

The remaining men who stood around sycophantically placating their leader laughed along with Mr. Wilkes.

Charlie only wanted to stand his ground, to appear unmoved. Though he was sure the man had lost his mind completely.

What the hell is he talking about? he wondered.

Trent, unnoticed by all, crept further and further to the back.

In spite of all the pageantry of the moment, all the bravado, the coils, and the machinery. The sheer hopelessness of it all. The only clear and consistent thought Charlie had was of Ellie.

Where is she? He kept wondering. She, after all, was the only reason he had come.

"Gentlemen," Mr. Wilkes said, as he pulled a chair into the middle of the room, "Shall we make our new *friend* comfortable?" Relishing in the power of the moment, something in him was let loose. For the first time in years, he was enjoying himself. And the more he released, the more his men seemed to feed off it, off him. Everyone's hunger grew for what was to come.

The men all cheered and Mr. Wilkes stood, dead center of it all, basking in what Charlie's mere presence had created for him.

Charlie focused in on the chair. He noticed the same decrepit and broken leather straps he had seen on the gurney upon walking in were fashioned to it. They, too, looked like they'd been well-used.

On cue, the same two men who had dragged Charlie downstairs came forward and grabbed hold of him again, then forced him into the chair. Charlie's knees buckled as he fell backwards right into it. Before he knew it, the straps were pulled over and around him, and he was fastened tightly into the confines.

He yelled and kicked and screamed, but it was no use.

"What the fuck!" he shouted. "Why—Why are you doing this to me? Tell me some—"

He was furious. He still had no clue why he was here or what role he was supposed to play. He hated being toyed with.

Mr. Wilkes took two steps toward him and motioned with his hands for Charlie to calm. "Charlie, Charlie, breathe, son. These just a precaution," he said, looking down at the straps.

Charlie twisted and fought against them.

"What the fu—" he struggled, grunting and flexing his whole body as he tried to tear himself free.

"Charlie," Mr. Wilkes said with a strange softness. "Charlie, if you cooperate with us now, we will explain everything. I swear. Now, are you going to listen and stop this *nonsense*?"

Charlie worked to still his exterior the best he could manage, but inside he fumed. Every ounce of his being burned to be freed of his restraints. He took in one deep breath and, as calmly as he could, asked, "*Why* are you doing this to me?"

"Charlie, how much do you know about the Fire of 1922?"

"What? What the—Nothing, I suppose—Why am I here, goddammit?"

"Charlie, you said you'd cooperate with us." Mr. Wilkes' tone slid back into one of playful control.

Charlie pursed his lips together to show he was trying to restrain himself.

"In due time, Charlie, I will tell you everything. You must have patience. I'm getting there, but I need to start from the beginning. After all, we have waited a century for tonight.

"And remember, too, that we want no harm to come to you. Though, I should also warn you again that we don't *need* your cooperation. Still, I feel obliged to give you an opportunity to understand your place in all of this. Will you please cooperate with us, at least for the moment, and stop all this struggling?"

Charlie shook his head to show that he would.

"Very good. Now, I ask you again, do you know anything of the Great Fire of 1922?"

"Here in Astoria, I suppose."

"Precisely."

"No." Charlie kept his answer short to curb his ever-bubbling frustration

"I figured as much. You see, in 1922, the city of Astoria was made up of a mere dozen or so buildings all constructed of wood, that stretched from the base of the hillside and ran its way down to the water, but not beyond."

"Okay."

"And did you know that the water came in further inland than it does now?"

Charlie shook his head to show that he saw no relevance whatsoever between this fact and the chair he was strapped to.

"The current downtown, you see," Mr. Wilkes continued, "was built out over the previous riverbank – the brilliance of human industry, really, making land where land didn't exist before. They were able to do this because of the *great fire of 1922*. There was a great *disturbance* on the night of December the eighth. There was mass devastation by the standard of the time that as far as the public was, well, *is* still concerned was brought on by the *fire*. *It* consumed the town and killed and destroyed everyone and everything it touched. The only original building left near where the water line was, The Flavel House, still stands to this day — the *whys* of which we don't have time to go into now. Everything else that has been built since, you see, has been constructed on cement pilings and was built or rebuilt by certain surviving industrious families. People with the foresight to be prepared."

Charlie stared at him. "Your family," he said.

"And yours, Charlie."

Charlie didn't like where this was going.

"But, you see, Charlie. This fire was not, and is not, the full truth of the matter."

Even Charlie couldn't help being intrigued by this. He was growing more desperate to understand what was happening.

"The picture you held upstairs and the copy you found in your attic proves the legacy of you and I, Charlie West. It was taken on the morning of December the eighth, 1922, a night that should have ended in triumph. A night that would have rewritten—No, re-started the very history of our world. It was to be..." Mr. Wilkes lost his words. "But it... it ended in a way that our forebears did not foresee. You see, the city wasn't destroyed by a fire. The fire was set later to cover up what had been done. What had *failed*."

"What are you talking about? *What* failed? What—" Charlie cut himself off.

Mr. Wilkes could see Charlie's interest was peaking.

I almost have him, he thought.

"What happened?" Charlie asked.

"You see, Charlie. Their aim that night, *our* forebears, was to call forth something from *beyond.*"

"*Beyond*?" Charlie laughed, his rising anger giving him the extra confidence he needed to push back. "Beyond what? What the fuck are you talking about?"

"Stay with me, Charlie." Mr. Wilkes took a step closer. His eyes widened as his excitement carried him forward. "For what I'm about to share with you is of the utmost importance. You see, The Order is—well, we are followers of a path. A path, Charlie, with an ancient and vital purpose. There *are* entities out there *beyond* the veils of our existence. Beyond even what we call *time.*" Mr. Wilkes waited for recognition to settle into Charlie before going on. "*The Nameless* we call them. And *your* grandfather was one of the founding members of our sect of *The Order*. He, along with my grandfather, took it upon themselves to take bold strides and, under grave, grave circumstances, they pushed through mockery and great resistance to accomplish their goals. *Our* goals. The night that photo was taken, each of the four men were cornerstones of a rite. Of a ritual that, for reasons unbeknownst to us, was not able to be completed. *But* something that night was started... something that now that you are here—the blood of *his* blood—we may bring to its culmination."

Charlie couldn't believe what he'd just heard or that *this* was the reason behind all the major shifts in his recent life. *This man is a fucking lunatic,* Charlie thought. Then, looking around the room, he saw all the men nodding along in agreement. These maybe once-rational men actually believed this. It baffled him.

Mr. Wilkes could tell by the look on Charlie's face that Charlie didn't believe him.

"It's a lot to take in, isn't it Charlie?" countered Mr. Wilkes. "But that's not all."

"What—" Charlie started. "What was the purpose behind this... this rite? What was so worth the cost of life?"

"Very apt question, Charlie. You see, these *Nameless*, these titans of old, they are bringers of destruction."

Charlie stood up a little up a little straighter in his chair, thinking he was starting to guess where this was going – but it seemed too crazy. He listened on.

"Destruction, but of *creation* too, Charlie. They are the *beings*, well beyond our understanding, tasked with keeping the ebb and flow of creation and matter and time. Of existence!"

Charlie, again, was stunned. He didn't know what to make of any of this. And his mind was swirling around in his head, turning itself over, cartwheeling from the strain of everything that was tugging at him.

"Their history, Charlie, is written in the night skies for those of us with eyes enough to see. *We* will harness them and bring them forth! *We* will usher in a new dawn for mankind! The birth of a *new* world!" Mr. Wilkes's intonation, an excited yell now, reached up beyond the cadence of his usual speech. He turned to face his followers, who hung on every word. He lifted his arms and spoke with such fervor they would have followed him through the gates of hell and beyond. This felt like the culmination of all the power he'd fought so hard to gather to himself. This was it for him, the eve of his mightiest and final achievement.

As the attention was off him for a moment, Charlie struggled and pulled at his restraints. He shimmied and worked to free himself, but it was no use.

The men of The Order, the fellow mindless drones, screamed in agreement with Mr. Wilkes with a blind and painful enthusiasm,

"Charlie, don't you see it?" Mr. Wilkes turned back to him, and Charlie stopped struggling. "Are you not tired of the toil? The pains and struggles of *this* world? Are you not tired of your broken and dreary existence?"

Mr. Wilkes' eyes lit up life fire, ablaze with the assurance of victory.

Charlie looked around the room, at how the madness had spread around to everyone there, except for one in the back. From across the room, he saw Trent and was overcome by a wave of grief, a discomfort that, given what was going on was nothing more than an annoyance, but a wound, nonetheless.

He looked back to Mr. Wilkes. These questions did ring with a certain amount of truth to Charlie.

Mr. Wilkes continued, "Are you not tired of looking out at the world and seeing nothing but a shattered surface with so many people, so many lives falling through the cracks?"

Charlie couldn't knock the cold reason behind these questions. They were questions that crossed his own mind from time to time.

Amidst all he was taking in, Charlie noticed that all of his alarms weren't even going off at these questions.

"You of all people should understand *our* purpose, Charlie. For the purpose you were born into. This is your birthright, Charlie." Mr. Wilkes paused, allowing his pleading stare to hang over Charlie, hoping he was getting through. "You yearn for an escape, do you not?" he continued, "To be free of it all? That pain that drives you, that drives *us*, Charlie, to the edge of madness? It could all go away and you, son, are the *key* to it all!"

Charlie was taking in too much stimulus now. He was feeling too much. His stomach burned. His mind thrashed. Pressure pulsed through the edges of his brain. There was such a power in him that he felt he could take on the whole room, but his body also felt strained and frail. These tensions fought and exhausted what little reason he had left.

"*This* is—" Charlie fought for focus as his temperature crept upward towards feverish state.

"It's okay, Charlie. It's okay," Mr. Wilkes said, in a tone which could have easily been mistaken for compassion.

"What do you need… from me?" Charlie asked. There was a calculated, cold steadiness in his voice. "You want to…"

"Charlie, we aim to remake the world as we know it. We will be the catalysts for the greatest change this world has seen in a millennium. We will call forth *The Nameless* from their sleep and they will wreak a havoc on the terrors of this world, the likes of which have not been seen since creation itself."

Mr. Wilkes paused to catch his excited breath. He didn't realize how heavily he had been breathing.

"And when they are finished, Charlie? A rebirth. Can you imagine it? A fresh beginning. The chance to start anew! A world free of this struggle, free of pain, free of—well, Charlie, the torment you grew up enduring." Mr. Wilkes was getting carried away, but he was sharp enough still to know which strings were the shortest to tug.

Charlie sat there, staring at the man, fearful only of the fact that some of what this man was hearing made sense.

"And me?" Charlie asked. "What role do I play?"

"Charlie, you play the most important role. Your great-grandfather was the cornerstone of this ceremony. And as the same blood flows in you, you are the key, the final piece in our mission that will allow us to set things right."

The room grew quiet but a busy tension hung everywhere.

Charlie said nothing.

"Take your time, Charlie," Mr. Wilkes said, breaking the silence with a soft and compassion-laced plea. "And remember, we hope you will join us willingly. But," at this word, any sign of tender understanding dried up, "we don't need your consent. In the end, we simply need *you*. And we will take what we want."

Charlie's chest constricted at what he took for a threat and he struggled to inhale his next breath. He was like a kicked dog, tortured and rabid with anger, backed in a corner. But at the moment, he was trapped, with no way of unleashing what fury flowed through him on his captors.

He had fight but not the means.

When all had finally been laid bare before him, the rage within him spiked, sending him just beyond the point where he could focus. Confusion settled in. All he could think about was getting out of here and getting even with every one of them for what they had done.

Right then, when it seemed to Charlie that all his power had been stripped away, he thought of his father. The anger. The rage that had driven him. He looked around as he was now witness to what had created his father, what had made him that way. He looked back into his memories and saw in his father what he saw in himself now. He saw what had been passed down. A composite copy of the same broken genetic structure. He'd worked his whole life to free himself of its grip. Maybe there was a time his father fought against it too. But what could Charlie do now, he wondered. What options did he have? Join them and bring about a promised destruction or stand his ground and commit himself to certain death. Charlie was unable to see reason amidst all his fury. All he felt was that he wanted to watch it all burn.

So Charlie leaned into his intrigue. "So, these *Nameless*?" he began.

"Yes?" Answered a forcefully understanding Mr. Wilkes.

"Would make a new world?"

"Yes, Charlie." Mr. Wilkes stood tall over him now, smug in his perceived triumph. "*Re*-creation, we have termed it."

Charlie shook his head. "But that's crazy. I mean, everything's already here."

"Yes, that is the awkward subtlety of it, isn't it? You see, Charlie. You're a sharp boy. If they are to re-create the world, one could only presume..." Mr. Wilkes lifted both hands up in front of him, palms facing up and showed a gesture of balancing scales. That was enough.

"They would... destroy... everything? Even you?"

"Precisely," Mr. Wilkes gently brought his hands together. "A sacrifice, most certainly, but a worthy one. And we, Charlie, you and I, and The Order here," he waved his hands to indicate everyone else who was still standing there, "we would have been the great cause of it. We would be responsible for the next step in the evolution of our world. Us, Charlie, harnessing that power, that brute cosmic force!" He was getting carried away again. "But Charlie, it doesn't end there. You see, *they* were created for this purpose. It wouldn't just be an *end*. It would be a *beginning*. *They* are the ones who brought our world into existence in the first place — and many others, for that matter. As such, *they* will be the ones who come back to close the door, so to speak. It is simply *their* function. But let's be clear,

Charlie. It's not an *end*, per se. It's a new beginning. It's about what will be *rebuilt*. What *could* be. *This* is the natural order of things, is it not? When something has come to its destructive end, does it not fall to its consequences? In this case, annihilation."

For the briefest of moments, a thought seeped into Mr. Wilkes' mind of the other sects of The Order, how, upon the evening's success, they would never really know the truth of Mr. Wilkes' victory, but he would at least die knowing that he had, in fact, won out. That was enough for him.

The same cold reasoning held true in Charlie's mind.

"Again, Charlie, look at the world around you. Pain. Destruction. War. Blinding inequality. What's to come of it all? What happens when all the oil runs out? When the climate is so changed that we as a species can't survive? Think about how things will go when we start the wars over the last drops of drinkable water."

These thoughts rang true with a certain amount of justice in them.

"Just look at the state of things, Charlie. The world, geopolitically. We are on the brink of collapse, son. Would this not be the humane choice?"

Mr. Wilkes stood before Charlie, waiting for his response.

Charlie seemed lost to one thought or another, but he was thinking hard, nonetheless.

At last, he spoke up. "This is fucking crazy, you know that?" He looked right at Mr. Wilkes, leaned forward and said, "You're fucking crazy!"

Mr. Wilkes exhaled long and his shoulders settled a bit. "So, Charlie West," he said, "you will not join us, then?"

Charlie thought longer and harder about this than made him comfortable, not that comfort was a real possibility for him at the time anyway. He knew his answer should have been an immediate no, but... he *was* tired of the pain, of the state of things. Both in his small existence as well as the big picture of the world beyond his own life. There were some seriously shitty things happening to people around the world. They had always seemed to cast a certain amount of weight on his already strained experience. But he thought, too, of all he'd worked to overcome, not that it was doing him any immediate good. His mind was reeling. But he considered his future, his hopes and dreams. He thought of his would-be career, of all the students he hadn't yet taught. His frustration was growing into a sort of rage and sharpened, bringing him to a strange point of clarity. He thought of the past few days, what he thought had been, and what he was now realizing really was. So much of it had been a sham, he knew, but *weren't parts of it real?* He hoped. *What about Ellie?* He thought. *At least she had been real.* She was why he was here now, after all. At the thought of her, his mind seemed to seize up, and heat flashed through his whole body. Anger rose and he began to grow unfocused again.

"*Of course,* I won't join you," he said, his words muffled by a flexed jaw and gritted teeth. "You're insane." He looked around at all the men standing around him, with their blank, lifeless stares. "I might have had a pretty shitty life at times, sure, but... *this?* I don't want everything *annihilated,* for God's sake. If we destroy everything... we... we..." Charlie thought about what the drive had been for the better part of his adult years – to grow, to overcome – "...we wouldn't have the chance... to make things... better."

"*Gods,* I believe you mean, Charlie. Plural, in this case."

Charlie's expression scrunched up. He couldn't believe the man could cast away rationality so quickly.

"So, you choose the side of foolishness then? Very well. We will try this *one* other way before we move forward." Mr. Wilkes turned, again, to the man standing next to him and, in a voice just loud enough for Charlie to hear, he said, "Bring her in." When he turned back to Charlie, he was smiling again, but this time it burned with a fury of a man who would not give in.

Ellie! Charlie thought.

A piercing flash of pain shot up from Charlie's gut up through his chest, landing sharply in his throat. He tried to sit up and strained his neck upward to watch the man walk through the crowd of men toward the small iron door that stood at the back of the room. He lost sight of him but could hear each echoing step leading up to a key jangling in a lock and the grinding of metal on metal as the wide door was opening.

Charlie thought he could just make out a series of muffled grunts and the sounds of a struggle when the crowd parted before him, making way for a prisoner, bruised, beaten, and gagged, and strapped to a chair similar in likeness to the one Charlie was sitting in himself.

It was her.

"Ellie!" Charlie screamed. He twisted and turned in his chair when he saw her, and shook with what violence he could channel, but it was no use. He needed to break free. He needed to get to her, but he was helpless. This worked only to fuel his already burning anger.

Ellie was visibly shaken and terrified, with confusion and regret fighting for which would become the dominant expression on her face. Blood was streaming down one side of her face and gone was the strength that Charlie had come to see as one of her defining traits. What sat before him now was exactly what Mr. Wilkes wanted Charlie to see: an expression of his maniacal and exacting power and reach. Through Ellie, Charlie would see how little control that he truly had.

"Now, Charlie," said Mr. Wilkes, bringing everyone's focus back. His voice bounced with a joviality normally reserved for trite banter. "Before this little reunion goes any further, certain things need to be made clear. Young Ellie here is present with us for one reason and one reason only, and that shall be explained in due time."

"What have you done to her!" Charlie yelled.

"What have *you* done to her, my boy? Hmm? *Your* decisions, right?" Mr. Wilkes was thoroughly enjoying himself now. "We were just having a little conversation, she and I. Catching up, you might say."

"What... what do you mean?" Charlie's anger was getting the better of him and he was finding it difficult to focus again.

"Charlie, Charlie, Charlie." Mr. Wilkes looked down toward the stone floors and took several slow steps over to Ellie, all the while never taking his raving eyes off Charlie. He pulled a pistol out from within his jacket.

"What the fu—" Charlie started, "what the fuck!" He writhed against his restraints again; he fought with all his fury.

Ellie sat there before them all, bleeding, her eyes tightly shut, holding in what tears they could. At the sight of the gun, her body started to shake and convulse, involuntarily leaning further away from Mr. Wilkes. Her whimpers echoed lightly off the concave ceiling.

She was restrained by fear more than anything else.

Charlie wondered what could have happened to have turned Ellie into the person who was sitting before him.

Motioning with the gun, Mr. Wilkes had Ellie brought closer to Charlie. Then he pulled the gag from her mouth.

As he touched her, Charlie kicked and screamed even harder than before.

"Don't you fucking touch her! Don't you even—"

Ellie erupted into a flood of sobs and tears. "I'm sorry, Charlie! I'm so sorry! I never—"

Mr. Wilkes backhanded her with the end of his pistol, silencing her.

She let out one quick yelp of pain before settling back into obedient silence.

Through more of a growl than a yell, Charlie screamed Mr. Wilkes, "Don't you dare touch her!" The veins in his neck bulging, ready to burst, the blood was pumping so fast through his body. The tone of his skin shifted again, phasing through various shades of purple and crimson.

"Let her go!" he screamed again, the building veins quickly moving up to his temples.

"Yes, Charlie!" Mr. Wilkes' attitude seemed only to be encouraged by Charlie's rage. "There's that fire again! Good. Good."

Charlie breathed in and out, trying to control himself with a methodical precision. It wasn't much use. The pressure was still building, and fast.

Some of the men standing near Mr. Wilkes took small steps back, as it looked that Charlie might burst through his restraints at any moment.

"Charlie... Charlie," Mr. Wilkes spoked slowly, trying to lull him back down – though his smile wasn't helping anything. "Charlie, my boy, listen to me."

Charlie kept breathing to the pulsing rhythm of his heart, and stared back into the wild grimace etched into Mr. Wilkes' face

"As promised, I want to explain to you the point that young Ellie is here to make." He turned and, with the gun, motioned for her to speak. "Ellie? Would you be so kind as to explain to young Charlie here the role you have played in our little game?"

Ellie was silent. Infinitesimally, she looked even further the other way, doing what she could to avoid what was to come.

Charlie stared back and forth between her and Mr. Wilkes, wondering what he could possibly be talking about.

"Ellie, dear?" Mr. Wilkes continued. "Would you be so good as to tell our new *friend* Charlie here who you work for?"

A handful of stray tears escaped her as she shook her head, indicating either that she couldn't or *wouldn't* answer.

Mr. Wilkes stood up straight, his face scrunching itself into a frown.

Then, Mr. Wilkes took a step closer and leaned in to speak to her. Judging by the way she shifted nervously, Charlie knew that she found the distance to be violating and too intimate. He said, "What was that, Ellie, dear? I couldn't quite hear you." Then he struck her again.

She let out another howl and the tears flooded in continuous streams.

"Ellie!" Charlie yelled.

"Come now, Ellie," Mr. Wilkes voice slid back to one of pleading understanding. "Ellie, he deserves to know the truth. After all, that's what tonight is all about, isn't it? The *truth.*"

"What the hell are you talking about?" Charlie yelled to him. He looked over to Ellie, but she was yet to allow herself to make eye contact with him.

Mr. Wilkes stood up straight again and looked over at Charlie. "Trust me, Charlie, this will be better coming from her."

Then, looking back at Ellie, he continued, "My dear, I'm going to give you one last chance to tell him and then I'm going to shoot you in the head. Do you understand?"

She shook with trembling fear. Her sobs reformed themselves into a series of choking heaves and wails as she worked clumsily to compose herself. She knew he would follow through with his threat and shook her head in acknowledgement to his demand in submissive understanding.

"Why are you doing this?" Charlie growled.

Mr. Wilkes ignored him. "Ellie?" she said. "Are you ready to tell him who you work for?"

With tears still pouring out of her and her head weighed down by a lifetime of guilt and shame, Ellie nodded that she would comply.

Charlie yelled out to her. "Ellie! Don't! Don't give in to him! Ellie… Ellie, look at me!"

It was no use. Right then, to Ellie, all that existed was Mr. Wilkes and the will he had over her.

"Very good, Ellie," Mr. Wilkes said, continuing to ignore Charlie. "Now then, who do you work for?"

She took a deep breath and let loose one loud, tear-filled sigh. It was a cathartic and apologetic purge, but even after it was over, she felt no less stained than before. She steadied herself, knowing now that there was no avoiding what was to come. And finally, she looked up at Charlie, whose eyes burned with a fire that, before, would have given her whatever push she needed to keep fighting. But, in that moment, when she looked at him, all she saw was what she had become.

"I'm sorry, Charlie," she said.

"No," Charlie pleaded with her. Images flashed through his mind of the two of them walking down the river front, getting drinks at the Portway, and walking back to his place. "You don't have to be sorry. We're going to get through this, okay? You don't have anything to say sorry about anything at all. Everything is going to be alright."

Mr. Wilkes let out a hearty laugh. "Such heroism, Charlie. And for what? Come on Ellie, goddammit!" His patience all but burned away. "Answer the damn question!"

He struck her again and she howled once more.

She flinched and caved back into herself.

"You fucking—" Charlie screamed, trailing off he was so furious.

Ellie dissolved into a low whimper. "I'm... I'm sorry, Charlie, but they—"

Mr. Wilkes stuck her again, causing Charlie to writhe and squirm, yelling to get away.

Her voice was barely a whisper.

Charlie had to lean forward as far as he could but still couldn't make it out.

Mr. Wilkes struck her once more. "Goddammit! Tell him!" he screamed at her.

Charlie was shaking in his chair, rocking back and forth, yelling at the top of his lungs. One of the straps around his arms was starting to loosen.

Finally, Ellie gave in. Blood and tears flowed in mingled streams down her arm and dripped from her finger as she reached up and pointed at Mr. Wilkes.

"Him," she whispered. She wanted to tell him why. She wanted to explain everything to him. She hoped beyond reason that she would have the chance to. She felt the need to make things right, a compulsion to make up for years of wrongdoing.

Charlie kept fighting against his restraints, not registering what he had just heard.

"What was that, Ellie?" Mr. Wilkes said loudly as he raised the gun to strike her again.

"I work for *him*, Charlie!" She yelled out before falling back into hyperventilation.

Then, crumbling back into hysterics, Ellie looked at Charlie again, eyes wide, and pleaded, "I'm sorry, Charlie. I'm so sorry. I... I didn't know what was going to happen... they made me..."

Tears poured down out of her like twin waterfalls, emptying into icy pools below.

A dizziness came upon Charlie again as he finally started to register what he had just heard. Everything around him faded away. All feeling and emotion. It was like something had siphoned it out. His face turned white and pale, but his shoulders tensed. He trembled. Every ounce of his being was attempting to wrap itself around this revelation.

He tried looking over toward Ellie but found that he couldn't bear to even see her and instead found himself gazing up at the fractured remains of Trent in the corner. A surge of confusion and an intense disdain flooded him.

Even Trent took another step back into the shadowy edges of the room. He wished he could have told Charlie that he hadn't known about Ellie either. He hadn't known how deep it all went, or what it had all been for. He would have given anything for the opportunity to explain himself to Charlie. But, most of all, he wished he would've acted when he had the chance. He was plagued by the reality that he could have stopped all of this but did nothing. He was sure, that no matter what happened to Charlie, nothing would be worse than whatever waited for him when all of this was over. The least of which being that he would spend his remaining years, however short they might be, living with *this*.

"Do you get it now, Charlie?" Mr. Wilkes yelled. "Do you see how little control you have? *We* have placed you exactly where *we* need you. You are truly alone." His laugher echoed of the chamber's ceiling. "Do you see it, Charlie?"

Charlie gave no response. He sat there, limp in his chair, ineffectual.

"*We*, Charlie, are in control. *I* am in control. And you are going to help us no matter what. Do you see? Whether you want to or not. It was your great-grandfather who tried to conjure the creatures forth all those years ago. It took the blood of the *willing* to begin this rite. And through the blood of that blood, as a family member, *you* will help us complete it. Your great-grandfather *willingly* gave himself to this great and true cause, and now we have you, Charlie, here! Exactly where *I* have placed you!" Mr. Wilkes reveled in the ceremony of how his plan was coming together. He basked in the glory of the power he had attained. "You see, Charlie, Trent and Ellie, they work for me. *It was they* who brought you to me. For you, my boy, there is no escape. No way out!"

Charlie, dizzy with disbelief, stared into the stone floor between his feet. He was still unable to even glance over to Ellie, or Trent for that matter – both of whom sat, broken, trapped within the weight of their similar but separate grief – though his thoughts at the moment didn't stray far from them as memory after memory from the last week streamed through his mind, all the depth of the assuming friendships he was building.

Ellie still sat there, bleeding now from both sides of her head, and stared blurrily down at the dusty floor at her feet.

As for Trent, he couldn't quite focus on anything at all. Instead, his gazed scurried throughout the room in a desperate and futile search for whatever it was he hoped would cure his regret.

Considering them both, Charlie's anger smoldered and only grew deeper.

Let it all burn, he thought.

"What do you say, Charlie West?" Asked the triumphant Mr. Wilkes. "This *will* happen. The Nameless *will* come. Will you not join us?"

"I don…" Charlie stopped short of answering as he considered his position.

The isolation. The true gravity of what the past few days had led to.

The life he thought he was going to lead, only to be torn to shreds, to *this*. His thoughts kept rounding back to one simple idea: he wanted to live a life untampered with, unrestrained from the wills of others. His head was spinning.

At last, he looked up to Mr. Wilkes.

"*Why?*" He whispered. "Why… why would you do all this?"

Mr. Wilkes didn't realize Charlie was talking about his solitary life.

"Because we must, Charlie. Because the world deserves better."

There was another long pause and the whole room seemed to breathe as Charlie sat there, considering his thoughts.

"What do you say, Charlie?" Mr. Wilkes pressed him, softer this time than the last.

Charlie looked away from everyone. He wanted to burn it all down. *Everything.* He wanted nothing more than to strike the match himself, but something rang deeper in him still. Something he couldn't quite explain. Something that rose above every other thought.

With a certain amount of finality, he looked up at Mr. Wilkes and shook his head. "No," he said. "Never. I could never willingly be a part of *this.*"

Then, ignoring everyone else in the room, he hung his head so his chin fell to his chest, and he gave a deep and accepting sigh. He knew his fate was sealed, as well as the fates of so many others.

"Indeed," said Mr. Wilkes, looking almost pleased. "Very well, then, Charlie West. As you wish."

Once more, the room grew quiet. All that could be heard were Ellie's soft whimpers echoing off the curvature of the ceiling.

And with an abrupt and premeditated precision, Mr. Wilkes lifted up his arm and pointed the pistol to the side of Ellie's head. He looked down at her and said, "Consider your debts paid, young lady," as he pulled the trigger.

The whole room jolted, shuddering at the burst, and then once more steadied itself into stillness.

Ellie's whimpering had ceased.

Aside from the reverberations of the blast that shot across the room, all had fallen back to quiet.

It took Charlie a moment to process through what had just happened, but then he burst out, "What the fuck did you just do!" Fury tore its way through him. Tears exploded outward but brought with them no resolve. He was shaking uncontrollably now. "What the hell is the matter with you?"

Mr. Wilkes' laughter echoed off every brick that held the domed ceiling together, seeming to channel it all back down to Charlie. "I'm surprised by your reaction, Charlie, my boy," he said. "Even after what she just revealed to you?"

Charlie was too enraged to even take in the comment, let alone process the complexity of it.

"Either way, she is of no consequence anymore." Mr. Wilkes held up the gun, as if to examine it, smoke flowing out of the barrel and rising to the stone roof above. It was the perfect symbol of his exacting hand. He set it down on the table next to him and spoke. "Now," he said, bringing everyone's attention back to the matter at hand, "would someone be so kind as to bring young Charlie here along to where his fate awaits him?" He looked at Charlie but spoke to his men. "He has made *his* choice, but we still have *our* final task before us. Come!" And with that, he turned and marched through the crowd as it parted for him back into the corridor that led up to the manor.

The same two men who placed Charlie into his restraints walked up to him. One of them pulled out a small club from under his jacket, lifted it up and brought it down hard onto the side of Charlie's head, knocking him completely unconscious. Charlie remembered nothing after that moment.

THIRTEEN

Charlie had no idea how much time had passed when he finally came to. It was night and he could barely make out the gentle fall of rain. The last time he'd been outside it was the middle of the afternoon, so waking up here was quite disorienting. His head throbbed and he remembered being hit, the club coming down upon him. It pulsed along with the steady heartbeat of his rage. Awareness settled itself upon him, reaching out to the surroundings. It picked up the lapping of waves crashing down upon a soft and welcoming bank of sand. Wind pushed itself past and through the immensity of a grove of leafy trees and branches, rustling then at every opportunity.

Charlie looked around, grasping for understanding. He could see that he was on a beach front of a sort, but it lacked that heavy salty air that accompanied the ocean. And even in the darkness, he could just make out another shore far off on the other side. *The Columbia*, he told himself, the mighty river that held the strong divide between Oregon and Washington State. He had to be on the river, somewhere on the outskirts of Knappa and Astoria.

He tried to step forward but found that he could not.

What the hell—

He looked down and a slow realization came to him. He was strapped to *something*, tight. He couldn't move or even budge. Whatever confidence and calm that had come over him beneath the manor was gone. It seemed now to be nothing more than a fading memory, one that he could not trust or rely on. The tug of his restraints brought him closer and closer to panic as worry drove him to look around with frantic jolts to gather whatever information he could about his surroundings.

He found that he was harnessed onto a platform, small and circular at the base, about four feet wide. Protruding up from the platform, just behind him, was a metal piece of framing cut out in the silhouette of a person. It was to this that Charlie had been strapped to at his ankles, knees, waist, and chest.

"What the fuck?" he shook with a wildness, his chest growing constrained with worry, and tried using his momentum to loosen it and break free, but it was no use. He wasn't going anywhere.

His hands were fastened out in front of him to an odd, translucent sphere, smooth as marble. It was no larger than a basketball. It looked, to Charlie, like an oversize crystal ball, like something he'd seen in a séance from some old black and white movie. Looking into it, he could see the reflection of the sky above swirling through it, in all its deep and murky streaks of grey and black. This otherworldly object, Charlie noticed, sat atop a stone pedestal, hewn from the same stone as the corridor underneath the manor.

Though it was difficult to focus, Charlie tried recounting the events that had led up to this moment, and the exhausting emotional ups and downs that had come with it. He still couldn't completely understand what was happening.

Moments flashed before him of being in Trent's truck and pulling up in front of the big mansion. Then he saw himself standing in the large room with all those men. He felt faint. Then he saw the long, dark corridor again, and the strange room that waited for them at its end. At this, Charlie's stomach clenched and turned over on itself. He saw Ellie and remembered the explosion of the pistol, its faint echo reverberating off the inside of that nightmarish lab within his mind.

As he slammed back to reality only to find himself still strapped to the nightmarish platform, Charlie flinched and shuddered.

He vainly fought to free himself from both his constraints and the memory.

Just then, he heard a rustling coming from the trees off in the distance, followed by the sound of several murmuring voices. A strange uneasiness cast itself over him, fueling whatever else was undermining his resolve. His mind, after all he'd been through, was thin and frayed, like the edges of an old quilt; it seemed it could unravel at any moment. He was ready for all of this to be done.

Then a voiced interrupted him.

"Ah, Charlie! Welcome back," said Mr. Wilkes. Charlie heard the sharp and commanding voice before he came into view, followed by a few dozen of the other men. "Gather around, brethren," he said to them. "Gather around. We are ready now."

The others followed behind him like blind and obedient children, bent by years of conditioning.

Charlie struggled, as if upon seeing them he would somehow be more apt to make an escape.

"It's no use, boy," laughed Mr. Wilkes. "Trust me. You are exactly where you're supposed to be."

Charlie froze at Mr. Wilkes' certainty and watched as everyone circled around him, all wearing dark robes, as if each had been cut out of the shadows of the cold night sky, as empty as the men who wore them. Mr. Wilkes stood at the center, facing Charlie, looking ready to pull down the heavens himself.

A smaller group of men, Trent included, stood a short distance away at the opening of a path. Each man, Trent aside, wore looks of eager anticipation.

Trent himself, so unused to the horrible pangs of regret, was working hard to discern what to do, swooning from the complexity of these feelings that seemed to be at war in him. Eager, too, but only in terms of looking for some way to intervene. He hoped beyond reason there was still some way to salvage the situation. Charlie would never trust him again, of that he was sure, but maybe, just maybe, there was something he could do for Charlie. He would have to try.

"What are... you..." Charlie started to say, still struggling with the restraints, before noticing what each man was wearing around his neck. "Those..." Charlie stuttered, "...what are... what are you..."

Catching what Charlie was staring at, Mr. Wilkes looked down and lifted up his own bronze medallion. "Ah, yes." He held it almost affectionately.

His eyes, Charlie noticed, were even more wild than before.

"These, Charlie," Mr. Wilkes continued, "are a key component of our rite. Very *interactive*, you might say. You would know better than most, though." This was followed by a haunting chuckle. "We don't exactly know *where* they came from, only that they've been passed down through the millennia, generation to generation, to us. Most likely a gift from *beyond*."

Charlie's worry grew, gripping his insides with a firm relentlessness. He could barely understand the words he heard.

"Your father wore one."

Charlie flinched at the mention of his father and held his breath. His cheeks flushed from the oncoming rush of emotion.

"And on that fateful night so long ago, your great-grandfather, along with my grandfather, wore one." Mr. Wilkes let his medallion fall back down to rest. "This location, you should know," he gestured to the scene around them, "is an ancient site of great importance to The Order and to those who came before us. The indigenous brothers – not the Chinooks, mind you, the true *first* people – this was their land. This is where they made their sacrifices." He looked up into the dark night sky and breathed in deeply. "Can you imagine it, Charlie? Even those savages understood the relevance of it all. Even *they* saw the truth of it.

"Here, in the very spot you stand, a *volunteer* would come forth and, through great sacrifice, *they* would shake the very heavens!" He grew more and more excited, his voice booming and fading off into far-reaching echoes through the river valley. "And tonight, Charlie, it is *our* turn! We will join our forebears in moving far beyond the normal reach of men. We will bring the heavens to their knees! We will accomplish a feat greater than any mortal has yet before!"

Mr. Wilkes walked toward Charlie. He took several quiet and slow steps through the sand, as if holding himself back as best he could. He wanted to savor every drop of these moments he could.

He wished he could see the look on Blackwell's face and all the others once their mission was complete. He wished he could have been there to witness the gravity of their shock that he and his *fallen and wayward brethren* had succeeded where they had not. But knowing the truth of the matter would have to be enough, he told himself.

As he walked toward Charlie, Charlie's feet scrambled backward to get away in several quick, futile bursts, but the straps were too tight and he went nowhere.

Mr. Wilkes drew closer and closer until he reached him at last, and from out of his robe he pulled out another of the bronze medallions.

"What's... that... for?" Charlie muttered, his feet still kicking to get away. He twisted and writhed, and his panic grew.

Mr. Wilkes reached up with both hands, the medallion hanging down between them. His eyes were like the sun, burning and sure.

"No! Stop! Please!" Charlie was powerless, but as the medallion drew closer, he felt a shift coming over him. His doubt transformed into a fiery assurance. His desperation, to anger.

"Can you feel it, Charlie? This is what we've been testing on you. Our sincerest apologies, of course, but we needed to be sure."

"Test... What?" His thoughts were bubbling as a blanket of heat seemed to pour over him. The pressure was building again. Just like the attic. Just like Trent's truck. Just like in his room that night. He could *feel* it.

"We were confident in who you were, Charlie, but one can never be too careful."

Just then, the evening's gentle sprinkle turned to a harder rain – not quite a downpour yet, but a storm was definitely on the way. A peel of thunder burst and rippled off in the distance.

Mr. Wilkes gave a short burst of laughter and, with exacting precision, aimed to stab Charlie in an already unstable wound. "Haven't been questioning our stability as of late, have we Charlie? Getting irrationally angry? Hmm? Haven't been losing our temper?"

His blood was pumping quickly again. In and out and back and forth through his body. It was a windy and chilly evening with the coming storm, but Charlie was sweating.

"What the hell? How do you—?" He felt he was hanging over the edge of exhaustion now, on the verge of collapse. If it hadn't been for the harnesses, he wouldn't be able to stay upright.

"When did you first begin to feel the rising fury, Charlie? The other night? With young Ellie?" Mr. Wilkes pressed deeper into where he knew Charlie's insecurities to lie, and twisted, wanting now to inflict as much pain as possible. There was nothing Charlie could do anymore.

Images flashed themselves in front of him. First of Ellie running out of his room. Then of his mother cowering on the ground beneath... Not his father... but him... then Trent smiling up at him, reaching out his hand. They came on fast, uncontrollably racing through his mind. One shadow loomed over them all: his father. It grew and grew until all else faded. The only thing he could see in his mind was himself collapsed onto an empty field of dust, completely enveloped by shadow.

"Fuck you!" Charlie screamed.

"That poor girl. I *think* she trusted you, Charlie. And to think about what happened to her."

"Don't you dare!" Charlie pressed.

The cackles of Mr. Wilkes' laughter carried across the stillness of the night.

"You had your chance, Charlie," Mr. Wilkes pressed back.

Charlie looked deep into the man's eyes and saw only madness staring back at him.

"But for the sake of clarity, Charlie," Mr. Wilkes continued, "I am interested to know. When did you start to unravel? Was it the other day, or was it before? Say, in your attic?"

Charlie eyes widened.

"What did you—how did you—?"

Mr. Wilkes gave him a surly grimace. He was loving every moment of this. "Surely, my boy, you're beginning to see."

With one final step, he reached up with the medallion, Charlie shaking with fury, and placed it around Charlie's neck.

Charlie thrashed and fought but it was still no use.

As soon as the medallion touched him, he let out a shriek. A piercing constancy burned through his whole body, like someone was holding up a match to every individual cell. Something within him fused together, like a circuit had just been made complete.

Mr. Wilkes just laughed. "That's it, my boy! That's it!" The men surrounding him followed suit and joined him in a sort of pre-celebratory hail of reveling yells.

"You are your father's son, aren't you, Charlie?" Mr. Wilkes said playfully. But then his face grew stern and grim, and he said, "Except your father had been trained his whole life for this. Primed. He lived under the weight of *this* moment. When Trent reported back what he had seen in you... and I..." he paused, "I knew the *time* was finally at hand!"

Trent, upon hearing this, was overtaken by the mounting shame and let his shoulders fall with his chin as he took a step further into the shadows. He couldn't even bear to look in Charlie's direction. He was sure now that no moment would present itself for him to act. It was too late.

Charlie opened his eyes. They were aflame with enmity. He looked at Mr. Wilkes who showed no sign of faltering. "You did this to me!" he said. "You made me this way!"

"Heavens, no, Charlie. Of course not. We didn't make you into this. This has always been *in* you. This *is* you. We merely tightened the screws a bit. Brought out what we needed, so to speak."

Shame moved over Charlie like a storm cloud over water; it settled right over him. He was shrouded by their shadows, a mirror of their inconsistent nature. He knew it. Deep down, he'd always known it. He'd fought so hard to become more than his wounds. To grow. To move beyond who he thought he was. But now he *knew* he was no better. At least he thought it, which meant it was practically a solid fact.

Charlie's heart wrenched at the thought that he would never be able to make it right. Any of it. Ellie was gone, after all. He would never get to explain to her what happened or say he was sorry.

But she betrayed me... he thought, and his heart reeled again within him.

He couldn't keep his thoughts straight anymore.

Then he thought of his mother. What he had done had probably destroyed her. And knowing that he probably wouldn't make it through the night meant he wouldn't ever be able to make it right with her either.

Anger blistered its way through his veins. This wasn't going to end well, but something in Charlie told him not to give up yet.

"Your mother, though, Charlie."

Charlie's eyes shot up at Mr. Wilkes, that wicked smile etched across his face again.

"Curiously enough, her reaction has been much more peculiar than yours."

Charlie's stomach dropped. His heart rate quickened and all the color disappeared from his face.

"My mother? What about her? What did you—"

"Nothing, *really*. Same as you, Charlie. We needed to see how people with a close history surrounding the event interacted with the *tools*," Mr. Wilkes indicated to his medallion, "You yourself have been a textbook case of exactly what we needed. It has a tendency, the medallions, once its imprinted onto a family or bloodline, to enhance or amplify, really, who that person is deep down—what they're capable of. It brings out... certain things."

"What did it do to her?"

Mr. Wilkes laughed.

"Charlie, I'm sure your mother is fine. She'll pull through if her strength holds—well, until the Nameless come, of course. We did to her the same as we did to you. We placed her in direct contact with one of these," he held up the extra medallion again, "and... she reacted."

"What!" Charlie exploded. "Where is she? Where?" He half-expected them to bring her out like they did Ellie.

"Charlie, calm down. Calm down, son. She's fine, relatively speaking. She's at home, resting, I'm sure. Our people are keeping tabs on her, just as we were with you. Though, I'm afraid she doesn't have much to hold on to anymore. She's quite the broken ball of fun, isn't she? And she seemed to become quite upset the other day after a certain... phone call..."

The veins bulged in Charlie's neck as fury flowed like he had never felt before. "Fuck you!" He screamed. It helped to burn away any guilt that had crept in.

"Have you ever seen someone just... *give up*, Charlie? Truly lose hope? It is quite an ugly affair."

Charlie looked as if he could break right out of his restraints, and that he nothing would have held back the revenge he yearned for.

"Why... why the... you should have left her out of this, goddammit! Just stay out of our lives!"

"Oh, we plan to, Charlie. In just a few more minutes, we won't be needing you anymore. Nobody will. In fact, in a few more minutes, none of this is really going to matter."

For the first time in Charlie's life, he felt filled with all the resolve and readiness he needed to accomplish what lay before him, but now here he was, still crippled and unable to act. It was a farce, almost Shakespearean, he thought.

He huffed and he writhed, breathing in and out in controlled bursts. Saliva built itself up around the edges of his mouth. If he could've thought straight, he might have considered how he could have gone back and avoided all this, but there was really nothing he could have done. It always would have come down to this moment. Eventually, he was always going to face this hell. The Order had made sure of that.

In a voice somber and taciturn, Mr. Wilkes asked him, "Do you feel it, Charlie? The electricity in the air? The power?" He looked around at his men. "The power that could have been yours but now belongs to *me*?"

At the last word, Charlie saw the true insanity of it all, the true reason for so much pain. This man didn't want to remake the world, to build it into a *better* place. He was no different than any other tyrant. He merely wanted to stand over others and know that he, even if for just a moment, had ruled.

"It's time, my boy," Mr. Wilkes said at last. The words were followed by a definite silence.

Charlie shook his head, the warm and angry tears starting to stream down his face.

Mr. Wilkes turned around and walked back to his place at the head of the circle. "Are we ready, brothers?"

In one singular and cohesive reply, they yelled out, "Aye!"

"No, stop!" Charlie sobbed. "This is crazy!" He was shaking. Still fighting.

Each man in the circle ignored him and steadied himself to a ready position.

Trent's chin dropped even lower and he took two more steps back.

"Brothers, it is time!" Mr. Wilkes bellowed over the wind.

"No! No! No!" Charlie's voice went hoarse. It was futile. There was nothing he could do to stop this. "STOP! PLEASE! NO!"

Still, the scene moved forward.

His mind spun in quick gravitating circles. It pulsed in and out, making it difficult to focus.

A sharp pain pricked near the front of his mind, just above his right eye, and an image flashed of Charlie standing in a storm. There was thunder cracking in the background and lightning flashes bursting with the potential for life every several seconds. Charlie saw himself standing in an open field of dust. Another crack of lightning. Then another. Finally, after one more burst, Charlie looked up and saw that his face had changed. It was no longer his own face plagued by worry. It was the face of his father, maniacal and filled with dreadful intent.

Charlie screamed in both real life and his waking dream.

CRAIG RANDALL

Still, the men pressed forward in their well-practiced routine.

"My brothers!" Mr. Wilkes yelled out. "Tonight, finally, we make our mark! We will reach up to the heavens and bring them tumbling down atop this wicked world! Today, it ends! Today starts anew!"

Cheers erupted en masse and the brothers raised their arms in celebration, shouting and hollering.

Trent's voice called out from amidst the chaos and yells and hollering. "Charlie! I'm sorry!" But it was useless. His plea was drowned out by the bestial screams and yells of the brethren. His last chance for absolution had been lost.

"Brothers, repeat the *focus!*" Mr. Wilkes ordered.

They obeyed.

Each man in their dark and sinister robes began to chant in unison. A crooked song they would lift high to pay homage to their dark gods. Those terrors from beyond.

Mr. Wilkes started it: "*Erae-elbereth-akalake-mellath!*"

Everyone else repeated: "*Erae-elbereth-akalake-mellath!*"

It had a deep resonant meter, a rhythmic cadence that punctuated the silence and was disrupted only by Charlie's feeble cries for help.

All together, they chanted: "*Elbereth-akale-aaiellaka-seett-allka! Elbereth-akale! Elbereth-akale-aaiellaka-seett! Elbereth-akale-aaiellaka-seett-allka! Aak-mella!*"

Charlie's screams trailed off. His eyes rolled backwards and then the lids closed altogether. His whole body began to shake. It wasn't like before, though. This wasn't him fighting against the restraints. This was something other-worldly. He fell into sharp convulsions.

Thunder peeled across the skyline and the light mist transformed into a turbulent downpour. As Charlie's screams died down, the chant continued, bringing with it an unnatural and unearthly calm.

"*Elbereth-akale-aaiellaka-seett-allka! Elbereth-akale! Elbereth-akale-aaiellaka-seett! Aak-mella!!*"

226

All the medallions, Charlie's included, began to vibrate and give way to a sordid buzz that undercut and added a morbid depth to the combined noises of the chanting and the winds and the rain. Then, as if in defiance of gravity itself, the medallions began to lift off the chests of the men and hung, floating in midair.

The buzzing grew louder and louder still. The chanting continued.

Charlie's body shook more violently. His body was on the verge of complete combustion, like the cells wouldn't be able to hold themselves together much longer.

The stones at the center of each medallion began to shimmer and, ever so subtly at first, they gave off a mild irradiation that grew brighter and brighter, baptizing the night sky in a crimson glow.

"Elbereth-akk! Elbereth-akale-aaiellaka-seett!"

Charlie continued to shake but with much more control. The rocks and pebbles at his feet began to lift off the ground and hover just off the surface of the earth.

Starting with Mr. Wilkes' medallion, the light from the stone grew fierce and shot out in both directions, like a rogue bolt of lightning fired with intent and control, contacting the stones in the medallions of both men standing next to him. This proceeded with the lightening reaching out to each successive man in the circle until finally the beams of light reached Charlie and both fired into his medallion with a force that, if he weren't strapped in, would have knocked him back twenty yards. Each collision of light sparked and sent out tiny explosions into the air and the ground shook.

The pulsing flow of electricity drowned out the chants of the men and ripped through the air as if it were breathing.

Several moments after the connection was complete, Mr. Wilkes intensified the delivery of his chants and directed his arms to where Charlie stood.

"Ellek-ama-mei-mel-Eila! Ellek-ama-mei-mel-Eila!"

From Charlie's medallion, a small sphere of blinding light grew and reached out with its edges further and further until finally the light burst into a cacophony of electricity and fluorescent hues. Sparks and tendrils fired out in every direction and in every pigment.

Immediately, the platform of which he was strapped was completely engulfed by this sizzling chrysalis of light.

More and more pebbles and smaller stones lifted from the sandy beach. The entire platform shook and creaked until several cracks could be heard and the whole platform shifted.

Electricity hung on every particle in the air, crackling and buzzing like a blanket of energy. Shifting swells of air whooshed back and forth. Anything not tied down – tarps, tools, one folding table – blew away with the bursts.

The phasing sphere of energy that surrounded Charlie pulsed and swelled until BANG! The chrysalis of light grew, consuming the entire circle of chanting men. It exploded outward, sending a rush of wind in every direction, knocking Trent backward along with the men who were hiding outside the circle.

Matter itself, each atom, froze hanging in their invisible magnetic fields.

For one moment, the sky itself took a deep breath inward and upon its exhale there was a thunderous and blinding detonation. A searing pulse shot upward into the sky, the blast sending forth residual winds kicking up sand from the beach below and streaked across the top of the river.

Following the pulse from the center of the growing sphere of blinding light, a thick beam fired upward into and above the clouds, the skyline itself, each molecule crackled and burned at its touch.

Multi-colored cumulus explosions followed the beam of light upwards, leaving a trail for anyone brave enough to follow. Its reach stopped just before the stratosphere's border bumped up against the cold depths of space.

If anyone could have seen that far, they would have noticed *something* starting to emerge. *Something* was starting to form.

In the sky, *something* was piercing the very fabric of existence. The beam of light, like a surgical knife, was cutting through reality's skin. There was a clear incision being made. And the tear grew, spreading from top to bottom, inch by inch, a domino of exploding atoms fizzling away as their integrity broke down and made way for what was about to come through.

This spot was becoming a doorway where two planes of existence converged. Little particles of energy burned and drifted down, falling to earth, only to dissolve before ever reaching its surface.

The incandescent and searing wound swelled, and its edges burned with torrid ripples. The incision stretched upward; the pace of its growth quickened. Fifty meters long, then sixty-five, eighty, one hundred, one fifty.

Down below, the chanting continued. The circle of men was nothing more than silhouettes of shadowed light.

As the tear continued to grow, the light seemed to reach down out of the sky, down to Charlie, the center of his own little cocoon. *It* called to him, *something* beyond the light, and his body went rigid and froze. His mind was alert and being made ready.

The platform he was attached to creaked and broke free from the base when something impossible happened. Charlie and the entire structure he was strapped to lifted from the ground and was raised by the light high into the sky. High above the circle of chanting men. High above Trent and the men who remained, cowering behind trees for shelter. He climbed higher and higher, picking up speed at every elevated gain.

He was drawn to the clouds and the stars in the sky as well as the storm of electricity that set them on fire.

And as Charlie was pulled further and further into the sky, *something* began to emerge.

Cruising through the air, Charlie gasped as if taking the first breath of air after being in a coma for months. Everything in him sharpened as if being channeled. His mind. His energy. His strength. Everything. The light grew brighter and brighter and illuminated the entire cove below. For him, time slowed down. The entire world was put on pause.

He wasn't necessarily conscious of anything around him. Within him, though, he *knew* what was happening. Somehow, he was connected with what was coming. He saw the truth in what Mr. Wilkes had spoken about. The frailty of mankind. The vapor of our lives. The inevitability of the end. He saw through the growing breach, the *in-between* area of worlds. And he saw, in his mind, the creature itself, this *Nameless* one. It was coming.

Holy shit.

It sought him in return. Somehow it *knew* Charlie as Charlie knew *it*. It reached out its consciousness and Charlie felt the tendrils of its mind on his, rummaging about.

The border between worlds blistered with power and continued to tear. The energy around it fluctuated. Even the air around it seemed to seek refuge from its weight and strain.

Charlie continued to rise through the air until he came to rest right at the center of the breach.

Charlie knew *it* was close, between worlds even.

Then, at the breach's center, something bulged and pushed outward toward him. The breach split and several objects emerged: tendrils. Long, viscous appendages of varying color and thickness all covered in a thick and soupy sheen. They burst forth and reached out, stretching themselves forward out into what, to them, was a strange land. As they continued to pour out, growing in length, their width proved to be massive. They spread and swelled.

Several at first, but then more emerged from above and below until hundreds of limbs reached their way forth.

Still, Charlie hung in the air, awake only in his mind.

The appendages continued to emerge – they looked more like something that would burst out of the great ocean depths ready to capsize old ships and pull them to their icy grave.

These great, beastie arms reached out and made their way to Charlie.

Eight-hundred meters long. Nine-hundred meters long. Then a thousand.

They cast fluorescent hues into the night sky. Their beauty curtailed by their destructive capabilities.

Charlie was an insect in comparison, an ant standing at the base of a mountain.

The threshold swelled once more as several appendages reached back and braced themselves against the walls of this world's reality.

They pushed with all their non-terrestrial strength. And then *it* emerged. The passage contracted and widened to push it through, making room for the body of the creature to show itself. It continued to push itself against the border of time, almost willing itself toward Charlie who stood, midair, as a speck of dust.

And then it was through. It was finally *there*.

It's massive, bulbous body defied gravity and hung in the air with thousands of tendrilous arms and legs hanging off, lapping up the air and the newness of a place it hadn't visited since its creation.

Charlie hung in the sky above.

The men of The Order were stuck, entranced by their obedient chant.

Trent and the other men hid where they could, insignificant in the scheme of what was taking place.

A calmness came over Charlie even as the storm raged on.

Trees swayed back and forth to their breaking point. Sand was flung all over by the wind. Nothing was untouched by the wet, cold rains.

The tips of the first tendrils that broke through reached out and stopped just in front of Charlie, hovering in the sky as if waiting for him to get used to them. From them, two bulges appeared on their surface. Pushed outward at first, but then they retracted quickly. Then they pushed out again a second time. Then a third. Something in them shifted and moved until out sprouted two smaller appendages, no thicker than the arms of a person. These stretched themselves out and reached right up to Charlie, feeling their way to him.

Making contact, they settled onto Charlie's temples and latched on. His body twitched but then fell back into a calming and restful posture.

The arms began to pulse and the creature spoke. Not in the assuming audible way that humans communicate; it simply *thought* and Charlie heard.

It didn't just speak *into* Charlie, it spoke *with* him.

Charlie West, it thought in a voice unlike anything Charlie had ever heard before.

Unsure how to respond, Charlie waited.

Charlie West, the creature thought again.

Charlie thought, *yes?* Then marveled at the realization that he was no longer angry. He no longer felt any sort of emotional pain at all. At that moment, he was filled with peace, almost reverie.

You have called out to us against your will, have you not?

Charlie wondered how the creature could know that before remembering it could read his thoughts.

Charlie West, have you not called out to us against your will?

Uh, Charlie thought, struggling. He was used to being able to formulate his thoughts before speaking. This was strange to him. *Yes,* he told the creature. *I... I have no idea wh—what's going on here or why.*

You have nothing to fear from us, Charlie West. I see in you that it was those below who have called upon us, but that you yourself are from without.

Without?

It means that you are not a part of them *or a part of* this *happening. That you are beyond their instincts and beyond their schemes. They have used you for their gain, have they not?*

Y-yeah—yes. I didn't know about any of this until today—I—

It is not yet our time to come forth.

What? Your time?

The time to live out our purpose. We were not yet supposed to come forth.

Your purpose. You mean... destruction?

That is one of our functions, yes. We are from before *and* beyond *your world, Charlie West, and your kind, and we are from* after.

What the hell, Charlie thought to himself.

Your confusion is understandable. Your mind is from within your world. Not intended for such depth and understanding.

So, you won't destroy everything now?

It is not yet our time. We are the trigger of existence, of all, as well as the triggers of the end. But until the appointed time is unveiled, we will simply be.

But that time isn't now? Charlie struggled to make sense of it all. *I don't understand.*

You would not, for you are a creature within time, of this realm. From within. All of you. And thus, bound within limits. We—

There are more of you— Charlie stopped abruptly, realizing his interruption.

We are many. And, like you, we occupy our expanse in order to live out our purpose. This purpose is simply different from yours. Our nature is reflected in that purpose.

Your nature, huh? Charlie thought about what Mr. Wilkes had told him about their intentions for calling these *Nameless* beings forth. *Destruction,* he thought to himself.

Our nature is not as crude as that.

Crude? Meaning?

We have a purpose. Like all things, we live to fulfill that purpose. At the beginnings and the endings of all things, we are present. What you call destruction, we see as duty, but we never act outside the appointed times.

Appointed times? You mean, it is all going to end someday?

All things have an end, Charlie West.

Even you?

When it is willed, we too will end.

But you came here now. Why, if you're not here to destroy everything?

We are not so crude as to destroy without purpose and it is not the appointed time. Nature dictates destruction with a purpose. We came, Charlie West, because you have called out to us. But not through your own purposes. It was through theirs *and it is not yet our time.* They *are contrary to our purpose.*

You knew this but you came anyway?

It is in our nature.

Charlie's mind worked to put the pieces together.

We were called forth, therefore we answered.

Charlie struggled with what was happening. The creature was so clinical in its estimations. Charlie thought of The Order and their purpose, of the nature of evil and hell-bent destruction. He thought of the pain in the world, in his own life for that matter. He thought of the intent that some had to inflict that pain. A flicker of anger rekindled in him. The creature sensed it. Charlie then thought of his father, of the order, of Mr. Wilkes and their ancestors working together to bring about so much destruction. At this, the pain erupted in his mind and fired itself quickly down through Charlie's entire body. He thought of Trent and of Ellie and of his mother. He thought of the world he'd grown up in. What he saw on the news. He thought of wars. Of famine. Of desperation. Of the mass amount of inequality out there. He thought of all the kids who didn't grow up with the hell that he had. Then he thought of all the kids who did.

The fires burned within him, but this anger was clear and precise. It was localized and given direction. There was a clarity to it. There was something *assisting* him in his ability to juggle the emotion.

Seeing Charlie's thoughts, the creature told him, *We have our nature, and you have yours.*

Charlie's anger flared at this.

So, we're the destructive ones? As soon as he said it, he knew it was the truth.

We only destroy at the appointed time.

Charlie's heart sank. It was true. He saw the senselessness of it all. *Humanity.* Even with all their laws and hopes and rules, they'd brought themselves to the brink of destruction so many times, even without the help of the *Nameless.*

It is your nature, the creature said.

Charlie wondered if it was meant as an encouragement or explanation.

Charlie thought about what Mr. Wilkes had said. *Maybe he was right about us. Maybe we deserve to step aside for what's next.*

That is contrary to our purpose, the creature said again.

There was a cold logic to it, completely cut off from emotion or human error. Maybe that was something to be thankful for. Compared to humans, *The Nameless* brought balance and purpose and consistency. There was a strange and common beauty to it. That in and of itself was something Charlie had always struggled to find in people. Perhaps that's because his earliest imprints were of pain, so no matter how hard he looked, or where, that's all he found.

He couldn't blame the creatures for what they did. They were following rules and pre-set bounds.

People, on the other hand? He knew he couldn't say the same. Unless that *was* our nature, to simply fall short, stray from the path. *But how could there be beauty in that?* He thought.

The creature was silent.

Charlie's consciousness was floating somewhere between pain and sorrow, then. Somewhere between reason and complete doubt.

He focused himself on the creature. *Surely, there must be something more to us? Right? As a species?*

Do you not understand your nature? It asked.

What?

Do you not understand your purpose?

Charlie's anger flared again. But somehow, he felt he was able to restrain himself, at least better than before. He wondered at where the precise ability to shift his emotions had come from, not thinking whatsoever about his connection to the creature.

Charlie thought of the men below. He thought about all the destruction they had caused and would cause. They had *made* his father, after all, and in turn had been the true cause of most of Charlie's pain. He thought of Trent and Ellie, how The Order had twisted their lives. And, lastly, he thought of his mother, what they had done to her.

Charlie struggled to maintain focus now. The fury thundered in him. Images flashed through his mind like gunshots, one after the other, of people screaming and bickering, yelling at each other; his father hitting his mother, kids at school, bullies, destruction on micro and macro levels. He saw wars and the destitution they bring. He saw his own life falling apart before him. The world burning. He saw the patterns passed down from generation to generation and their wicked and broken legacy. Over it all he saw his father's shadow looming above – but instead of his father's face, Charlie only saw himself.

His breathing quickened.

No!

You are in distress, Charlie West.

Even in his sedated state, he twitched and began to shake.

Charlie West, you are not calm.

Are we even worth saving? Charlie internally yelled out.

It is not yet the appointed time, was all the creature said, in its cold and distant clinical manner.

Fuck your time. Charlie told it. *Now or then? Does it even matter?*

As time foresees, so will it be done at the appointed time.

What the—? He was too emotional for the creature's logic. *So... you have the power to stop all this, and you won't?*

Deep down, Charlie realized that he was *disappointed.* Completely driven by emotion though he was, he *wanted* this.

It is not yet the appointed time, was all the creature would say.

Even after all the injustices? All the wrongs? All the atrocities that go unchecked? The pain and the destruction freely reigning in the world. After my father. The Order bel...

I sense in you deep pain, Charlie West.

Even though connected to the creature and barely conscious, Charlie's body shook and was in the early physical stages of hyperventilating. He thought of all the people who had ever hurt him, and he thought of what he'd like to do to them at that moment. With that fury and that power. Never had his thoughts fallen into such darkness. His mind was racing and reeling for options, for answers. He was concocting plans for revenge and ways to get back at all those who had destroyed his chance at peace.

Then the creature said: *I know what it is you would have us do, Charlie West, and yet you question me about nature and destruction.*

Charlie ignored it and more and more images flashed before him: His father screaming, drunk and raged; his mother's face being struck; her frail body hitting the floor; images of their years of torment; Trent and Ellie, smiling, their assuming friendships and eventual betrayal. Lastly, he saw Ellie pleading with Mr. Wilkes, then the shot, the bullet entering her skull, and finally silence.

Guilt shot through him like an arrow through an apple.

At that, Charlie thought of himself and the choices he had made. He thought about what he thought he deserved. He saw the patterns of his own destructive behavior painted with pain across the night sky like an open wound.

The air shifted around them and the electricity it carried moved about, searching for a conductive source.

Before, it had been the creature that connected himself to Charlie. It established their connection and had been its keeper. The creature reached out and felt Charlie, the entirety of his person, his *being*. It truly *felt* him. His pain. His suffering over the years. His anguish. That deep yearning for justice. After a certain moment, the creature opened this connection between them, allowing Charlie to influence the connection the other way. It did this in seeking to understand his pain. It let the energy and thoughts flow into him.

This fueled Charlie's feelings, accelerated them in a way. His agony and pain. The remembrances of traumas and heartbreak. Even his guilt and shame.

Charlie thought of the men below. What they were attempting. What they were willing to do to remake the world. To destroy everything that Charlie had ever known. He thought of what he was willing to do at the expense of revenge. It boiled through him and poured itself into the creature.

You are distressed, Charlie West, and in deep pain.

I... He couldn't even finish the thought. His whole body was tense. All his emotions ran wild and his anger flowed freely. It streamed out of him and into the creature in a great cathartic purge.

Just when he didn't think he could hold it in anymore, that pressure broke and he began to cry. *Something* in him broke free. The tears flowed unrestrained.

Pain is a mighty weight, Charlie West, the creature said. *A burden no one need carry. As is the same with anger.*

With each tear shed, a weight and burden were lifted from his shoulders and placed on the creature. Still the anger and loathing flowed. Charlie could feel the channel connecting him to the creature. He swam in it. He felt understood by it, at peace with it in a way. As if he knew, with the creature here, he would be safe. He was protected. But he hoped that not all was protected. He felt a certain peace, but true peace was still far out of reach. He bled in hope for the execution of his dark desires.

I know what it is you would have us do, the creature repeated, *but it is not the appointed time.*

Charlie struggled against whatever was pushing against his thoughts. There was what he wanted and there was what was right and he couldn't tell the difference between the two anymore.

He wanted justice and he wanted peace. But could he have both?

With each bounce back and forth between this forced spectrum, his brain stretched and strained, spinning his mind out of control. Charlie was losing it.

I can't— Charlie stopped himself.

I know what it is you would have us do, the creature said again, *but it—*

I know, goddammit! Charlie tried to breathe calmly, but his whole body was tense. His blood was pumping fast within his veins. The pressure was still building in his mind and his chest.

The creature took more of the strain from him onto itself and, arms shaking, gripped by an unearthly strength—a gift bestowed on him by the creature—he let out an ungodly scream, savage, and beastie. His whole self was in flex. With unequivocal ease, he ripped himself free of the straps and restraints that had held him. The platform and metal silhouette that had held him fell to earth below, like a falling star, lonely and quiet. No one heard it or saw it land.

Now, held up only by the creature's arms, Charlie hung in the heavens, caught between the tensions of the physical world. He himself had become a conduit of power and change.

Plagued by pains and visions, his mind spun and moved well beyond his control.

In the end, he would never fully remember making the decision, or that it had even been his decision to make, but Charlie would never forget these words: *As you wish, Charlie West.*

That was all it took.

What? Charlie's thoughts were pulled out of his frustrating wails, caught off guard by the electricity moving through the air.

Maybe it was compassion or empathy for the pain it had felt in Charlie. For a long time, Charlie wouldn't know. He would only remember the aftermath.

In a moment, each particle of the air, each molecule and atom buzzed and rattled. The surrounding energy and all its potential reverberated and echoed off the wind, rain, and sky. The interconnectedness of existence had never been so apparent. Everything danced together for that one moment. It could have easily been misconstrued for harmony.

And then it happened.

The air murmured. Its hum grew and grew, building to a pounding decibel until, without warning, it retracted inward, concentrating itself to a singularity and potential of destruction.

The entire scene, just for that moment, breathed. The leaves and loose sticks, anything not held down that had been adrift by the wind, it all just hovered in the air, as if someone or *something* had hit pause.

Charlie, too, hung in the air, his expression pained and his face tear stained. His arms stretched out to his sides.

The singularity drew in its deep breath, expanding itself outward. Like a balloon filled with too much air, it would burst at any second.

And then, *it* let go.

Boom!

The earth shook.

The concussion could be heard for miles in each direction down the river valley, echoing up the coastal mountain walls. An imminent alarm of impending doom for all who heard it. It was sheer momentum let loose to flood down onto the unsuspecting and serene calm of the Columbia river valley.

Tidal forces burst out in every direction regardless of what impediments stood in the way.

The power of it surged through Charlie as his chest was pulled tight, but he was alive with its fury. With all its destructive potential, Charlie was not in danger himself. He was caught within the confines of that chrysalis of light, seething with vitality. Somehow, he knew he was protected.

A light shot out from the blast, blinding and terrible. Its horrific beauty could only be compared to the pangs of the universe as it gave way to the birth of a new star. A clear display of raw, destructive function.

A second concussion fired out a gleaming pulse in every direction, picking up speed with every step it took. In droves, trees were ripped right from the ground and carried off at great distances, hundreds of yards, in an instant. Entire forests just disappeared. Gone in seconds.

As the pulse ripped forth, all that was left in its wake was the gentle falling of dust – the remnant carbon particles left over from whatever molecular exchange had taken place.

Trent and those men who had stood by him didn't stand a chance. So close to the blast's center, they became nothing more than vapor. Just dust that floated back down to the scorched ground below.

Nothing could stand in its wake.

Mr. Wilkes and the others taking part in the dark ritual stood their ground, wrapped in power, and were unaffected for a prescribed amount of time. Protected by the thin veil of crimson light. Like having blood smeared across the door post, the plague moved right over them.

Though they themselves were unaffected, the blast blew a crater in the sand below them. Tethered by the blazing medallion's light they, like Charlie, hung in the air, a fiery ring of oscillating light burning underneath the creature. With nowhere else to go, the excess sand compressed into itself and fused together under the heat and pressure. It formed a perfect bowl of glass, a feature that would confuse the recovery workers for years to come.

River water was vaporized and spewed scalding hydrogen gas upwards into the atmosphere.

Tidal waves hurdled forward, carrying water for miles in whatever direction they could.

Power continued to surge through Charlie, fueled by his anger, his indignation. He wanted to be free of it, but no matter how far the burst spread out, it clung to him tighter and tighter. The further it reached out in the world, the greater it grew in him. Vengeance was his.

Waves of heat followed the initial blasts. What they didn't destroy was simply scorched out of existence. No trace was left behind of anything that tried to stand in its wake. Whatever roads weren't ripped out of the ground simply melted apart, like water poured over a sandcastle and turned to congealed muck. Tree roots and shrubs that had – by whatever miracle – held on were torched to dust. Even rocks and stones were just wiped away in seconds, like spilled juice on a kitchen table.

Nothing could withstand the harrowing fury of the conflagrant glow. It burned too hot and too bright.

Beyond the blast zone, the pulse pushed outward at its devouring pace. Tearing through highways and protected forests and the odd periodic deer, it made its way to the edges of the Astoria and Knappa border, wrapping itself around the geography of the land, mountain sides, hills and gullies. It moved through and around whatever obstacle the terrain put forth. Nothing was spared.

Resentment and scorn continued to rise in Charlie, even though his body was well beyond exhausted. It was his mind that was held in constancy and gave strength to the purging wake.

241

The first breaches of destruction were the homes on the outskirts of both towns. They were incinerated instantly, rendering them inconsequential to the gravity of what was spreading.

Still the blast moved on, indifferent and without prejudice, to the various and scattered homes that populated the random nooks and backroads it destroyed.

Parked trucks and boats. Dirt bikes and four wheelers. Those big garages that men spent lifetimes populating with toys and tools that often towered over the family home. Gone.

Still the blast carried on through the smaller neighborhoods that clustered together as it grew closer to the center of the towns.

The quiet houseboat community that had always minded its own business under the Gnat Creek bridge. Gone.

Home after home after home was laid to waste. There wasn't even time for the people to scream. One minute they were there, and the next they were just gone. They ceased to be.

Showing no sign of slowing down, it reached the center of Knappa first. The Chevron station, the logging offices, the cafe, the tanning salon, The Logger. In seconds, gone.

And still it spread, burning its way through the trailer park, the high school, and all the neighborhoods the wound their way around the bends and roads.

In less than a minute, the town of Knappa had been completely removed from the surface of the earth.

Being the populated area, the destruction of Astoria was both more starkly and gravely pronounced and, for those who would venture forth into the destruction later, more noticeable.

There, too, it hit the neighborhoods on the edges of town first. The trees and homes burst into splinters, shattering before collapsing into dust.

Finishing there, it moved on to the more populated areas, hitting the hillside neighborhoods and downtown.

Everything was decimated.

The Astoria Column was gone. All the local businesses. Gone. The piers. Gone. The school buildings. The ball fields. Parks Grocery stores. All the little mom and pop shops. Art galleries. The local library. Daycare centers. Cafes. The bars and Pubs. The arcade. All of it. It was all gone.

The Megler Bridge, the longest free-standing bridge in North America and true testament of man-made ingenuity and power, was pulled apart like balsa wood and, like everything else that was not built last through eternity, it was gone.

The house Charlie had rented and his chance at a new life. It, too, was consumed and gone.

It took the inferno less than a minute to consume it all. Everything was gone. Not to mention the people. All those souls who slept cocooned within their peaceful dreams, those who would never wake again, were all gone.

Families. Grandparents, parents, children, aunts, and uncles. Everyone was gone.

And still the blast moved on, carrying its dark mission forward until the rage finally quieted.

Such were the consequences of the justice that had burned so poisonously in Charlie. The ends brought on by the acts, he told himself, of those who had wronged him.

The blast didn't stop at the sign that read Astoria City Limits. It moved on further down the highway and tore its way through the neighboring community of Warrenton. Down as far as Gearhart and Seaside. All of which, as communities, were equally as ill-prepared for the coming slaughter.

The Jetty where Trent and Charlie had howled into the night sky was pulled apart. The boulders, the foot holds of the gods, were wrenched from their places, crushed by pounding force and turned to dust. The platform didn't stand a chance. And the sea line, when it finally receded back, had made up for those long years of lost ground taken from them by the reach of men.

From the epicenter, for twenty miles in all directions as it was later measured, everything had been completely atomized. Acreage and miles of existence, of history, of life, of trees and animals and homes, and of lives, was devoured and unmade.

What was left behind was a horrid and desolate field of dust. The byproduct of the creature's wrath, of Charlie's unbridled fury.

It had only taken a minute, that was all. In that short time, so much and so many were affected, so much and so many were lost.

Mr. Wilkes and his men, having served their purpose, were dealt with justly, and in a way that would have, to Mr. Wilkes, seemed prejudiced. A small and singular burst of light shot forth from the creature and wound its way through Charlie and down the beam of light to the circled men below.

Somewhere just inside his realm of consciousness, Mr. Wilkes saw what was coming and knew, beyond any doubt, that it was outside of his control. A deep and immediate panic grew, but there was nothing he could do. He and his men were now intricate mechanisms in the rite that should have been his triumph; but, in that moment, he feared what end would come. One by one, starting with Mr. Wilkes, the burst struck each man as they stood oriented in the circle of crimson light, and they each, in a sudden flash of blue flame, went up into a quick burst of smoke and simply vanished, as if they had been completely erased. Even their screams seemed to evaporate into chaotic atmosphere. The last thought that crossed Mr. Wilkes' mind, or what was left of it, was an image of himself sitting around a large round table with the other Elders of The Order as they had each recast their votes to keep his sect expunged from the collective group. That had been the moment he had fought so hard to undo and he had failed. And now, he would never know what the fates had in store.

Afterwards, only their medallions remained and fell to the ground, unaffected and void of any illumination.

With the connection broken, the beam that had led upward to Charlie flickered and traced in the darkness and started to fade. Then it was only Charlie hanging in the heavens, held up by the will of the creature. Both the sun and the moon, together, lighting up the night sky.

It was finally over. Charlie was avenged.

But what that meant for him in the future, only tomorrow knew. Whatever wounds Charlie had carried before had not been healed. His heart had been ripped open anew, with new cuts over old scars.

One day he would have to face them, but that would be a while yet down the road.

Charlie hung in the air, his arms spread out wide, the creature still attached to his mind. He was no longer screaming but was barely conscious and far from a state of peace.

The creature considered him for a moment, and though he knew how Charlie felt, it went against its nature and said to him, *Be at peace, Charlie West, and live.*

Charlie, lost to the delirium of unconsciousness, gave no response.

We all must learn to live within our nature and come to terms with the repercussions that it brings. With the consequences.

With that, the creature lowered Charlie gently down to the ground with gradual ease. His body floated, like a leaf falling slowly, caught in an early morning autumn breeze.

It set Charlie down onto the ground, a soft bed of dust. He was unconscious and completely unaware of anything that had taken place. To him, for a time, it would never be anything more than a nightmare. Just distant memories that would never fade but were difficult to grasp.

There he slept.

With its purpose fulfilled, the creature began to retract itself slowly through the threshold from which it came, held open now completely by its own power. It moved with a slow certainty as its limbs reached back through the in-between sections of existence, pulling itself into the cosmos, back to where it would wait until the end.

It pushed and moved through those temporal boundaries until its final remaining tentacles barely protruded out of what remained in the tear in the sky.

Just as it had come into this world, it was gone.

The tear in reality fused and began to merge itself back together again. First from the ends at both top and bottom, as if someone was sewing it tightly shut from the other side. It shrank and shriveled until it went from looking like a gaping wound to a gash, to just a small cut, and then it too faded from the sky. There was no evidence that anything was ever there. Just the wake of its destruction and of its doom.

Charlie lay below on a bed of dust and ashes, asleep and twitching from the terrible dreams that plagued him. A nightmare where thousands of voices were screaming out until he saw a blinding flash of light, and then he heard no more. All that was left was silence.

Ash fell from the sky all that night and most of the following morning. It was carried off in alternating directions by the various weak bursts of wind.

Charlie lay where he had the night before, motionless but breathing in the center of the ring of medallions. Next to him was the platform and straps that he had been harnessed to, burned and scorched. These were the only objects not pulverized to dust.

When the investigators would later show up, though, they would not find Charlie. They would only find the footsteps he had left behind, and they would never know to whom they belonged. That, to most, would remain a mystery.

Ninety-eight miles away, in the house where Charlie grew up, his mother lay sprawled out on her bedroom floor. The room could only be noted by its stillness, by an eerie quiet. Nothing moved. Not even she stirred, for she had stopped breathing sometime in the night, and her body now, just starting to grow stiff, had lost whatever little vitality it had previously held. It looked, now, the color of bleached bone, paled by an abandoned desert sun. She'd never had much life or color in her cheeks to begin with.

When she had finally given out, she was in a state of delirium, knowing fully well that she needed sleep. She needed a deep, deep rest. She'd spent the final hours of her life wandering aimlessly around her house, lost to the world she knew, muttering to herself indecipherable ramblings that may or may not have been connected to any thoughts. Periodically, she would cry out, but then, as if she'd forgotten why she'd started in the first place she'd quiet again and continue her aimless pacing about the house.

The darkness ruled the house. It guided her, like water through a funnel, calling to her with its soft and gentle invitation to the rest she needed. And she gave in, following its beckoning call.

She followed it to her bedroom. Upon entering, she swooned and almost lost her step but caught herself on the edge of the bed. She was so tired. The bed had never looked more comfortable. Using her hands as a guide, she navigated her way around the corner of the mattress toward her nightstand and took a deep breath. With a strange and ominous acceptance, she seemed to be aware that that breath held what little spark she had left and, upon her exhale, she fell forward onto the nightstand, knocking over the lamp and the pile of books that now would never be read. Everything came crashing to the floor and was suddenly still.

The lamp was still on, its light casting its shine into the darkness underneath her bed, revealing a finely folded up piece of white linen cloth. Something was protruding out of its end: a circular, bronze piece of jewelry. A medallion with a matching bronze chain hanging from the top. At its center, a crimson jewel was embedded. It lay dormant and covered by shadow. Like her, it sat lifeless and dead.

The expression on her face didn't speak of suffering or pain, nor did it give the impression of peace. It simply *was*. It spoke of a journey's end. It spoke of the fact that she would no longer have to live a life of struggle. No more would she need be defined by pain. But as well, no more would she need to worry about her son, for he was beyond her hands now in the land of the living. She had never had the chance to warn him of what was coming, and she would never again be able to explain herself or make him understand what she did or didn't do. If she had been able to process it, she would have been shattered by the reality that never again would she be able to share her life with him, even if he'd wanted to.

Her burden to him, and his to her, was gone. Now, they would each have to find their own way, wherever their paths lead.

Just before dawn, a man walked into the room, surveying it and looking around, as if assessing the damage to a car. There was a distance and a preoccupation to his demeanor. He stepped over Charlie's mother's body, pushed away the fallen books and lamp and, kneeling down, retrieved the medallion from underneath the bed. With a painfully inhuman nonchalance, he stood back up and, without looking back at Charlie's mother, walked out the bedroom and back down the stairwell to the front door of the house, where he slammed it shut behind him as he left. The sound of a car starting and the subtle tension of tires on pavement could be heard as he drove off.

Finally, silence returned, the only companion that would remain by Charlie's mother's side as she passed on from this world to the next.

FOURTEEN

By mid-morning, the sun had steadily followed its normal course and was resting at the center of the dusty, soot-filled sky. Its heat tried to work its way through the cloudy mantle, in hope to bringing warmth and life to anything that sprung up below. But here was none.

Charlie had been walking for hours.

Sore and confused, he trudged through endless field of ash, following the newly formed geography of the valley. He was walking toward what he hoped was the distant tree line miles ahead. This green band of a horizon was the only thing that separated the slate tones of the ashen ground from the stone-grey skies overhead.

Charlie covered his mouth and face with his sleeve as he walked to keep from inhaling all the toxins and dust. It was irritating his eyes his eyes to no end, and for the past hour he had been coughing uncontrollably.

Pain and soreness were circulating through his whole body. Everything hurt, and he was broken and dispirited by the fact that he had no idea what had happened. The last thing he remembered was Mr. Wilkes walking toward him with the medallion in his hand, reaching up to place it around his neck – that and the slow, muttering chants of The Order.

As he walked, Charlie found his thoughts lingering always to Ellie and Trent, and the role they had played.

What happened to them? He wondered.

The thought gnawed at him.

He assumed they, too, were gone, just like everything else in the region, lost in the wake of whatever had caused the destruction.

Was any of it even real? Charlie winced as he considered what he thought to be the friendships he had been developing with both of them. He had felt a connection with each of them, and a depth that he was very much not used to sharing.

He'd let them both in, and he *thought* that they, in their own way, had let him in.

Still, Charlie didn't have much experience with friendships, so maybe there was something he was missing.

He thought of that first night, Trent introducing him to everyone at the bar. The two of them drinking beer after beer. Or their time at the Jetty and the strength that he had found there. Was that a lie too?

And all the time he'd spent with Ellie: their shared pints and walks. The trust he'd felt seed and bloom. There were those few precious moments where he had let his guard down and allowed her look at who he really was; and he was pretty sure she had invited him in to see those not so often shared parts of herself.

All of his insides shifted and turned over within him.

Grief was a dead weight, a burden that he was beginning to care very little for.

Charlie remembered the anguished looks they had both worn at the end. Those looks of shame and regret. He knew them all too well, for he had worn them often himself.

Some of it had to have been real, Charlie found himself hoping.

But like the desolate scenery around him, he couldn't quite hold those hopes together and they too dissolved into arbitrary and distant pains.

The more he dwelled on these memories, the more his chest tightened and gave off the effect of carrying more and more weight, something Charlie could not afford at the time. So, he pushed them away.

His head throbbed and his heart was heavy with grief. He seemed to be wearing the world upon his shoulders. His slouch grew deeper and graver with every mile he walked.

Something had happened and it was big. He felt the cracks around the foundations of his mind, the way you feel with your hands when searching for something in the dark.

Terrible flashes invaded from time to time. They drifted back and forth with the wind, cutting off his thoughts as he was desperate to put the pieces together. He hoped they weren't memories.

How could they be? He reasoned.

He trudged on for hours through the desolation, never taking a break. There had been no sign of anyone else at all.

A weight gripped at his gut, tugging on the dull and numbing grasps his mind made.

As afternoon turned to evening and evening into night, Charlie finally passed beyond the threshold of where the most destruction was wrought and found himself walking amid a varied section of forest, populated with debris strewn about and trees half-ripped from the ground. The remnants of whose roots were unearthed and left open to the wiles of nature. Everything was covered in a thick coat of sand. This was in contrast to the previous few miles, the haunting no-man's land of hazy dust, as if all life had been ground up and left as a fine powder.

This new section went on for about a mile, and the further Charlie walked, the more trees he noticed were standing.

Eventually, he made it to where the scenery resembled more of what could be described as a forest. The destruction there was almost nonexistent. There were mere and subtle traces of ash and soot that blanketed certain sections of the road or a branch here or there.

This left him with the feeling he was a man out of place and time, like someone who'd just walked off the trenches of WWI and back into the village he'd grown up in.

He walked on for another hour or so when, off in the distance, he heard a sound, alien to his more recent experiences. At first it was a cause for fear. Charlie panicked. He couldn't see it right away and his brain was still recovering from whatever had taken place, but something in him recognized what it was. Staring down at the center lines of the highway, he focused himself and was finally able to identify the noise. It was the hum of an engine.

His body told him to run and hide, but he froze.

Before he knew it, a truck had emerged from around the bend in the road and the hum grew loud and fierce.

Shit, Charlie thought. He didn't want to see anyone. He didn't know what to say. How was he to explain what was going on?

But it was too late.

At the last second, the driver of the truck saw Charlie and slammed on the breaks. The truck swerved, narrowly missing him. And Charlie clenched his eyes shut, looked down and prepared for impact, hugging the centerline.

When it hadn't come, he looked up and heard the sound of the truck's engine turning over. The hum faded into the quiet rustling of the wind.

The truck's door screeched open and a man emerged.

Charlie found that he still couldn't move.

"Whoa, shit, buddy. You okay?"

Charlie didn't answer. He waited, then tried taking a step back. He felt like he'd forgotten how to speak.

The man raised his arms as a show of peace and looked Charlie up and down.

"Seriously, bud, are you okay?"

All sorts of alarms were going off in Charlie's brain. He didn't want to trust this man, but he didn't know why. He did manage a shake of his head, expressing that he was in fact *okay,* which was not true. Charlie could tell the man didn't believe it as he expression only grew more worried.

The man looked Charlie up and down, considering his physical state. Charlie was a mess. His clothes were thrashed. He looked like a mountain had collapsed on top of him. And he had been so focused on Charlie, he hadn't yet noticed the change in geography in the distance. Where there had normally been hills and the smaller peaks of the coastal mountains, now only housed a long graveyard of devastation and unelevated soot.

"What the hell happened here, son?" The man couldn't take his eyes off the scene that lay beyond Charlie.

"I dunno," Charlie said.

"Holy shit, holy—" the man said. They were the only words either of them managed for some time.

Then the man took a step closer to Charlie, and with every step he took Charlie managed one back.

"Whoa, it's okay, buddy. It's okay. *Seriously,* are you okay? You look like shit! I mean… you—you don't remember anything that happened?"

Charlie's chest heaved and something broke; he burst into tears. "I don't—I don't know," he sobbed.

The man walked up to him and Charlie finally let him close the distance. The man put one arm up around Charlie's shoulder gently, and with his other hand grasped at Charlie's forearm to help hold him steady.

"It's okay… it's okay, buddy. We're… we're gonna figure this… shit out. Okay? Let's just… get you into the truck?"

Charlie wept and virtually collapsed into the man's arms. He allowed himself to be led, all the while feeling a strange resistance to the action. Together they crossed the road. The hours of walking and thinking had worn on him, so what else was there to do?

"Do you remember where you were headed?" asked the man. "I'm coming from Portland, myself. You see, I was gonna visit my brother and his wife, but—" The man looked back up the road, searching for his own understanding of what was going on. "…but I don't see that happening."

Portland… Charlie thought. *Mom…* He wanted to go see his mother. He wanted to go be with her, to be home.

The man guided Charlie over to the passenger seat of the truck and lay him into it to rest.

Off in the distance, ash and smoke continued to plume and drifted off through the air.

Still weeping, Charlie rubbed at his face and looked up at the man. "Portland?" He asked

"Yeah? That's where you were headed?"

Charlie was lost for a second and didn't answer. Memories of the last week filtered themselves through his mind, though foggy and disconnected. He just couldn't remember everything. *I had just moved to Astoria*, he told himself. *I… I was going to… teach.* Then Trent's face appeared before him. He smiled at first, thinking of their time at the bar, and the Jetty. But it was washed away by the pangs of betrayal. Charlie shook the memories away. Then he saw Ellie. Her face was smiling at first, free and alluring, but it quickly turned into one of pained anguish. Charlie yelped and twitched and pushed it from his mind. Other thoughts tried to invade, but he fought them off. He needed rest. He needed to get home and see his mom. He needed to rest and figure this out, then he could deal with the rest of it.

"She's in Portland," he whispered.

"What's that?" asked the man.

"Portland?" Charlie said through a muffled sniffle. "I think that's where I was headed."

"Okay. Okay," said the man, nervous and agitated. He looked at his phone. There was no service. "Look, ah. I'm not sure what's going on here, but we need to get you somewhere safe and figure this shit all out. You want to come with me? I mean, I can't just leave you out here."

"Back to Portland?" Charlie's voice was feeble and void of hope.

"Sure, yeah. Back to Portland," the man said, reminding himself. "Back to cell reception first. I dunno." The man looked to Charlie thinking that Charlie looked how he felt, lost and unsure.

Charlie thought about it, a difficult process at the time. What else was there to do?

"Okay."

"Alright," the man paused again, almost unsure of how to leave. "Let's go," he resolved.

He buckled Charlie into the passenger seat, then ran over to the driver's side, hopped in and started the engine. It roared to life.

"Hold on," said the man as he backed up the truck onto the gravel lip before pulling back onto the highway. "O-okay," he stuttered. "Let's get out of here." His voice trailed off with a strain, sucked away by his rising worry.

Charlie was silent through it all. He gave no response and let the truck carry him down the road, away from the fallout of the event he could not remember.

Neither man spoke. The driver chewed on his lip while mulling over what he had seen. He strained to rationalize the irrational.

All the while, broken by the weight of unknown burdens, Charlie wept. He couldn't stop. He was raw like an open wound and wasn't sure what the future held for him. As the truck pushed on down the road, he actively worked not to think about the thoughts that pressed themselves inward, the fierce reminders of what had happened. Charlie felt he'd rather not know. They crept up and hid in the crevices of his exhaustion and worry. What he knew was that the plans he'd made had been destroyed. Whatever *new* life he thought he was building didn't exist anymore. He wasn't even sure anymore if they had been his in the first place. He didn't want to deal with any of that right then, so he pushed it all from his mind. It was the only thing he could do to keep himself from falling apart. *Calm down, Charlie, and breathe.*

Lost and unsure, he wondered where the road ahead would lead.

And the driver, too, gripped with worry himself, confused by the situation, kept looking over at Charlie, feeling equally lost and unsure of how to help.

EPILOGUE

In Portland, a warm summer rain sprinkled down from under a scattered and uneven sky. Strange and unpredictable clouds had rolled in the night before from over the coastal mountains. They'd been funneled in and driven south to an unsuspecting and fertile Willamette valley.

The Willamette River wound its way through Portland, dividing the East and the West ends, snaking its way up through valley, eventually dumping into the Columbia, the shipping channel that linked Portland to Astoria.

On Portland's west side, just where the 405 came to an end, a little beyond Union Station, there stood a trio of tall buildings the city had coded as apartment complexes. They stood just inside one of the bends in the river. They had been constructed several years before as part of the city's initiative to curb the oncoming housing crisis and homeless issues. They had become the crown jewel of a city overhaul, refurbishing, or in some cases rebuilding completely, and over-looked Portland's Pearl District.

Nobody lived in these buildings, which would have come as a great surprise to many, seeing as they looked very inhabited. The rents for each room were always paid and the parking lots were bursting with gleaming new models of cars. People could always be seen entering and leaving the buildings, mostly those dressed in fine suites or clothing suitable for the location. It was bustling.

Plants and hammocks hung from balconies, and bicycles from hooks. There were always dozens of bikes parked at the entrances of each building.

They looked lived-in and habitable, as they were meant to. The top floor of the seemingly subsidized high-rise tower closest to the water, however, *was* consistently occupied. The morning after Astoria had been wiped from all but memory, there sat a man in this office, engrossed in the morning edition of *The Oregonian* behind a rich mahogany desk and seated comfortably in a neo-modern, tanned and oiled chair, all of these indicators of wealth. His monthly planner was open before him with several of the day's appointments scratched out and, next to it, an untouched, steaming cup of coffee waited to be drunk. He poured over an article overviewing the aftermath of the devastation in Astoria, or at least what little they knew at the time. They were still trying to figure out if it was geologically linked, like an earthquake, or whether or not it was connected to climate change. The authorities were as lost as everyone else.

This man's jaw twitched as he read. He carried with him a confident yet anxious weight, like he knew more than to let on.

There was a knock at the door that startled him.

"Come in," he said, making no attempt to hide his annoyance at the disruption. He also didn't take his focus away from the newspaper.

The door swung open swiftly, and in rushed a man who bore a subtle and subservient gate, panic written across his face.

"Sir? I—Have you—?"

"I've heard all about it," said the man, not taking his eyes from the morning edition.

It wasn't difficult to tell who was in charge.

"I've just got off the phone with our—"

"*Our* operation has not been connected with the party in question in over ninety-seven years. *We* are unharmed by this. Now what do you want?"

"Well, sir—" The man droned off and took a moment to straighten his tie and attempt to stand up a little taller.

"In fact," the man behind the newspaper continued, not worried that he'd cut the other man off, "this event is quite fortuitous for our operation."

"But sir, how do we even know that—"

The man finally put the newspaper down. "What is there not to know? Haven't you watched the news reports? Haven't you read the morning's paper? Read about the level of destruction? It was *them*, dammit. I know it!" He paused for a moment, gathering himself. "That damnable *Wilkes* and his so-called *brotherhood*."

"But, sir—"

"It was *them*. They, somehow, found a *key*, what we've all been looking for. And they were, *somehow*, able to succeed, in a manner of speaking."

"I just don't see how any of this can be a good thing, sir."

"You wouldn't."

The lesser man went to open his mouth again to speak, but quickly shut it and took a step back instead.

"Get Travis' team together and get them out there now. Use *any* favors we have. Pull *every* string you can. Do *anything* necessary, do you understand me? Local authorities, or whatever's left of them. Politicians. State police. The feds. Anyone. *Everyone*. I don't care, do you hear me? Use who we have on the inside. I want a retrieval team out there now!"

"Of course, sir. Right away. But for what?"

"They'll know it when they get out there."

"Who?"

"The tea—Travis, goddammit! Get them out there, now!"

"Of course, sir. Right away." The man gave a bow and turned to walk away.

Halfway to the door, he was called back. "One more thing before you go."

"Yes, sir."

"Put in a call to The Head. It's time."

The man stopped, and his whole body stiffened. "Th—the Head, sir?"

"Yes," the man folded his hands over his lap. "Is that going to be a problem?"

"N-no, of course not, sir. Right away."

"Good. Very good."

The man walked out of the room and closed the door behind him. As his footsteps faded down the hallway, the other man stood up from his desk and walked over to a painting on the wall. He lifted it off the wall and set it down onto the floor next to him, revealing a small safe. It was high-tech, befitting of the surroundings. He punched in a seven-digit code then scanned his thumb and index finger. A pressurized release could be heard and the door to the safe swung open.

Two objects lay inside. The first was a very old book with a cracked and faded red leather binding. The other was a medallion: bronze, with a thick matching chain that was looped through the top. It was small and rectangular, but one of the short ends was curved. Inset into the medallion was a very large crimson jewel.

The man picked up the medallion and held it up. He considered it with great interest and in a tone both vicious and combative, filled with enmity, he said, "Wilkes, what the hell have you done?"

"So full of artless jealousy is guilt,
It spills itself in fearing to be spilt."
—William Shakespeare, *"Hamlet"*

AFTERWORD

This story gestated in me for a long time. It was born of pain. My own pain, but pain is an interesting thing. Some of it is brought on by others, isn't it? For instance, the initial pain we experience in life is often brought on by the people closest to us, friends and family and such. It's not necessarily a bad thing, though it can be. We're supposed to experience pain, and—I would argue—we're supposed to learn how to overcome it. I think that's what this book is about. Although Charlie's story isn't over so I'm not 100% sure yet.

At a certain point in our lives, once we become a little more responsible, doesn't it become more dependent on *us* what we do with that pain? It's less on the *other's* shoulders, isn't it? After a while, that pain becomes truly ours and we have to decide what to do with it, to minimize it, place it where it needs to be so we can move forward, or blow it up. I think we all ebb and flow on that spectrum every day. I know I do. And I will for the rest of my life.

This story has been a saving grace for me. It's been a liberating experience to enter another world and, in a way, physically—at least mentally—grapple with these realities. I've learned a lot. About pain, struggle, and anger, but also about perseverance, love and hope. I have come to love Charlie as a part of myself. Probably because he is a huge part of me.

For the record, it should be stated that the locations in this story are all real. They all exist. I lived in Astoria for seven years and I taught at both Knappa and Astoria High School. It was a time of immense growth in my life, and a time of pain. Like I mentioned above, some of this pain was brought on by others, but if I'm being honest, a lot of it was brought on by myself. Sure, there were several wounds that I didn't ask for, nor did I even realize I had committed to, but in the end I made certain choices, doing the best I could with what I had at the time and what happened.

When you look back, isn't it so much easier to see what you could have done differently? That's just the way it is, isn't it? That is the case with my time living there too.

Sometimes in life, we're blessed with the opportunities to make things right. And sometimes, were blessed with the foresight enough to dive at those opportunities. At other times, it just doesn't seem to happen.

In a way, this book is the remedy to that. It's an apology in one way, strangely enough, and an acceptance in another. In a completely different way, it's an indictment to all involved, myself included. But where an indictment comes, justice will follow, and my hope for myself and others is that with that justice will come forgiveness and mercy. I think this book strives for that too. Ask me again in five years, especially after I've written the next part. Or maybe even the third and final part of Charlie's story.

We'll see.

In the end, just note that this book was a massive step toward healing for me. And after its publication, I hope it can be that for others too. Beyond myself, I hope this book resonates with anyone who feels or felt like they don't or didn't have a voice. For anyone who has had to fight to be themselves. And for anyone who has been crushed by the various circumstances in life and have fought bravely—which is all of you—to stand in the light free of shame, this is for you.

For me, writing this book brought a tremendous amount of healing and hope. I had to travel back in and through dark memories to get there, but on the other side I found hope. A hope I wanted to share and will forever be thankful that I had that opportunity.

Thanks for reading.

Thanks for walking with Charlie as he navigates his own journey.

I can't wait to experience where he goes next with you.

Thanks.

Craig
Amsterdam, The Netherlands
February 20th, 2020

AUTHOR NOTE

This is a work of fiction. Though each location in this book exists – they are very, very real – none of the characters within the story bare any direct resemblance or connection to any person(s) in real life, except Charlie, who has been a metaphor and extension of myself as I have been investigating my own emotional journey.

I lived in Astoria for seven years. My children were born there. I loved it, and still love it dearly to this day. While living there, I went through some immense changes, both emotionally and mentally, that I'm still working through. As a result, I'm sure that flows in and through the text, but in the end, Astoria was simply the ideal location for the story to be set.

Thank you. I hope you enjoy.

Acknowledgements

First and foremost, I would like to dedicate this book to those who inspired it. Namely, H.P. Lovecraft, Mike Mignola, Neil Gaiman and Haruki Murakami. An eclectic group of authors who have helped shape my literary landscape for years. Thank you.

Next, to my wife and children and their endless love and support. To my parents, siblings, and extended family, for whom those first bonds of relationship are formed. And to the friends who have been there with me since the beginning. Thank you for those long walks and even longer conversations.

A very special thanks to Jamie-Lee Kelly, Kevin Randall and, again, my wife for being the first readers of this book and for encouraging me to continue long after it seemed a hopeless cause. Thank you for the encouragement, the edits, the conversations and the many thoughts and ideas. Thank you for putting up with me!

A huge thank you to Anna Druse and Andy West (no relation to Charlie), my 9th, 10th and 11th grade English teachers. Two of the most incredible and inspiring humans I know. You two laid the first bricks in the foundation of my love for literature and writing, and teaching. You introduced me to poetry. Steinbeck. Shakespeare. Whitman. Dickinson. Salinger. Bradstreet. Morrison. Lawrence. And so many more of the greats. You pushed me. Encouraged me. Inspired me. And most importantly, you showed me something in me that I didn't even know was there. I have spent the last twelve years of my life following your example. Thank you.

Thank you to Danielle Robertson and the Morrighan Publishing team, or family as it's come to feel. Thank you for taking this chance with me! I am forever grateful.

Lastly, and with all my heart, thank you to all the students I've ever had out there. From my time at Knappa to Astoria High School, Farm Home School in Corvallis, all the way to my current post here in The Netherlands. In pushing you to find and follow your dreams, I have stumbled upon mine. I can say, without a doubt, that I would not be who I am today without every one of you. Thank you for persisting, for your courage, your flare and thank you for letting me be a part of your lives. This one, and hopefully many more to come, is for you. Thank you for believing in me.

CPSIA information can be obtained
at www.ICGtesting.com
Printed in the USA
BVHW082329070921
616209BV00007B/142